Gold Mad

Gold is where you find it.

Michael Maser

To Larry,
Gold is where you
find it!
Michael Maser

Gold Mad

And may you find
the gold you are
seeking.

BOOKS

Cover and book design Włodzimierz Milewski

Note for libraries: A catalogue record for this book is available from Library and Archives Canada at www.collectionscanada.gc.ca

ISBN: 978-0-9868776-5-0

BOOKS

MW Books
Garden Bay, BC
V0N 1S1
Canada
mwbookpublishing.com
info@mwbookpublishing.com

10 9 8 7 6 5 4 3 2 1

CONTENTS

BIG BLUFF MINE

NORTHERN CALIFORNIA

1894

Dank air mixed with blasting powder tickled Pat Parrot's nostrils. Bathed in flickering light thrown from a torch jutting from the mine wall, he hoisted a scaling slick and gouged a fist-sized chunk of quartz vein from the rock face in front of him. He paused to wipe a dirty broadcloth over his dripping forehead.

Except for his breathing, the air was still and the darkness mute as he studied the rock. His grimy, callused fingers traced over rough-formed blebs of gold.

A cut torn open on Parrot's knuckle leaked blood that trickled down his thumb. "Flesh, stone, eternity," he muttered before licking his thumb then tossing the rock toward an ore cart parked in a curtain of shadow. He continued to stare down the dark mine tunnel, listening. A splashing noise in the distance preceded two men who emerged from the darkness, walking toward him.

"You're still here," one of the men grunted. "Your shift ended more than an hour ago."

"I like it fine when nobody's around," Parrot said. "How come you're late?"

"Big boss man's hanging around, asking all kinds of questions about the vein."

"I bet he's planning to tunnel in from the north creek," the other man said. "Hoping to find some new ore."

"More likely he's thinking about shuttin' down," Parrot said. "There's too many faults and splits here. Not enough mineral."

"Well, I don't know about that," the man continued. "I seen lots of color in the rock I've been bustin' up."

"You don't know piss," Parrot told him, handing him his pick. "I've been chasin' veins for nine years and I know when a streak is playing out."

Parrot stepped away from the rock face and picked up a shirt lying nearby. He started walking down the tunnel, stopping briefly to pick up the rock he had tossed and drop it in the ore cart.

"You'll fill this up in a couple of hours," he said aloud. "I'll tell the chinks to come and fetch it."

Without another word, Parrot continued into the tunnel. The light from another torch glowed dimly in the darkness ahead and he walked slowly and deliberately toward it, lifting his boots to avoid stumbling on rail lines that wound along the tunnel floor like string left behind by a child.

He followed the twisting tunnel, splashing through puddles and past piles of rock that slumped into the drift from the mine walls. He heard the sounds of men talking as he walked past the juncture of a smaller tunnel that angled into darkness to the side. Eventually the main tunnel widened into a large cavern that he and others had mined out months before. On the side of the cavern, Parrot climbed up a series of ladders and started along another tunnel. In the distance he saw a thin aperture of light that slowly enlarged as he approached.

Closer to the entrance, the walls of the mine were supported by squared timbers hammered together. Parrot was walking through this latticework when he heard a faint rumble. He paused. The ground shook slightly. Then the timbers groaned and a puff of dust shook down from above. Parrot started loping toward the entrance. The rumbling surged in intensity and the ground began heaving. Timbers broke away from the latticework and dropped into the tunnel, kicking out clouds of dust and rock that obscured the light. Parrot staggered forward a few steps when a swinging timber smashed into his side, sending him sprawling against the wall. He raised his arms to protect his head as debris poured onto him. A large rock caromed off his shoulder. He yelled but his cry disappeared in the noise of the cave-in.

The ground stopped moving. Parrot lay unconscious - pinned among a pile of broken rocks. Hours later, he regained semi-consciousness, his body wracked by pain when he tried to shift around. His thoughts drifted through torn moments, bodies, houses, rock. The face of his mother. Gold oozing from milk-white quartz like candle wax. More pain and thirst. He was able to move one hand and he gripped a fist-sized rock and began knocking it against the boulder on which he was pinned. The tapping merged with his groans until he was reclaimed by darkness and pain.

GOLD DISCOVERY

YUKON TERRITORY

August 1896

Seeking relief from swarming mosquitoes, the adamantine beast melted into the black water, first dunking its head to quench the searing pain that ringed its swollen eyes, then to drink the cool liquid.

It lay submerged in the pond for more than a minute. Then it moved again to lift its snout above the water and blow a foaming spume from its nostrils. Head swinging, it stepped onto a shallow shelf and stood with the sun reflecting from its hind flank, a shining mat of fire.

The surrounding forest was still, engulfed in mid-summer humidity that encumbered the living like a yoke. The mosquitoes were not discouraged, though, and swarmed the moose again.

A light breeze swirled over the water and a raven squawked from atop a nearby spruce tree. The moose opened its nostrils wide to sniff the air. Detecting a molecule of something strange, it fought to leave the water and return to the forest cover. As it emerged, an explosion shattered the air and something smashed into the animal's side, knocking it to the ground. Its hooves gouged sand and rock from the water's edge, but the connecting tissue to one of its front legs was severed and it was unable to stand.

It writhed on the ground for a couple of minutes then lay gasping, its energy spent, blood choking its airways and dripping from its nostrils. It made no attempt to displace the flies gathering on its eyelids.

A shadow fell on the beast and a white man, thin and thewy, wearing deer-hide leggings, blousy shirt and a grimy, rumpled hat bent over the body. He pulled with all his strength on an ear to turn the great head. The head would not turn.

"Hey, Indian," the man shouted. "Help me dress this goddam moose."

Another figure walked up to the beast that continued to stare, though it was dying.

A rifle barrel pressed against the skin just below the moose's ear and a second explosion rent the air.

The white man whirled and gave the Indian a hard shove on the shoulder.

"What the hell are you doin', wasting bullets?"

"I got more," the Indian said.

"Yeah, I gave them to you, too. Remember that, you sonofabitch."

Another Indian slowly walked out of the bush and up to the dead animal. "You shot a doe," he said, flatly.

"That's the truth, Jim," the white man said. "And tonight we're gonna eat our faces off, aren't we?

"Shouldn't shoot a doe before it's calved," the first Indian responded.

The white man rummaged in a shapeless backpack until he produced a length of rope.

"Piss up a tree, Charlie," he replied. " There's more moose in this country than mosquitoes."

He squeezed the hooves of the moose together and looped two hanks of rope around them. He pulled the line taut, and threw an end to one of the Indians. Turning back to the moose, the white man made a deep incision with a large knife in the softest part of the underbelly. Pulling erratically on the knife, he slowly cut a slit large enough for the intestines and organs to slide out onto the sand. They lay there, a glistening, steaming mass without form.

He grabbed the rope and struggled to drag the carcass toward the forest. "Charlie. Jim. Gimme a hand here. Put your back into it, and we'll string 'er up to drain."

Later that night, the three men sat around a fire that cast undulating shadows across their faces. Their stomachs bulged from moose meat, half-cooked. The slaughtered carcass was cached away from the fire site, hanging above the ground between two spruce trees where it would be safe from predators. The white man rocked forward for a moment to probe the fire with a long stick, then settled back down. Eventually, Charlie spoke without turning his head or wasting words.

"I think we're gonna see more colors tomorrow."

"Colors like that last pan today'd be good," the white man said, unhurriedly. "A sign there's real gold here, not just a sniff. We'll stick to the main fork tomorrow but jack up to the creeks running off that south ridge. Camp back here at night."

All around them the darkness smothered the sounds of the forest. The men sat in silence for several minutes before speaking again.

"You gonna leave a message for Henderson?" Jim asked softly, as if someone might be listening.

The white man drew in a long breath, thinking, then speaking without any extra emotion. "No, I ain't. Sonofabitch doesn't like the company I keep, let him find gold on his own. Wouldn't sell you no tobacco, neither, though I seen his pouch was bulging."

He thought a moment before he spoke again. "I guess I met a lot of white men like Henderson. Don't like Indians."

Jim canted his head towards the white man but said nothing. Then he rolled onto his side and pulled a blanket over his shoulders. Charlie did the same moments later.

"You wake up in the night, you throw some sticks on the fire, okay?" the white man said. "I don't want to wake up bein' squeezed out some bear's asshole."

He chuckled to himself then lay down on the ground, too, with his hands tucked under this face. "Hey, Jim," he said, remembering something.

The Indian shifted around but did not speak.

"Find a good strike, we all get rich together. Hear me?"

The Indian rolled back onto his side.

The white man persisted. "Well, whaddya think of that?"

The Indian lay mute.

"Sonofabitch, maybe you'd rather work for three dollars a week," the white man muttered, pulling a blanket round his ears and tucking up his legs.

The three men awoke soon after dawn, the forest amplifying the morning calls of a hundred birds. Without talking, the Indians lit a small fire and the white man gathered a handful of elderberry leaves that he rolled between his palms before throwing them into a pot with some water. He knelt next to the fire where he balanced the pot between a burning stick and a flat rock, keeping watch until the water heated. When it started to boil he pulled a battered tin cup from a formless, gray rucksack and scooped up half a cupful of the hot tea. He waved his hand over the steam and drank intermittently.

"It's coolin' down at night," the white man said. "Sonofabitch but summer ain't gonna be here much longer."

Jim held his hands over the small, darting tongue of flame.

The white man continued. "I tell you, Jim, I had the damndest dream last night. I was trampin' through bush, in a hurry about something I can't remember now. Then I skidded down a mud bank into a river. The water was real dark but I could see salmon swimming all around, some of them bumping my arm and starin' at me with green-gold eyes. I can tell you, I got some kind of weird feeling. When I came to I looked up and saw the sky just full of stars. 'N the wind hissin' up the trees."

"Maybe a bear was chasin' you," Charlie said, chuckling. "White man's always dreamin' about bears, 'cause you don't understand 'em."

"I don't know, sounds like a good dream to me," Jim countered.

"It probably weren't anythin'," the white man said. "Just a crazy dream."

He scooped more tea from the pot. As he sipped, he tilted his head and slowly scanned the forest canopy.

"Tell me, Charlie, you ever dream?"

The Indian stared into the fire.

"Well, do ya?"

"Maybe."

"Whaddya dream about?"

The Indian tossed his remaining tea into the fire then stashed his cup into a dirty rucksack.

"You wouldn't understand," Jim said, rolling to his feet. "Indian dreams belong only to Indians."

The white man rose, too and kneaded his thighs.

"I'll bet I know what you dream about. That squaw of yours snuggled under a big moosehide. Hey? Ain't that about right?"

Charlie kicked dirt onto the fire and nudged apart the smoldering logs with the toe of his moccasin.

"We gonna do some work today?"

The white man tightened his muscles at the challenge and his narrow brown eyes lost their warmth.

Both Indians turned and walked into the bush.

Throughout the day, the white man and the Indians followed a routine they started weeks before. Working slowly, they leapfrogged up one side of a creek, digging wedges of sandy gravel out of shallow overgrown creek beds, some of them only two feet wide. Hiking up one side of a stream fork until they were satisfied the prospecting was weak, then crossing over, they beat their way back through the bush, repeating the sampling process in all the creeks they intersected. After working down three or four pan loads, their backs ached and their hands and feet were numb from the gelid creek water. Mercifully, the gurgle of the creek drowned out the noise of the unrelenting, ever-present mosquitoes. At times, the noise of the creek pulsed in hypnotic rhythm, and pushed into their ears with a sharp intensity, a symptom of prospecting fever that afflicted all gold panners.

No strangers to the chronic discomfort of goldpanning, the white man and the Indians eased their strain by kneeling in the gravel and splashing icy water on their heads. In a few moments the tremors dissipated and the noise of the creek returned to a sustained and steady pitch.

On this day, pan loads of creek sand were showing colors - flakes of gold - as they had the previous day. The yellow metal lay in arcing tails of sandy residue that remained after lighter minerals were washed away. Enough colors to jar the imagination and send a jab of adrenalin rushing through the blood, further cauterizing the senses.

More so than the Indians, the white man was captivated by these sparkles. His imagination fixated on a desire to discover a pocket of gold that would make him as wealthy as a king and relieve a dizzying ache in his head and heart. He knew the probability of such a discovery was minute - years of prospecting, tramping through bush, plunging his hands into icy creeks, and crippling backache had brought him scant rewards - but a dream flitted in and out of his consciousness until it guided all his actions. In his mind's eye, he pictured himself huddled under a great bearskin coat, protected from the cold and rain, safe from the rigors of prospecting. Again and again he saw his gold pan disappearing beneath black waters and he felt comfort flowing into his body. The dream ended there.

The Indians did not share the white man's anxiety to discover gold. They were comfortable living in the forest that had been the home of their ancestors, secure in knowledge and skills to survive from season to season. White people thought very differently about the forest and the animals and how to live. Working with the white man added to their security and increased some pleasures - tobacco, whisky, a new rifle and tools like axes and knives, but those were the only benefits they counted in their association.

An alder branch snapped back against his face, jolting the white man from his reverie as he plodded from creek to creek. Cursing, he tore it from the trunk and hurled it away. Underfoot, spongy, head-sized knots of moss twisted his ankles and vexed his balance as he plodded on. He sank into a carpet of lichen for a couple of minutes beside a small streambed, cupping a handful of water to his mouth and wiping away the sweat that burned his eyes and dripped from his face.

Rested, he stumbled a few steps to a bar in the middle of the stream where he scooped out a pan of sand, then crouched to wash it in the current. Each time he dipped the pan into the water he would rock it from side to side, working with gravity and the energy of the stream to sort and wash away the lightest particles, usually mud and clay. The heavier particles, including any gold flakes or nuggets, would sink to the bottom of the pan.

At first, the pan of sand the white man washed down on this site was no different than the thousands of pans that had preceded it.

Initially, the composition was fine gravel, sand, clay and water. Then came a moment when what was left in the pan represented a small fraction of the initial scoop, the true concentrate. With a deft flick of the pan, the white man swirled the concentrate into an arc for analysis and final judgment.

Of all the judgments the white man had pronounced on all the panloads of sand and gravel he had rocked back and forth into concentrate, only a few revealed enough gold to suggest he might turn a profit by working the main stream bed with a sluice box or other placer mining gear. Even fewer were the times he'd seen a tail of gold flakes painted on the bottom of the pan.

This time, when he turned his pan towards the sun, what he saw in the residue was not so much a tail of gold as a ribbon, wide and long as his thumb. Textured with fine flakes and nuggets the size of baby's teeth. A richer sight than he had ever dreamed.

Instinctively, adrenalin flooded his body and knotted his stomach. He dropped the pan and lurched to the stream bank where he fell onto the moss. The sound of roaring water filled his head until he thought he would scream. Instead, he retched violently. Then he pressed his hands into his temples and lay still to catch his breath.

A few minutes later a hand reached down to rock his shoulder. The white man jerked back in horror.

"Hey, are you okay?" Jim asked him. Charlie stood behind him in the bush.

The white man stared back, speechless, trying to remember recent events. He saw his gold pan lying upside down in the middle of the stream and wondered if he had dreamed the ribbon of gold.

He pushed past the Indians and splashed into the water where he scooped out another panful of sand that he furiously rocked back and forth.

The Indians watched from the bank, certain that the white man, surrounded by a cloud of mosquitoes, had become sick with a summer fever.

In a few moments, the white man stopped his jerky motion. He stared into the pan then suddenly lifted his head and looked at the Indians with a curious expression. His mouth hung slack and his chest heaved to suck in enough air. At that moment he felt nothing, not the icy water that numbed his feet, nor the aching spasm that ran the length of his spine. He was entirely consumed by his imagination.

"Look yourself," he said, stepping across the stream and carefully extending the pan as he might a delicate flower. Together, the three stared into the pan and pawed at the sandy gold with gnarled fingers. Then the white man lay the pan onto the moss, pulled the Indians out onto the gravel bank and, crunching rocks and cobbles underfoot, danced a clumsy jig.

Later, as the fading Yukon sun transformed the scrub forest into a skein of sinewy shadows, the white man and the Indians finished the task of staking new mining claims. Using a short brush axe, the white man squared the sides of a balsam fir tree, then knelt in the forest duff to write the details of his claim on the fresh shaved surface with a stubby wax crayon. With careful strokes it was born into history:

NOTICE

I DO, THIS DAY, LOCATE AND CLAIM, BY RIGHT OF DISCOVERY,

FIVE HUNDRED FEET, RUNNING UP STREAM FROM THIS NOTICE.

17TH AUGUST, 1896

GEORGE. W. CARMACK

Then all light drained from the sky, leaving the three men to face another night and grapple with mosquitoes and their dreams.

GOLD RUSH

YUKON TERRITORY

Fall 1896

The gold of the Klondike gravels was unique, richer in quantity than any mineral deposit mined on earth. George Carmack, Skookum Jim and Tagish Charlie merely tickled the surface with their discovery in the creek bed.

After staking their claims, the three men trudged through bush then paddled along the Yukon River to the small village of Fortymile, where they filed a record of the claims and announced their discovery in a nearby saloon. By next morning, Fortymile was deserted. Within a week, every prospector within a hundred miles had rushed to the area and staked the creek bottom for miles, laying claim to the gold below and then laboring to extract it.

During the winter of 1896-97, the mining claims yielded flakes clumped together in layers thick as saddle leather and nuggets scattered in the creek gravels like birdseed. With gold valued at sixteen dollars an ounce, some miners cleaned up four dollars of gold from a pan of gravel, some found forty. Some found four thousand dollars worth in a single day. Sweat and blood were traded silently for gold through the early autumn blizzards and under the frozen grip of endless Arctic winter darkness.

Fingers and toes throbbed with pain or froze solid as stone and still the hunger pumped strong. With empty stomachs and aching muscles, somber men shook gravel and pawed into muck until their eyes burned with fatigue. Beside the light of flickering candles or moving amphibiously through ice fog, the living resembled the dead, only the dead were thought to be more comfortable. Time was marked by sleep or a semi-conscious period when men ignored the most urgent instincts, subsisting instead on one reward - the slow accumulation of gold as it trickled over numb fingers onto rusted scales and into cotton socks, tin cans, glass jars.

After months of winter darkness, a subtle change crept over the frozen land, a link to the cycles that had molded the gold pockets for ten thousand years. Daylight slowly returned and rising temperatures greeted chattering birds. Dozing bears pawed through the rotting snow of their ice lairs and emerged into bright sun to begin foraging for spring roots. Fresh breezes carried the intoxicating perfume of balsam fir and cedar.

Under the warming spring sun the men of the mines, hording gold fortunes, longed for escape to the south so they might eat fresh meat, take a bath or gaze at a woman.

Finally, the Yukon river, frozen for more than six months, split open with the fury of Zeus and flowed again. A month later, the first riverboats of 1897 paddled upstream to berth alongside the collection of cabins and tents where the miners gathered at the confluence of the Klondike and Yukon rivers, now known as Dawson City. Whisky poured into throats desperate for drink and men shook with delirium. Clutching their treasure, many abandoned the land of gold and navigated more than a thousand miles down the serpentine, muddy river, past endless acres of scrub forest, to where the Yukon spilled into the Pacific Ocean nearby to the village of St. Michael, Alaska.

There, the air thick with fishrot, lay the *Excelsior*, a nondescript, rusting steamer that would deliver the fortune-laden men of the Klondike, and the first news of history's largest gold discovery, to the rest of the civilized world.

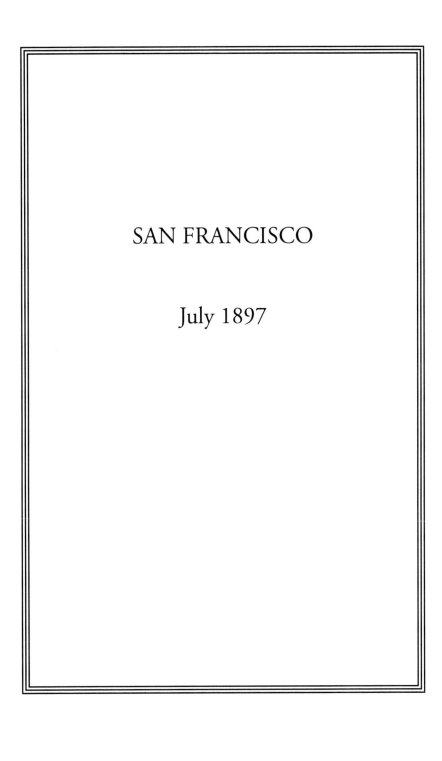

SAN FRANCISCO

July 1897

Following San Francisco Bay inland by wagon road, the terminus of city development was about three miles from the downtown core. Beyond the city, the land was shared equally between clutches of buildings hugging the water's edge and, for the most part, treeless hillside. On the valleyland, pioneers had excised farmland from coastal forests, nurtured crops, or raised cattle, hogs and horses. Tradesmen, merchants, blacksmiths, sawyers, veterinarians, midwives and all people, young and old, serviced the industries and workers of the fertile farmlands and the growing city.

Such was the case in Manzanita, a collection of buildings located a twenty-minute ride from the city limits by horse and wagon. Though human activity habitually diminished with the setting sun in most communities, Manzanita was an exception. Here, energies were directed to the *Oasis*, the entrepreneurial establishment of the most gracious matriarch between San Francisco and Sacramento, Madame Rosalba.

Born in the French Caribbean, Madame recited to all who inquired of her heritage that she had completed finishing school in Buenos Aires and Patagonia at fine, respectable establishments and married two different gentlemen. Despite her yearning for a long and happy marriage, each husband was struck down by tragic circumstance leaving Rosalba in solitude, though cushioned from misfortune by a healthy inheritance. She eventually sailed from South America to find a drier climate and to establish an enterprise by which she might help ease the burdens of life that fell on young women less fortunate than herself.

Arriving in San Francisco fifteen years earlier and "preferring country mice to city rats," she chose the valley to make her new home. After years of upgrading and developing, her estate now boasted an airy Colonial courtyard, resplendent groves of fruit trees and flowering verges, and a beachfront promenade from which one could look eastward across the tidal flats towards the ramshackle dwellings of Oakland or northward past the island of Alcatraz to the forests of Sausalito.

The *Oasis* stabled up to as many as two dozen young ladies who earned their keep entertaining and satisfying all the desires of a robust male clientele. They came from all sorts of backgrounds - one was a blacksmith's daughter, another the niece of a governor, and another was a half-breed Cherokee Indian. In Rosalba's care, they were fed and schooled in graces, and she arranged for medical help when they contracted a virus or when birth control failed. All babies were cared for up to three months, after which they were adopted out to good homes.

On this late afternoon, a breeze fresh from the water lightly jiggled the rhododendron bushes flush with blossoms and relieved the stifling heat of the afternoon. Several ladies, dressed elegantly in button-down shoes, flouncy gowns, feather boas and plumed hats, walked, not quickly, along a rough-hewn walkway toward a short flight of stairs that led down to the sand. The procession was led by a man carrying a cumbersome box camera and tripod balanced uncomfortably on his shoulder.

"Just beyond the planking a short ways will be fine, ladies," he said, checking back to make sure no one had dropped behind.

"I do hope this will not take up a great deal of time, Mister Cobb. I have chores to finish," one of the ladies chirped.

"You're not done chores, Aster?" admonished another. "Madame will skin your backside."

"It shouldn't take but a few minutes to set up and complete," the photographer replied.

"Madame says she'll withhold my earnings if I don't soak my sore foot before tonight," said another girl who was walking with the help of an ebony cane.

"How did you hurt your foot, Miss?" asked the photographer, assisting her down the stairs.

"I picked up a sliver from those rough floor boards and it's become painfully infected."

"I'm so sorry to hear of it," he said.

"That must've hurt something crazy, Maryanne."

"It was just awful. Course it still hurts like stingin' nettles. That's why I've got to walk slow, Mr. Cobb."

"I understand, Miss. And I'm sure Madame appreciates your making the effort to join us."

"Oh I'd do anything for Madame, Mister Cobb. She's been an angel in my life."

"Now don't go overdoin' it, Maryanne," one of the ladies urged.

"What're you talking, Gina? Madame has given me a home and a career. More'n I ever dreamed of."

"If you can call strokin' a dozen different peckers a week and getting smacked up like I did a few weeks ago a career, I guess you got it, honey. One day I hope to do something else, run my own business. What do you think, Myrtle?"

"I think what that bastard did to you was terrible, Gina. And I hope the Lord boils his balls in acid. But in general, and I mean compared to some places I've worked, the *Oasis* is a first-class whorehouse."

"Please don't call it that," Maryanne pleaded. "That sounds so demeaning. I think Madame goes to great pains to teach us the most important things we need to know to please a man, even cooking and keeping house," Maryanne interjected. "Look how many girls she's married off to fine men."

"For the right price."

"And after they pass the most important test."

"Now ain't that the truth," Myrtle giggled.

"I think you girls are talking shamefully," Maryanne admonished.

"Maryanne, perhaps we could talk about something else, something that doesn't offend you so," Aster suggested, winking at Myrtle.

"Ladies, this will make an excellent site for a photograph," the man spoke up. "There's no need to go further."

"We're grateful, Mr. Cobb. We do have to conserve our energy," said Gina, bringing a snicker from the others.

Posing the ladies against a dune, Cobb hovered over his camera set-up, first aligning the legs of his tripod, then preparing the light-sensitive picture plates. Huddled beneath a black drapery he adjusted the focusing ring and called out.

"Please look over my shoulder and smile, ladies. Stay absolutely still. Excellent. Thank you, you may relax. I'll set up for one more, though, so please don't wander off too far."

None of the ladies moved away. Aster waved a large hand fan to create a cooling effect.

"Lord but it's fiercely hot today," she said.

"Hotter than Felicity's boodle for Mr. Malcolm?" Myrtle inquired.

Aster laughed aloud.

"That old turkey! Now there's a slow ride."

"Ain't she just hopin' he fixes title from one of his mining properties to her name before his great big heart winds down."

"A dream we've all had at one time or another, I dare say," Maryanne volunteered.

"Mr. Cobb, what'd you say Madame is going to do with these photographs?"

He poked his head from beneath the cape.

"She's going to print up a handbill and affix a photograph to the page. To advertise the *Oasis* a little further abroad."

"Lord, I wonder what she won't think of next."

The photographer disappeared behind his camera again.

"Alright, ladies," he called out, "I'm ready when you are. Can you please smile once more and stand completely still? That's perfect. Hold that now. Thank you."

The ladies began walking back from where they'd come. At the top of the stairs waited Madame Rosalba herself, a spreading hillock of flesh and fabric, exotic smells and potted colors. Her countenance, however, reflected singular impatience.

"Well, Mr. Cobb?" she inquired.

"I believe the photographs will turn out fine, Madame. I'll develop the plates straightaway."

"For which I'd be most grateful." she pronounced heavily. " I don't know what I'll do if I can't attract more business soon."

The ladies immediately stopped walking.

"You wouldn't turn us out would you, Madame?" Maryanne asked plaintively.

Madame moved beside Maryanne and draped a soft, waxen arm over the girl's forearm.

"*Pobrecita*, I didn't mean to frighten you, I just want to be honest with all of you. The money's just not coming in fast enough to pay the bills."

"We'll do our best to help out, Madame," Gina said.

"You always do," Madame Rosalba soothed. "You know how proud I am of all of you. My beautiful girls. We have all seen quite enough of this economic depression. At least today is payday for most surviving businesses."

They continued slowly along the boardwalk, their footsteps mixed with the sound of waves nudging the beach and the caw of seagulls cavorting nearby.

"Madame," broke in Myrtle. "I've scuffed my new kid shoes

and was hoping you might know how I could remove the stain."

"They're white?" Madame Rosalba inquired.

"Yes, Madame."

"Dip a clean flannel in a little ammonia, there's some in the kitchen. Then rub the cloth over a soap cake and polish the scuff away, though not too hard."

"Thank you, Madame."

"Madame," Aster next inquired. "I was wondering how to perk up my dark velvet dress. It's starting to look a little dusty."

"Sprinkle a little beach sand on it and brush it away," Madame offered. "Mind you don't brush too hard, velvet is much more delicate than cambric."

"Yes, Madame. Thank you Madame."

"De rien."

From the side of the house an elderly man approached the entourage and bowed humbly before Madame Rosalba. He extended a silver tray upon which was placed a business card.

"What is it, Abram?"

"A businessman, Madame," he said, "waiting in the drive out front."

Madame read the card aloud. "Mr. James Robinson, bicycle salesman and riding instructor." She turned to her followers. "Well ladies, are you interested in viewing his merchandise?"

"Oh yes, Madame," Gina said enthusiastically, "bicycles are such fun. I'm thinking of taking lessons."

"You aren't," Aster reproached.

"I am, too. So I can ride to the city."

"A gentleman told me the city council's planning to build a tremendously long bicycle path near the water's edge," Maryanne said.

"Bicycles are a fine way to break your skull. Or damage other parts," Aster warned Gina.

"I quite agree, Aster," Madame interjected. "They're nothing but a passing fad. In any event, girls, go and see the bicycle man but be quick about it. See if you can lure the gentleman in for some ..." and here she paused, "tea. After he's completed his business. Now I must attend to some accounting."

With that she turned into a side door. The ladies paused.

"Please excuse me," Myrtle said. "I'm not much interested in bicycles. I think I'll go inside and clean my shoes." She turned and followed Madame into the house.

Near to the front entrance, James Robinson waited nervously atop a rouge-colored bicycle to see who might emerge. Though 23, Robinson led a sheltered life and experienced little contact with immodest or coarse persons. His life and character were beginning to change however, thanks to new confidence from a budding career selling bicycles.

The idea of venturing to the *Oasis* had struck him the day before when he was brainstorming with another company agent about where he might expand his sales territory. The agent snickered when Robinson, in jest, suggested stopping by the *Oasis*, but then he pledged that if Robinson didn't tempt the devil, he would. Robinson, who had never previously visited a house of ill repute nor even come face-to-face with a prostitute as far as he was aware, determined that he would breach the *Oasis* though he could only vaguely imagine the acts of carnal knowledge that the bordello represented.

Catching sight of the ladies approaching from the side of the house, Robinson's heart began to cannonade within his chest. He swiped a comb through his hair and stared a few extra seconds before sucking in a measure of air and removing his hat as he had practised.

"Good afternoon, ladies," he said, bobbing his head. "James Robinson at your service. Bicycle salesman and riding instructor."

"Good afternoon," Aster proffered. "We haven't much time, Mr. Robinson, so please don't dally or Madame will scold us all."

Robinson paused nervously before continuing. "You're in a hurry, I can understand that, so I'll show you some of the features that make Weiler bicycles the greatest pieces of engineered machinery known to the world." Robinson flipped the bike upside down and gave the back wheel a spin. "You can see for yourself the wheel spins flawlessly. That you won't find on any other bicycle except a Weiler." He rubbed his sleeve across a sweaty face.

"But the most spectacular accomplishment found in this machine is in the frame," he continued, righting the bike and bouncing it on its tires. "Ladies, the frame of this bicycle is made of precision-forged, diamond steel. This frame has been especially designed by Weiler engineers so that you can ride a bicycle for hours, even days, without feeling tired."

"Mr. Robinson, could you slow down a little, please," Maryanne requested. "It's so hot today, my head just can't keep up with your speech."

"Yes ma'am, I understand perfectly," Robinson acquiesced.

"Mr. Robinson," Aster interrupted. "Why would anyone ride a bicycle for an entire day?"

Robinson stared hard at Aster, struggling to retain composure. "That's a very good question. The answer is, ma'am, the bicycle is going to replace the horse as a method of transportation."

"It is?"

"Yes, ma'am. It's already done so in many European cities, where thousands of people, women, too, are riding bicycles everywhere, to work, to the country. And soon you'll see the same thing here."

"Are you sure you're not just stretching the truth a little bit, Mr. Robinson?" Maryanne cut in. "I mean, there's hardly any roadways around here to ride one of those bicycles."

"That's right, Maryanne," Aster said. "And how do people ride those things up hills and mountains? I'll bet it's very difficult."

"I can't imagine riding a bicycle around San Francisco," Maryanne continued. "I'm certain the hills are much too steep."

"You girls aren't giving Mr. Robinson a chance to finish," Gina said. "I think bicycles have a very promising business future. And I'll tell you another thing. You don't have to look after a bicycle the way you have to mind a horse."

Robinson nodded enthusiastically. "Thank you, ma'am. That's so true. If you've ever kept a horse, you'll know that they're big and they aren't at all like a bicycle."

Aster smiled. "I appreciate the obvious differences between a horse and a bicycle, Mr. Robinson. And I imagine that riding a bicycle, like riding a stallion, as we sometimes do in our business, requires a lot of stamina. Don't you think so, ladies?"

The other women giggled but said nothing. Robinson looked perplexed but continued.

"Yes, ma'am, and I can tell you that right now Weiler engineers are designing a bicycle that will help people ride up mountainsides with no more effort than taking a promenade."

"Well, that is fascinating," Aster spoke up, "but now you'll have to excuse me, Mr. Robinson. I must tend to my chores."

"And I must soak my foot," Maryanne said, "though I have enjoyed myself. Are you coming, Gina."

"Not just yet. I want to hear more of what Mr. Robinson has to say."

"Alright. Bye then. Nice to meet your acquaintance, Mr. Robinson," Maryanne volunteered.

"Maybe you'll come inside for some nice cool lemonade when you're finished here, Mr. Robinson," Aster offered.

Robinson studied the women intensely as they walked away, his jaw hanging slack.

"Mr. Robinson," Gina said. "I have never driven a bicycle. Is it difficult?"

He turned to stare at Gina. "Sorry, ma'am?"

"I asked if it is difficult to master the bicycle?"

"Not at all. A young child can ride a bicycle. Watch me."

Robinson jumped astride the bicycle and wobbled forward for a few strokes. "See. It's easy as lard."

"You're very accomplished," Gina called out to him. "Would you be able to show me some basics?"

Robinson came to a halt and jumped off. "Why yes, ma'am. Just hop on the seat and I'll have you riding this bicycle in a few minutes."

Gina lifted her skirt and delicately positioned herself upon the seat. "It's not at all comfortable for a woman," she complained, wriggling her bottom.

Robinson tried to determine what she could possibly mean by this. "Sometimes it takes a little getting used to, ma'am," was all he could manage by way of reply.

"Very well, what do I do next?"

"Well, ma'am," he said, placing one arm upon her hips for support and using his other to help guide the handlebars. "You just pump your legs and drive forward. Why don't you try it slowly?"

Together, they made cautious, unsteady progress over six feet. Robinson laughed nervously under his breath.

"It would be easier if you stopped shaking so much, Mr. Robinson," Gina said.

"I'm sorry, ma'am. I'm just so hot," Robinson chattered, wiping an arm over his sweating brow.

"Let's keep trying," Gina urged.

After sundown, gentle, loping waves glided forward under moonlight, signed brief signatures in the beach sand and then retreated to opaque depths. Onshore, cooling vapors that rolled in from the bay relieved the sticking heat and blended with the scent of evening primrose. The air also supported the sounds of the pulsing tide, calling birds, coyote yips and a steady tattoo beat out by cicadas.

Nighttime at the *Oasis*, a din of human activities muted the sounds of nature. Jagged piano chords punctuated bellowing laughter, stories stoked by thunderous embellishments, shrieks and trills of surprise, doors opening and closing and drink glasses slamming down on hardened, polished wood. In darkened rooms, velvet and silk rustled against dusty linen, rough cotton and dirty wool, mixing with the sounds of hurried love-making, fleshy smacks, kisses, grunts.

The main parlor, furnished with dark-stained tables and chairs, was filled largely with brash, horny men discussing mining, railroading, banking or timber, weaving stories about gangs of Chinese thieves, and carefully studying the ladies who breezed in and through the room. Anxiety and relief charged the atmosphere, creating friction as when a thunderhead arises in a blue sky.

James Robinson sat alone at a table, a mixture of nervous tension and lassitude. His hand gripped an empty drink glass while his head bobbed around the parlor or stared into space. At times his mouth dropped open and the ends of his lips curled up into a half-smile. His eyes were glassy, unfocused.

An excess of gin had reduced Robinson's recent memory to a jumble of tangled events. The bicycle lesson with Gina had not continued long before she was summoned inside. He started back toward the city but stopped to rest by the side of the road and eat some bread he had carried with him in a shoulder pack. As the sun began sliding from the sky he rode back to the *Oasis* where he leaned his bicycle against a tree and ventured inside. Greeted by Madame Rosalba, he asked after Miss Gina and was directed to the parlor where he drank down several shots of liquor in giddy anticipation.

Eventually Gina appeared in a white dress trimmed with blue stipples and pink brocade, a radiant mirage to Robinson. She told him she would be occupied for some time but would return later. Since then, Robinson continued to sip at the gin and consume the sights and sounds around him.

Two men entered the parlor, boisterous roughnecks who steered each other about arm in arm. As per regulations posted in the main foyer, the men had secured curling ties about their necks but the rest of their fashion was rumpled and indelicate, grimy and dust-caked.

"Lord jinglin' Jesus, I could use a drink," one of the men said, reeling about.

Madame Rosalba hustled into the room after them.

"Gentlemen, might I help you to a table?" she asked, pulling out a chair.

"That's real nice of you, ma'am," said the noisy one. "And would you send around the bartender real quick. We're thirstier'n desert nomads."

"It's the truth, ma'am," said the other one, at a lower volume.

"You're not already drunk, are you?" Madame Rosalba asked sternly.

"No, ma'am, we haven't touched a drop," said the second one. "My friend here, he's wound up like this all the time. A real coyote."

"What're you talking?" said the noisemaker. "You'll be sorry if you get lippy with me."

"Sir," Rosalba interrupted, "what would you like to drink?"

He grinned up at her from a bearded, sun-toasted face. "Whisky, ma'am. A large glass of whisky."

"I'll bring you a bottle," she said, studying him for an additional moment before turning away.

"Another thing, ma'am," he bellowed after her. "Send us out two of your fillies soon as we're finished our drinks."

A room was set aside in the rear of the *Oasis* where the ladies washed up and freshened their perfume after they had finished with their customers. The room had been partitioned into a series of private alcoves in which were stationed washing basins, full-length mirrors, chairs and dressers. An ornate wood stove for use during cool weather perched in a corner and several plush chairs and a comfortable divan rested nearby.

On this July night, traffic in the back room was moderately brisk. Several of the alcoves were occupied and Maryanne reclined on the divan, faintly pumping a sandalwood hand fan to cool her face.

"What I wouldn't give to be a fish swimming in the ocean tonight," she said.

"Or to be sitting on a mountain top, next to a big sheet of ice," said Aster, emerging from behind a bamboo door.

"I think I'd rather be a fish," Maryanne continued, "swimming this way and that, floating along. You'd have to climb your mountain first to get to the top, and Lord I don't feel like climbing any mountains tonight."

"That's a point," Aster added, standing next to the divan. "Maryanne, would you be a sweet thing and button me in the back?"

"I guess I could do that," Maryanne said, slowly getting to her feet. "Are you keeping busy?"

"I've been busier."

Madame Rosalba came through the door into the room on a pulse of bustling satin. She frequently checked on her girls through the course of business and sped things along whenever possible.

"Hello Maryanne, Aster," she announced, on her way to a window which she tried in vain to open wider than its capacity. "Isn't it hotter than Hades tonight. I only wish I could cut away the roof for a few hours. Then we'd get some relief."

"What a wonderful idea. Then I could lay in bed and watch the stars," said Maryanne.

"After you were finished with business," Aster said.

"Speaking of business, do you have anything new to report?" Madame Rosalba queried.

"I was just going out, ma'am," Maryanne said.

"I finished with that railroad man. He was real serious, but he gave a five-dollar tip," Aster said.

"Excellent. I hope he'll visit again. Now I know that Sarah is occupied. But have you ladies seen any of the others?"

"I'm right here, madame," said Gina, from behind one of the partitions. "I'm just fixing up."

"That's fine, precious," Madame Rosalba continued. "I wanted to tell you there's a young, anxious looking man in the front parlor who has asked after you."

"Oh, I completely forgot. That's Mr. Robinson, the bicycle man."

"And there are two newcomers sipping whisky at a table as well."

"I'm going out in just a minute, madame," Aster said.

"There's no rush. They're a little excited, is all. Maryanne, perhaps you could freshen drinks. Thank you, ladies."

Her brood accounted for, Madame Rosalba turned and exited the room. As if on cue, Maryanne turned and slumped into a chair.

"Oh Lucifer, it's too hot to think about working tonight," she said with finality.

In the front parlor the noise level had attained a steady pitch, jagged and mesmerizing. Over the chatter of honky-tonk piano, men laughed raucously one moment, then strained to focus through the smoky fug at a woman or a painting on the wall.

Into empty glasses the two new men poured large second measures of whisky. The quieter man rolled himself a cigarette and lit it with a flaring match. Periodically, the other man twitched, as a train locomotive might belch out a puff of smoke. He gulped half a glassful of whisky to help control his pent up energy.

"Where the hell are those whores?" he demanded.

"Take it easy, Parrot," his friend said. "They'll be here. Do you see the one you got tangled up with last time?"

"No, I ain't, but I tell you partner that dolly was the sweetest piece of business I ever plugged. Had skin soft as a cow's udder."

"Ooo-eee. And I'll bet you can't wait to get a-milkin'!"

"You got that right, partner."

Gina emerged from a darkened side of the room and hustled up to Robinson's table where she placed a hand upon his arm. He pushed a chair back and struggled to his feet, trying to focus his eyes.

"Mr. Robinson, I am sorry for having kept you waiting. I was helping a friend with a personal problem."

Straining from the confluence of alcohol and adrenalin, Robinson elected his words carefully. "And is everything alright now?" he inquired.

"Pardon me?"

He tried again. "Your friend. Is she feeling better?"

Gina briefly considered the question. "Yes, thank you for asking. Much better. And have you been enjoying yourself?"

Robinson leaned over the table to be heard more clearly. "I've been thinking about you, Miss Gina."

"That's very sweet, Mr. Robinson. Would you like to go to another room where we could enjoy more privacy?"

Robinson could only stare as he puzzled over the meaning of the sentence. Gina tugged him by the arm. "Come with me."

Together they slowly wove their way through the room, Robinson wavering, Gina smiling stoically and coaxing him along. As they passed by the table where the new men were seated, Pat Parrot looked up and a pulse suddenly drained the color from his face. He jumped to his feet, grabbed Gina by her arm and wrenched her around.

"Hey, dolly, how're you doin?"

Gina was paralyzed by the bear-like grip on her arm and a jabbing pain that took her breath away. Parrot continued, oblivious to Robinson.

"Let's you and me go for a walk."

Released from Gina's hand, Robinson reeled around next to the stranger and bumped up against him.

"What're you doing? This lady's with me," he insisted.

The stranger glanced at Robinson only long enough to find his face with his free hand and push him away. He released Gina's arm for a second then re-clamped it. She yelped.

"Come on, honey pot," Parrot said, trying to drag her along.

Gina summoned her strength and cried out.

"Stop it, you're hurting me!"

He made no motion to loosen his grip so Gina leaned over and bit him on the hand. He squealed and released her momentarily, his eyes flashing like embers.

Madame Rosalba appeared nearby.

"What's the problem here?" she demanded.

Gina backed against a wall, holding her arm and pointing towards the man. "He's the brute who beat me."

Madame Rosalba stared fiercely at the man. "Get out of here, now, before I summon the marshal."

The man tightened like a spring, muscles rippling, and turned to Gina. "You bitch!" he roared and made a move to kick her.

Robinson shoved the man from the side and spoiled his kick.

Like a cat, the man whirled, grabbed Robinson by his hair and drove a fist into his face. Blood spurted almost instantly. A collective gasp went out from people standing nearby. A moment later the stranger drove another fist into Robinson's face. Then another, and another, as fast as he could swing his arm. Robinson collapsed onto the floor and the man fell on top of him, pummeling him.

At first the crowd remained transfixed, inert. A second later Madame Rosalba stepped forward and swung a chair against the man's head. He sprawled on the floor then turned and glowered at his attacker. Pulling himself to his feet, he made a move towards her.

"Somebody stop him," Gina called out.

"Parrot, give it up," the other man called out.

"Bitch!" the man yelled again, collecting himself and lunging towards Madame Rosalba.

He didn't make it. His friend grabbed him from behind and another man blocked him from the side. For several seconds they whirled around before tumbling to the floor. Still the man lashed out.

"Hold him!" Madame Rosalba ordered, stepping in to swing a vase high in the air and smash it against his head. He yelled loudly and tensed his muscles before lying still.

"My God, It's the devil himself," she said, slowly rising to her feet and surveying the now-silent parlour. "Please, ladies, one of you rouse Abram and tell him to fetch a marshal."

"I'll do it, ma'am," someone offered.

Another man spoke up. "Better get a doctor, too. Kid's a real mess."

"Yes," Rosalba added. "Tell Abram to summon the doctor." She pursed her lips and crossed herself. "*Hijo de puta*," she muttered.

Gulls looped lazily over San Francisco Bay under clear skies. All around, boats bobbed up and down like duckpins and maneuvered in and out of berths, belching plumes of smoke, ringing bells and blowing sonorous whistles.

Three blasts blew from the single stack of a rust-smudged steamer nudging into port. The wooden pier lurched slightly at the ship's contact and a ship hand leaped down onto the planks and quickly whirled coils of greasy, limb-sized rope around dock staves. The pier creaked and strained under the stress but halted the boat's momentum. The ship's captain summoned a final whistle blast that emerged as a shock of black smoke and the ship bobbed slowly to rest.

From inside a pocked, squat building next to the berth a man wearing a blue uniform emerged and shuffled toward the bow of the ship, a sheaf of papers pinched in one hand. He squinted, trying to make out the name of the vessel, then approached the ship hand, still yanking on the rope.

"I can't make out the name of your boat for the rust. Who are you and where've you come from."

"We're the *Excelsior*," replied the ship hand.

The agent cocked his head to hear but the answer was lost in a cacophony of laughter and shouting that drifted down from the ship-board crowd gathered at the top of a short gangplank. The agent studied the crowd uneasily for a second then turned back to the ship hand.

"I'm sorry, I couldn't hear. Tell me again," he said.

The ship hand moved closer. "The *Excelsior*. From St. Michael, Alaska."

The agent scribbled down the information. "Alaska. I guess I'd be happy gettin' back to civilization, too, after living in that fiendish wilderness. One fella told me the bugs were so fierce up there he couldn't never drop his pants and have a decent crap. And what he wanted more'n anything else when he first stepped off that gangplank was to find a place where he could sit down and have a dignified shit. Don't ask me why but oh, Lordy, I laughed some when he told me that!"

"These men are happy because they've made a fortune," the ship hand retorted. "Most of em' will never have to work another day in their lives."

"What're you talking'?" the agent queried.

"I guess nobody's heard the news. These here prospectors are bringing out more than a ton of gold."

Wide-eyed, the agent turned to stare a moment longer at the mottled crowd on board the ship. The noise increased as the passengers began disembarking.

"A ton of gold?" he asked, incredulous. "Where the hell'd they get that?"

"The land of dreams," the ship hand shouted. "The Klondike."

Late afternoon traffic on Merton Street was light. Brilliant summer sun bore down on the southwest-facing buildings - Creeman's Rigging and Tackle, Buscanti Brothers Freightage, Millen's Apothecary, the Merton Tavern and Canteen, and an office of the Klamath and Siskyou Metallurgical Company. The intense sunlight had blistered the previous year's paint from the buildings' cedar plank facing, bestowing a shredded, moth-worn appearance to each, the exception being the freightage shop which the brothers had not painted for some years save for a gold-trim sign that curved across the front window.

Each afternoon the sunny side of Merton Street was abandoned in favor of the shady side where human, horse and wagon traffic made its way along knobby cobblestones or spiny boardwalk.

On the roadway a young Chinese laborer pulled on a tump line and struggled beneath a cubic block of dry goods twice his size. A step behind trotted a panting blond and brown mongrel. Looking up, the Chinese noted a buckboard approaching from the opposite direction, re-shifted his load and swerved toward the boardwalk.

"Hey, chinaman, watch where you're goin'!" a rawboned voice bellowed from behind.

Turning his load, the Chinese jostled against a horse and range rider trying to pass.

"Get the hell outa my way, Slant Eyes. Move!"

Jerking hard on the reins, the rider twisted the small horse's head around, causing it to stumble. It fought to regain its footing on the cobblestones. Beside the horse, the small dog started to bark, increasing the horse's frenzy and causing it to retreat.

"Get on, ya bastard," shouted the rider, lashing a short rawhide quirt against the animal's flank. The horse pawed at the air and pumped its head around.

Hoping to snatch the dog away the Chinese dropped his bundle at the side of the road.

"Get the cur, chinaman, or I'm gonna shoot it," demanded the rider.

The Chinese crouched down and stalked forward to grab at the dog. But under a final blow of the whip the horse jumped forward, kicking out. Its hoof struck the Chinese on the forearm, knocking him back. He collapsed on the roadway writhing in pain.

The horse reared, its rider barely hanging on. He lashed the quirt against the animal's neck and yanked on the reins to jerk its head. In a battle of strength the rider won. He directed the horse away from the accident site, spurred its flanks and rode on.

The incident had taken less than half a minute and caught the attention of only a handful of passers-by. No one made a move to help the Chinese lying on the ground as the man and horse trotted off.

Coming down the roadway, the burly, bearded driver concentrated on guiding his horse the horse and wagon around the injured man. A young girl standing in the wagon stared in horror and tugged on the man's arm.

"Pa," she shouted, "that man's hurt."

The man glanced over his shoulder, first at the form on the street then into his daughter's eyes. "He's a chinaman."

looking contemptibly at the Chinese. He pushed past the wagon man. "This here's a bar, not a surgery."

The Chinese suddenly squealed in pain. His face was slick with sweat and he made a move to roll to the side. The wagon man gently laid him in the shoeshine chair.

"That chair's not for chinamen, my friend. It's for paying customers," the server announced from behind the bar.

"Who said I ain't a customer," said the wagon man, wiping a cloth across the injured man's face.

"You haven't bought nothin' yet," the server chipped in.

"Then bring me a glass of water and a whisky." The wagon man turned back to the Chinese. "Rest easy friend, we'll keep lookin' for a doctor."

He stood up and wiped the cloth across his forehead. The server approached with the drinks on a tray.

"Twenty five cents," he said.

The wagon man reached for the drinks. The server pulled the tray back.

"I'm sure you do things differently out on the farm," he spoke sarcastically, "but in this bar you pay up before you drink."

The wagon man glared at the server before digging into his pocket and fingering several coins. He slapped them down on a nearby table then removed the drinks from the tray. He took a gulp from the water then emptied the whisky into the glass and turned to the Chinese.

"Okay partner, drink this down. It's good to kill pain."

The Chinese sipped at the water then choked up. He rolled his head to the side and refused to drink more.

"Come on now," the wagon man urged. "Drink a little more."

"Perhaps he'd prefer a little opium," said a man with a thin mustache wearing a brown suit who had approached and now stood nearby observing the business.

The wagon man turned to appraise the stranger then turned back in frustration. "Well, I don't got no opium," he retorted, "just dog's breath whisky."

"I'm sorry," the stranger said. "I thought perhaps I might be of some help."

"Are you a doctor?"

"No, not a medical doctor. I am a scientist, however, and I am familiar with many details of physiology and anatomy."

"I don't know what the hell you're talkin' about," the farmer said, puzzled.

The suited man looked at him a moment before stepping forward to cradle the injured man's arm and twist it gently.

"He appears to have a radial fracture," he announced, without expression.

"Can you help him?" the farmer asked.

The suited man furrowed his brow and gently bobbed his head. "I believe I can set his arm. Though I'd advise the patient to drink down that whisky before I realign the bones. We'll also need something to support the limb." He swiveled around scanning the nearby tables. "Your broad cloth will have to do for now."

The wagon man undid the mottled cloth draped around his neck and handed it over.

"You're a farmer, aren't you?" the stranger asked.

"Yes, I am. Henry Jacobs is the name. How'd you figure I was a farmer?"

"By your clothes and your hands," he said, refolding the cloth. "They're filthy."

"Yes, I guess they are," Jacobs said, studying them. "I was just comin' from the market when I seen this guy get kicked by a horse. Next thing I know, I'm carrying him door-to-door."

"Perhaps you'd help him imbibe that whisky now," the other man interrupted. "Then we'll set the fracture."

"Sure thing," the wagon man agreed, kneeling next to the Chinese and holding the glass up to his mouth. "Drink this down quick, buddy. That's it. All of it now. He's finished," he said putting the glass on the table.

"Fine. Now you get behind him and restrain him tightly when I pull on the forearm. Ready? I'm straightening the arm ... now."

The Chinese writhed and moaned as though he had been jabbed with a knife. The dog whined in empathy. Customers at the bar watched for a few seconds and then moved away.

"Hey mister, I told you this ain't no surgery," the server shouted out. "You take that heathen Chinaman outta here."

The Chinese suddenly slumped over in the chair.

"There, he's blacked out," said the man in the suit. "It's for the better." He turned to the server and spoke curtly. "We'll be finished here momentarily. Don't bother us again."

"I'm going for Mr. Merton," said the server, walking quickly out the rear of the bar.

"The people of this city have worse manners than the cowboys of the plains," the man in the suit said, wrapping the cloth around the injured man's arm.

"That's just who got this business goin' with him," said Jacobs. "A cowboy."

"I might have figured as much. They're a scroffulous breed."

Jacobs looked confused.

"Tell me, Mr. Jacobs. Where do you live and what do you farm?"

"I sharecrop a few acres in Santa Clara county, a few miles outside of the city. Beans 'n corn n' hogs. Maybe berries next year."

"Sounds very bucolic."

"What'd you say your name was, mister?" Jacobs probed.

"I didn't. But since you're asking I'll tell you. I'm Isaac Fayne of Boston, Massachusetts." He looked up at Jacobs.

"What're you doin' in Frisco"?

"I'm acquiring supplies for a northern expedition to Alaska. I shall be leaving within one or two weeks."

"That's really something," Jacobs spoke sincerely. " I gotta tell my wife."

Fayne got to his feet. "There, the bone has been set and supported. I expect your friend will not have the use of his arm for several weeks however."

"Oh, he ain't my friend," Jacobs said. "I was just driving by with my daughter when I seen ..."

"Get out of my tavern," an older man suddenly shouted from

behind the bar, waving a wooden spindle and approaching quickly. "Hear! Get the hell out or I'll fill your ass full of splinters."

Fayne stood and intercepted the man.

"We are leaving," he said icily, "though I have found the food lacking taste and the ambience of your establishment primitive. Save for a dockyard rat, I wouldn't commend it." He turned to Jacobs. "Are you able to help him out?"

"That'll be no problem," he said, clutching the Chinese and offering him support toward the door.

"I bid you good day," Fayne said, scowling at the owner and tossing a coin to the ground in his direction before he turned and walked to the door.

Just before he reached it, however, the door opened from the outside and a small boy pushed his way inside excitedly and ran head first into Fayne.

"'Scuse me, mister, but there's a whole group of men comin' up here from the water," he shouted, "cayusin' and crazy as bats."

"Whoa, lad. Slow down and tell us your story," Fayne urged him.

"They've just come from a boat, and before that, way up north. They found gold. Some nuggets as big as your fist. I seen 'em myself."

Merton came forward. "And they're comin' here?"

"They're comin' up the street now," the boy shouted. "You can hear 'em."

The men paused and cocked their heads. They heard a noise of boots tromping onto the boardwalk before the door burst open and a soiled, leathery face pushed into the tavern, grinning as wide across as its lips could stretch.

"Yeeeeeeeeehhhaaaaaaaaawwwww!"

Mitchell Toffan ran his hands through thinning gray hair and attempted to focus his thoughts on the white page lying flat beneath his nose. He repeatedly dipped a plumed pen into an inkwell but suspended a motion to continue writing. The words on his tongue could not be coaxed into text. In frustration, Toffan deposited his pen into the well, pushed his body back from the desk and rose up, unfolding as a great blue heron. He strode to a mahogany cabinet on which rested a massive mine rock streaked with fingers of silver, a fine crystal decanter and a plaque acknowledging the contribution of Toffan's newspaper, the *San Francisco Shield*, in a fund-raising drive for orphaned children.

Toffan removed a small glass from within the buffet, lifted the decanter and poured out two fingers of amber-colored rum. Holding the glass delicately, he turned and walked back toward his desk where he again studied the page resting upon it. One hand reached out to scratch a large, black cat that was curled up and sleeping on the edge of the desk. Toffan's head jerked up and he broke the silence with a barking laugh.

"I tell you, Judas, It doesn't matter a cobbler's last if I tell the Commerce Association unmitigated piffle or quote New Testament scriptures, the scruffy rodents'll make plans tonight to string up another chinaman. The best I can do is help their piles along before they lynch me!"

He hurled back the contents of the glass into his mouth and slammed it down on his desk. Snatching up the piece of paper, he waved it through the air and began a rehearsal of his speech with dramatic arm movements.

"Esteemed gentlemen of San Francisco. I am honored to stand before you this evening. To share with you my optimism that the current economic recession will reverse itself and that a new era of prosperity will soon be sweeping through our fair land. I know this for a fact because today I had lunch with the devil and he told me it was so. And he told me to extend his personal greetings to each and every one of you!"

At his joke Toffan again burst out laughing and turned to retrieve the decanter.

"I'll bet they wouldn't flinch if I told them their seats were reserved in Hell."

He poured another drink and inhaled the strong thick vapor before gulping it down. He sat back down though he made no move to resume writing.

"I wonder what this world is coming to, Judas. Everybody as reckless as dinosaurs and headed for a fiery afterlife. Including the honorable women of the Church League and their poodles!"

Toffan started to laugh once more but was interrupted by a knock at the door.

"Friend or Foe?" he shouted out.

"It's Bunty, Mr. Toffan. I've heard of a big story breaking on the waterfront."

"Then come in, Bunty," Toffan ordered, "and enlighten me."

The door opened and Frank Bunty, a young man wearing a light brown suit, his face bisected by a curling, waxed mustache and ragged pink scar, stepped across the smooth wooden floor into the office. Toffan waved his hand.

"Pull up a chair, Bunty, and tell me your story."

Bunty remained standing.

"A steamer has just docked from Alaska, Mr. Toffan, the *Excelsior.*"

"That's grand news, Bunty," Toffan interjected. "I'm glad I can count on my reporters to keep me informed of the most significant events in the western hemisphere. In this case, a boat from Alaska has taken a berth in our dockyards and a second moon has risen in the afternoon sky. Am I correct?"

"Well, sir, apparently the passengers are quite rich with gold. A lot of gold."

"How much gold, Bunty?" Toffan demanded, still irreverent.

"The report I got said more than a ton of gold. In flakes and nuggets."

Toffan parsed this information in his head, then rolled his eyes to the ceiling.

"Flakes and nuggets. So these people are prospectors, common unwashed bush monkeys. Only now they're rich." His eyes sparkled. "For centuries, Bunty, people have searched for elusive riches in the wilderness. And it's still a story when one of the suckers gets a strike. Matter of fact, it keeps people like me in business."

Toffan pushed himself to his feet and strode to the door.

"Come on, Bunty. Let's walk together in our scuffed boots

down to the docks to hear the latest from El Dorado. Who knows, I might write a story for the morning edition myself."

Liam Minney rubbed his eyes with dusty palms to discharge the stinging sweat crimping his vision. Instinctively, he reached into a back pocket low down on his hip and tugged out a ragged, filthy cloth to wipe his glistening brow. He felt limp under the blazing sun and craved rest.

A guttural voice bellowed nearby.

"Get off your ass, Minney! Hoist this crate or go hungry. I thought you knew how to do a day's work."

"I'll hoist it when I can see what I'm doing," Minney wheezed. He squinted at the figure standing in the back of the oversized buckboard. "Why don't you help, Harlow? I signed on for this job as a worker not a slave."

"Slaves don't get paid, Minney," Harlow retorted. "I'm paying you for the heavy lifting around here, remember."

"Five dollars a day ain't any wage, Harlow."

"Fuck you, Minney. Go back to scrapin' up fuckin' potatoes out of that gravel bed you call a farm if you don't like my wages. Who do you think you are, Thomas fucking Edison?"

Minney flinched. Gripped by frustration built up by years of too much work for too little return, by failure piled on failure, by four children and mounting stress, he rued the day he emigrated from Ireland for a new start in America. He wanted to seize Harlow and shake him and bellow in his ear for a change. Instead he channeled his anger into his shoulders and thighs and gripped the bottom of the crate and heaved into it. The crate slid up the planks and into the wagon as if it was greased, slamming into the load already parked.

"Watch what you're doing, you slut!" shouted Harlow. "If any merchandise is damaged I'll take it out of your pay, Minney."

"I've earned a break," Minney announced, again wiping his brow and then rubbing knuckles that ached with arthritis.

He walked over to a crude pine bench under a gabled awning. He splashed water on his face from a rusty bowl and then sunk face down onto the bench. The anger drained out of him and was replaced by fatigue the moment he shut his eyes.

After a few minutes Minney reached under the bench and slid out a dirt-encrusted haversack. As he rummaged inside for the knob of bread he had thrown inside that would serve as his lunch, he unearthed a crumpled newspaper underneath the bag. His burning eyes scanned the headlines and he slowly ciphered the words. He read them a second time and then stared at the photos etched in fading ink. His mouth felt as dry as sand and his heart began to pound as he read the headlines again: "World's Richest Gold Strike Discovered in Klondike – Common Men Now Millionaires". The photo showed nuggets piled high on a miner's scale.

"It's immoral and must be stopped, Reverend. There has been no peace for two days now. Sin has overtaken us."

Reverend William Benning listened to a diminutive, plain woman sitting across from him while passively observing a shower of dust glittering in a shaft of golden light slanting in from a rooftop window in the ceiling of the church rectory. The sultry heat of late afternoon in combination with the fusty air of the rectory blunted his senses. He shifted his weight atop the pine stool on which he sat to refocus his attention and cleared his throat.

"I agree, Miss Kettle," he recited. "The arrival of the prospectors has triggered the most licentious and disagreeable behavior."

Kettle poked a waxen finger into the dust shower. "Though I have not yet borne my own, I am gravely worried for the children of our city, Reverend. There is no haven or refuge within our geography that has not been victimized by this plague. Children are in danger of being recruited into Satan's legions."

Benning nodded. "Yes, that is always a possibility. One must be strong to resist temptation."

Kettle prattled on. "All this talk of gold erodes morality. It creeps into the spirit like a rotting fungus and weakens the righteous character. Men and women are perverted by its very essence, Mr. Benning, don't you agree?"

"Amen, Miss Kettle. Amen," said Benning, toweling his face.

Her voice rose in defiance. "We must face the horned beast, Mr. Benning. We must banish it from our midst and drive it back into its cave. That's what the other ladies and I have decided."

"And how do you imagine you might perform this feat, Miss Kettle?" Benning queried.

A Bible appeared in her bony hand. "The Word of our Lord will prevail, Mr. Benning. With your help and with exhortations from this temple and these pews we shall banish the beast. You will help us, won't you?"

"Indeed I will, Miss Kettle, though I noted very few goldminers attending yesterday's service."

"Then we must trumpet The Word from the street, Mr. Benning."

Kettle paused then pleaded with him. "We must rout the beast from the dark corners where it hides. We must or all is lost."

She covered her eyes and a haunting wail arose from her shaking body.

Reverend Benning rose from his stool and placed a hand on her shoulder. "Console yourself, Miss Kettle."

She continued to sob. "Don't you see?" she shrieked angrily. "The dark days are upon us, Reverend. As it says in Revelations, we shall all perish."

"There, there, Miss Kettle. We have strength to draw on."

"Oh my Bible comforts me, Reverend. But when I think of the children .... I ... I am so gripped with fear, I want to lash out and grip someone tightly about the throat until their breath is extinguished. Is that natural, Reverend, or am I in Satan's grip as well?"

Reverend Benning stared again into the golden dust shower but did not answer her question. "There, there, Miss Kettle," he recited.

"Oh, Reverend, I am so afraid," she sobbed spasmodically. "I see only darkness around me and I'm so afraid."

From the moment the prospectors trundled down the gangway of the *Excelsior* they proved a disparate lot. Returning to civilization carried different meanings to each of them. Many were returning with what they considered fortunes, ranging between ten thousand dollars in dust and nuggets earned in wages working placer gold holdings to many more thousands of dollars. All appeared satisfied. Some paused to pitch their belongings into the oily harbor water, a symbolic gesture in keeping with crossing the threshold from common laborer to millionaire. Some clutched their fortune in dirty canvas rucksacks, shook hands with traveling companions and stole away quietly to safeguard their treasure and privacy. Others who had stowed their share of gold in the ship's safe waited as a group while the captain of the *Excelsior* oversaw the unloading and transportation of the safe to an office of the First American Bank a few blocks away. A couple of men knelt down and kissed the grimy pier, while a few others yelled and yipped in celebration. Some asked directions to the nearest hotel and tavern to consummate their arrival partaking of pleasures they had done without for many months.

Word of the ship's arrival and the remarkable story it carried spread through San Francisco like a telegraph message, transforming the city in a few hours as an anthill stirs to chaotic frenzy when it's prodded by a stick. Crowds of people surged through the streets, absorbing the stories of the Klondike like arid soil soaking up rain. Few got close enough to hear a real prospector tell his tale so shards of stories were repeated among friends and complete strangers. Banks exchanging gold nuggets and flakes for paper money had to hire extra men to guard the caches of golden lucre accumulating in safes. Within two days banks ran out of paper currency and printed authorized notes as substitutes.

San Francisco newspapers created their own bonanza in the wake of the *Excelsior's* arrival, competing with each other to get stories out on the streets where they sold out in minutes. Greasing facts with liberal dollops of fantasy, the papers quickly elevated the news of the Klondike to mythical status, self-fuelling the story-lust that gripped the port like a typhoon.

The *San Francisco Shield*, guided by veteran editor and publisher Mitchell Toffan, quadrupled its circulation and printed special 'Land of Gold' supplements. In a deft move to scoop or match the competing papers, Toffan booked a suite of rooms at the elegant *Jade Pacific* hotel and enticed several prospectors to book in as guests of the *Shield*, provided that they recounted their stories exclusively to the *Shield*. It was an astute strategy that paid off handsomely in the *Shield's* favor, with Toffan personally overseeing or interviewing the prospectors-turned-gentlemen each day over a sumptuous meal in the hotel's *Redwood* dining room.

Two days after the docking of the *Excelsior*, Toffan arrived in the *Redwood* room in early afternoon and strode to a polished table where two other men were seated. One was reporter Frank Bunty, who had been toiling under Toffan's supervision taking notes, writing and editing copy for the paper and delegating tasks to a trio of cub reporters newly recruited to keep up with a demand for stories; the other was well-known author and traveler A.E. Chester.

"Hello, Ambrose," Toffan said, seating himself, and extending a hand to Chester. "I thought you were kicking around Mexico, regaling the public with tales of bougainvillea and cactus liqueur."

"I've been back a couple of weeks. My gout proved too much to bear in that damned heat."

"What can I do for you, Ambrose? If it's medicine you're after, you'd best try the druggist."

"You always were succinct, Mitchell."

"Hell, we're going flat out telling the world the most important news story in twenty years, Ambrose. Two days into the story and this town's almost out of booze and I'm running low on adjectives. Any chance I can buy some from a skilled wordsmith like yourself?"

"I'm spoken of for the moment, Mitchell. Of course, I'll be traveling to the Klondike to see it myself. In fact, I've been hired by California's finest congressman to complete a preliminary report on the gold strike.

"Excellent. Braithwaite and that lickspittle band of rogues he appointed deserve a good yarn now and then just like the rest of us."

"When I learned that you'd corralled some of the fortune seekers I thought I'd ask you a favor."

"I'm listening. Just don't ask me to part with a bottle of rum or borrow one of my reporters. It's damn hard work keeping up with men who are trying to spend their fortune."

"Well, I need to catch up with these prospectors, to ask them some questions."

"So would every other paper in the country, Ambrose. But the *Shield* is always open to the right business proposition."

"What do you think is fair value for chatting up these unwashed bush rats holed up here."

"You'd best be careful how you describe them, Ambrose. Some of San Francisco's finest whores have scrubbed hard on those dirty parts. I know, I hired them, too, to help keep those bush rats satisfied for a few days until they wander off to God knows where, if they haven't spent all their riches. But I'll tell you flat off, if you want access to the men stuffed in here on my account, it'll cost you a share of my expenses."

"I told Braithwaite this was going to cost him so you bill me what you think is fair."

"And your account will reflect the very high respect I hold for that band of highwaymen protecting the interests of this nation."

"Just don't bill me for any disinfectant."

"Agreed."

"I should tell you, Mr. Toffan," Bunty cut in. "we're down to eight prospectors still checked in. Filmon and Dickinson were recently piled into bed after drinking themselves and a group of saloon rats into a stupor. Filmon threw up his guts by the side door before he passed out. For most of the morning, Swenson has had three girls locked in his bedroom and he recently rang for food and drink."

"It's important for a man to keep his strength up in times of warfare," Toffan said sarcastically.

"I can't interview a bunch of drunks," Chester said, emphatically.

"Oh, no?" Toffan retorted. "Then perhaps you'd care to make a suggestion on behalf of the United States government as to how exactly one learns about the greatest gold discovery since Forty Nine? These men are drunk because they've earned it chipping their nuggets and flakes in Hades. I tell you, if a fraction of what these men have told me is true, the Klondike is going to make the Sierra Nevada and Pike's Peak look like a church picnic. But don't take my word for it. Here comes one of our intrepid argonauts now, and he looks surprisingly composed. Hello, Schmidt!" Toffan stood and waved at a man with slicked-down, short hair and new denim coveralls walking through the restaurant.

"Good day, Mr. Toffan."

"I'd like to introduce you to a friend of mine. Will you join us?"

A humble looking man with a bony, taut face approached the table. "Alright. I'll have some food while I'm here."

"Excellent," said Toffan. "Ambrose, this is Gram Schmidt of Klondike fame. Gram, this is Ambrose Egerton Chester, A.E. Chester the writer. Perhaps you've read one of his best selling books, like 'Sagebrush Stories' or 'Land of the White Buffalo'."

"Sorry, I've never been much of a reader. Not in English or German."

"Don't worry about it, Schmidt. Mr. Chester is now in the employ of the United States Congress, charged with the task of informing our esteemed government about the fabled land of gold. Ambrose, you'll be interested to know Mr. Schmidt has remained respectfully sober since returning to civilization."

"I'm pleased to meet you, Mr. Schmidt," Chester said. "I expect you've earned a rest."

"I've pretty well caught up on my rest. I expect I'll push off for home soon."

"And where is your home?" Chester asked.

"Well, I've been away from Wisconsin for several years now. But I'd like to return there."

"Tell me, Mr. Schmidt," Chester continued. "Are you a wealthy man?"

"I suppose I am, Mr. Chester."

"You've cashed in your gold?"

"I did. Yesterday."

"Can you disclose the amount of gold you returned with?"

"I'd prefer to keep the amount secret, Mr. Chester. I will only say that I now have more money than I ever imagined."

"Wouldn't you rather travel the world? Visit Paris or London?" asked Toffan.

"That's not for me, Mr. Toffan. I'm a working man and I've dreamed of starting a farm all my life. I can do that now."

A woman approached the table. "Can I get you gentlemen something to eat or drink?" she inquired.

"I'll have a glass of beer," said Toffan.

"I'd like a meal of potatoes," said Schmidt.

The other men declined and the woman retreated from the table.

Chester continued asking questions. "Mr. Schmidt, do you think the Klondike will yield more gold?"

"I think there's gold enough up there for any man willing to dig down into the frozen muck to find it. I never seen so much gold as some men found in their pans. Like that Dickinson fellow, his claim on Forty Mile Creek cleaned up two, three thousand dollars a day for nigh a month or more."

"Three thousand dollars," Chester said, incredulous.

"That's right. His paystreak was the richest I heard of. But he sold his claim, like me, and now there's hundreds more men crawling over the hills and workin' the creeks. Some of them'll come out rich men. Not many. Some will die trying."

"I've heard that some men just dug into the muck and shoveled out gold. Or was that just a story that Mr. Toffan authored."

"For a few men it was that easy. But I worked hard, Mr. Chester. Harder'n I ever worked in my life last winter, when the temperature was sixty degrees below zero on days dark as night and our food supplies was wormy flour and navy beans. Those were the good days. We went hungry on the others."

"We?"

"I had a partner. I sold my share of the claim to him when I had what I figured was enough gold. He's still there."

"Mr. Schmidt even sawed off three of his partner's toes that froze solid," Bunty added.

"That's right. I had to, before gangrene took his foot and maybe his whole leg. Or killed him."

"Please be sure to inform Congress, Ambrose," Toffan interrupted, "on the importance of counting one's fingers and toes in the land of gold."

"Evidently," Chester said. "Tell me, Mr. Schmidt, what is the most expeditious route to the Klondike today"?

"Well it's a long, long ways into largely uncharted territory Mr. Chester. Over the tallest mountains you've ever seen or up the blasted Yukon River. A dangerous route, no matter how you try. No doubt many men will try to reach it now that word of the strike is out. Many of them won't make it."

"How do you know?"

At that moment the waitress returned to the table with a plate of food that she deposited in front of Schmidt.

"I can't tell you for sure, Mr. Chester, but it's an infernal journey." Schmidt stared into space then lowered his face to the meal below. " Excuse me, if you don't mind, I'd like to eat my dinner."

"Let the man enjoy his repast in peace, Ambrose," Toffan chimed in. "He's earned it."

"I've never heard of anything like it. It's incredible. But you know as well as I do, Windy, these newspaper stories have had more make-up applied than the clowns in the circus. You don't know what to believe and what's a load of tosh."

"I know what I need to know, Phinius. There's gold up there and we need to be angling for a piece of it. If we miss out now, we might not get another crack at it."

Phinius Grant and Windy Woolner stared hard at each other. Woolner sat rigid as a cat in a hard-backed hickory chair and ran his fingers through a thatch of gray hair atop his head. Grant rocked slightly on his heels. Both men were resting in the Reno offices of the Olympia Mining Company. On Woolner's oaken desktop rested a wrinkled copy of the *San Francisco Shield*, graced by the headline "How They Did It – and How You Can, Too".

Woolner lifted his six-foot four frame from his chair and with the help of a silver-tipped cane hobbled over to a yellowing mine map adorned with colored, wriggling lines tacked onto his wall. He rapped the map with his cane.

"You and I know that unless we find an extension of the #8 vein, we've got another 2-3 years left in the *Silver Chalice* and then we're dry. The great mines have all been discovered in this area, Phinius. We need to look abroad."

"There's plenty of ore for us in Australia."

"Ore, maybe. But we don't have a work force. I received a wire two days ago from Franklin in New South Wales. Cholera has killed more than two hundred in the Ibo district and he can't find men to fill a shift. Thinks it might be a year or more before the epidemic slows and they can find new miners."

"How about Chinchilla?"

"The army hasn't secured the area in months. The papers are talking about a full-scale revolution. Look, dammit," he said hobbling to his desk and waving the newspaper in the air. "A boat docked in San Francisco with a helluva payload. Exactly how much gold was on that boat isn't important. I say we need to be up there and get in on this play as soon as we can. Where in Alaska is this blasted discovery anyways?"

"The Klondike is actually just inside of Canada. The Yukon."

"I don't care if it's at the North Pole. I'm ready to go myself."

"Windy, you've brought in more than your share of mines. But

I don't think it would be practical or wise for you to go sprinting off to the Klondike. Besides, this company needs you here."

"You don't think I'm up to it?"

"I didn't say that. Windy, you're a smart mining man but you're sixty-two years old. You've got a bullet lodged in your back and a bad leg. Do you really think you can hike up mountain ranges and out-hustle a crew of young bucks?"

Woolner stamped his walking stick on the floor. "I'm stronger on one leg than most men with three, Phinius, and you know it." He turned and stared out the window. "I tell you I want some of this action."

Grant walked over to Woolner and gripped him round his elbow. "That settles it, Windy. We're going to Frisco on the train tomorrow to see if this gold rush is for real."

"Yes, we need to check it for ourselves." Woolner looked again at the folded newspaper he held in his hand. "I know for a fact that Mitchell Toffan is a whoring scoundrel who wouldn't report the truth to his own mother. But if even a tenth of this story is true, then it's worth finding out."

He put the paper on his desk and looked through his dusty window and up and down the main street.

"You know me, Phinius. It's not just that I hate sitting behind a desk. But when I hear of a gold strike somewhere, I've just got to be there." He knotted his fist and pounded it into the wall so that a sprinkling of plaster dust trickled down from the ceiling above. "Goddam, but I wish I was twenty years younger."

"So do I, Windy. So do I," Grant chimed in. "Now I'm going

to go and get us tickets for tomorrow. Plan on catching the early train."

Grant picked up his hat and strode out of the office.

The morning breeze puffed a lace curtain and fluttered a newspaper in the elegant bedroom where Garton Rood lay sleeping. The noise caused him to retract his legs to his chest and groan. A moment later he fought to free his legs from the blankets and then kick out a bare foot that he retracted just as quickly. "Get away!" he yelled, before resting again. He lay still a moment before propping himself on an elbow to survey the room anxiously. "What the hell …?" he said to no one in particular, before flopping his head back down on his pillow.

Rood stared at the tin-patterned ceiling, gathering his thoughts and reflecting on events that had conspired to place him in room 314 of the *Jade Pacific* hotel on this sunny morning in July. His eyes flicked around the room as he worked to convince himself that he was not still dreaming.

The dream that had startled Rood was no strange apparition but a familiar sequence that had troubled him since the previous winter. Rood, a 26-year old Albertan had tired of working on the family farm three years previously and joined up as a rail-line laborer on a northern spur of the Canadian Pacific route between Edmonton and Vancouver. Quitting his track job in Vancouver the next season, he worked as dockyard stevedore for more than a year before signing on as crew of the *Maddie Hart*, an 85-foot steamer that ferried supplies up the Pacific Coast to several isolated ports and returned with furs and people half-crazy and desperate to escape the bush for the bustle of Vancouver. The same people he would often ferry back up north on the return journey within 10-days of docking. "Had enough city for this year," they would tell him, often recounting what they could remember of spending their hard-earned money after cashing in their furs or socks filled with gold. The prudent ones would buy supplies immediately after being paid out before they would head to the hotels and taverns where their remaining money would quickly disappear.

On one trip north he met André Bedard, a French Canadian twelve years his senior who seemed to have endless stories of fortunes won and lost trapping and prospecting in the Canadian north. Bedard knew how to survive in the bush very adequately and on this trip north he was determined to find enough gold so that he could quit the bush and travel south to join up with relatives living in the French colony of Louisiana. In Vancouver he had cashed in a year's supply of beaver, fox, wolf, seal and sea otter pelts for the best bush gear he could buy, betting that in Alaska lay the fortune he would find. He limited himself to one good bender before he sobered up and dedicated himself to watching out for the right man that he could tempt into partnership. He was unsuccessful in finding an earnest partner before the *Maddie Hart* sailed, so he left anyway, trusting that he would achieve this goal on board or in port at Juneau before he headed inland.

He chatted up Rood once the boat sailed and was impressed when the young man told Bedard he enjoyed working in the wilderness and wasn't frightened off by cold weather or similar discomforts. When he got the opportunity, Bedard urged Rood to leave the ship in Juneau and join him on his prospecting venture in a 70-30 partnership, with the chance to increase that to 50-50 if things worked out between them over one year.

Rood accepted the offer and disembarked with Bedard at Juneau in May of 1896. Within days they were hiking the Katchit trail with a load of 110 pounds apiece on their back, including food staples, bedding, rifles, prospecting picks and shining steel gold pans. Working from crude maps purchased at the U.S. Geological Survey outpost in Juneau, and embellished with hints Bedard had gleaned from fellow prospectors, they struck out for largely unknown and unmapped wilderness close to the U.S. border with the Canadian Territory of the Yukon.

It was rugged, unforgiving land where a slip on a wet rock could easily lead to painful injury or death but Rood soon proved an adequate partner for Bedard. By day the pair leapfrogged up creeks, sampling sand bars and gravels for gold and hiking up and over mountain passes when they sought new watersheds to explore. Occasionally, they shot a ptarmigan and enjoyed fresh meat but generally they ate the beans and hard tack they packed with them. Bedard sang French Canadian folk songs to keep himself amused and warn bears off, a habit that comforted Rood. Rood enjoyed the company of his mentor and acquired ample knowledge of bush living and prospecting. Bedard thought the mountain rocks were very promising hosts for mineral deposits though they discovered nothing of exceptional value save for occasional fine gold flakes.

One day they reached a large river flowing north and decided to hike it to see what they might encounter. A day and a half later, they first smelled, then saw a plume of smoke rising in the distance. An hour later they came to the confluence with a larger river and a broad, green delta where four log buildings were erected. Dropping their packs outside they entered the main building, a supply depot for the Northwest Company. Inside they strode past a family of Indians who eyed them suspiciously and then exchanged greetings with the Chief Factor of the depot.

Welcome to the Dominion of Canada he said, before pouring them each a cup of coffee and sitting down at a rough-hewn table to tell them some news. There's been a recent gold strike, he recounted, a big one, about three days hike up the larger river. Every prospector in the vicinity who'd heard about it was headed there, to a place up the Klondike River. The first mining claim had been staked by George Carmack, who recorded his claim with the Factor on August 21st and was packing a shotgun shell of gold filled with flakes and nuggets.

The Factor, who doubled as the mining recorder for the district, said, regretfully, that he'd been cleaned out of all supplies save for some lye, rope, rubbing alcohol and sailcloth. He was expecting another steamboat load of supplies in about two weeks, but his advice was to move on to the strike and take their chances that they could purchase supplies in a few weeks time. Other miners that had headed up to the Klondike and returned to record their claims had said there was lots of good real estate remaining on the creeks.

Bedard thanked him for the news and advice before turning

to discuss the situation with Rood. They agreed to push on to the gold strike immediately.

They left the settlement and began hiking steadily along a muddy, rocky trail that followed alongside the big river, making the Klondike in two and a half days. There, they met several other prospectors who told them Bonanza creek was staked solid for six miles until it disappeared, but the next creek over the hill was also proving up and there was unstaked ground upstream. A day later, Bedard and Rood staked claims covering a 1,000-foot length of the upper end of Choker Creek, where the water ran no wider than eight feet. When they tested it, they turned up gold the likes of which Bedard had only ever dreamed.

Rood's memory of what happened during the next few months melded into a hazy recollection of dogged work, exhaustion, hunger and bone-numbing cold. He and Bedard erected a rough cabin out of knotty spruce alongside the creek, raced back to the Factor's post to record their claims and buy a few scant supplies. At the site of their claim they devoted most of their time to scrabbling in the creek bottom to locate and extricate pockets of gold. With each day, the length of sunlight waned and the weather turned colder.

By early October, a foot of snow lay on the ground and the creek was solidly iced over.

They learned from other miners that a fabulous pay streak was to be found by sinking a shaft twenty feet down into the permanently frozen gravel, then tunneling horizontally along an ancient winding of the creek. They sunk their shaft by building a fire on top of the frozen ground, waiting for the heat of the fire to melt the ground a few inches, shoving the burning embers off to the side and shoveling off thawed muck before kicking the coals back into the hole, building up the fire and repeating the procedure. As the hole got deeper, they needed to build a ladder out of tree branches to get down to muck out the hole and rebuild the fire. In two weeks, they had sunk their glory hole down to the level of the 10,000-year old creek bed and they started tunneling along it.

In the tunnel, where a single candle burning in a cast-off lard can threw the only somber, flicker of light, Bedard and Rood picked at the gravel until they won enough muck and water to swirl about in their pan. Even in the dim light they could see a ribbon of gold. "Dis is de pay streak, Garton. De big one." Bedard said enthusiastically. "I tink de devil 'imself left it 'ere for us to find." At the top of the shaft they built a crude windlass around a spruce log that allowed them to hoist up a bucket of muck at a time. They dumped the muck in the snow on the bank of the frozen stream, planning to wash it with running water when the creek thawed in the spring and collect their gold from a sluice they would construct.

Grubbing inside the mine, they often found a slender tail of gold flakes that they scraped up with a knife and spoon and carefully accumulated in another can. On a few occasions, they found a paystreak an inch or more in thickness, amounting to several hundred dollars worth. They also prised gold nuggets out of the muck ranging in size from that of a corn kernel to an adult thumb.

By December, daylight disappeared entirely from the sky so that when they emerged from the tunnel they had little idea whether it was night or day. Stepping off their ladder, they stumbled a few feet through snow drifts and piercing sixty degree below zero cold to their shack where they would build a hasty fire and then collapse onto the moss and spruce boughs and sack cloth that served as their beds, pull a heavy woolen blanket over their heads and sleep for three or four hours before cold and hunger jarred them awake.

Rood began experiencing a shift in consciousness as the paralyzing work wore him down. He felt the biting cold burning his toes, fingers, face and ears, and the fatigue at the end of a shift in the tunnel washed over him like a cold ocean. But as his energy drained, he also experienced a detachment from his body. He would hold out his hands a few inches or a few feet from his eyes and ponder for a few moments whether they existed at all. He became equally uncertain about judging distances to other objects like the shovel or gold pan and about recollecting details of his past life. He noticed it required increasing concentration to focus his thoughts and recall special memories, like the faces of his mother, father and siblings, which used to easily come to mind.

In the cabin, Rood often held up a handful of gold, wishing it could be transformed into food. Then he would widen his fingers and allow the flakes to trickle through them like sand before his head collapsed and he sank into sleep.

Christmas came and went with little recognition by either man, though two neighbors paid a visit and offered to share a pot of their last coffee grounds. These three men looked exhausted and described how they had lost their other partner two weeks before when he was overcome by smoke working underground. They couldn't bury him so they hoisted his body into a tree where it would remain, frozen, until spring. The visit did little to cheer up Bedard and Rood, and they continued working in their mine into the new year.

In the last week of January they needed to procure additional food supplies. They agreed that Rood would take half the remaining food and set out to try to purchase food or kill game. It took several days for Rood to return with some supplies after tromping to the campsite at the confluence of the Yukon and Klondike rivers and having to wait until food supplies were hauled in by dog team from some depot to the south. At the village site now known as Dawson City, Rood was shocked to meet so many ghastly, gaunt men stooped and huddling against the frigid, Arctic darkness. Peering into a mirror for the first time in months, Rood saw that he was no different than the other specters he encountered and he came to believe that he had arrived at a place where he and the others would soon succumb to quiet, solitary death.

After exchanging several handfuls of gold, Rood filled up his pack with a month's worth of flour and beans for two, eight dozen candles and ninety matches. As he labored through fresh snow back to the cabin, Rood noticed for the first time the inky sky lightening with a slender band of daylight, though the surrounding land radiated only somber hues of white, gray, brown and black.

Rood repeated the trip again as the winter dragged on into spring. By March, the back of winter had broken and the frozen land began to thaw. By April, the snow drained away in spring rains and Bedard and Rood began washing their winter's bounty in the muddy torrents that roared down the creek bed.

Each day the gold piled up in their tin cans, though by now they had stopped thinking about the meaning of accumulating wealth. By this time their labor was habitual and vacuous, like that of oxen.

After one trip out and back from the now-booming Dawson City for hard-to-find supplies, Rood swept aside a spruce branch from the cabin walkway and pushed against the door into a cold, dark interior. After fumbling in the darkness to light a candle, he started to haul supplies out of his pack before he turned and saw Bedard stretched deathly still on his bed, his face and head covered with matted, dried blood.

"André!" Rood shouted, as he rushed to kneel beside the shrunken, prostrate form that resembled more a cadaver than anything living. Rood detected Bedard's heart beating weakly as he rubbed his arms and rasped again over his blood-stained face. "André, what happened?"

Bedard grunted slightly and Rood moved to cover him with another blanket and build a fire. Ten minutes later, the cabin warmed and Rood heated water in a bucket next to the flames. He brought Bedard a cup of water and with a wet rag he began to dab at his blood-caked face. Bedard remained limp, however, slowly rolling his eyes and barely swallowing a couple of spoonfuls of water. Finally he whispered, "Be careful. Dat mine cave in on me."

Bedard's eyes rolled shut after he spoke. Rood propped his head up higher and continued to moisten his dry lips.

"Don't worry. I'm going to take care of you."

He finished cleaning Bedard's head and examined a long ragged gash and a lump above his right eye the size of a duck egg. The skin around it was bone white, laced with a filigree of blue and red veinlets. As the room warmed up, Bedard began to tremble slightly and Rood stroked his head.

"You're going to be okay André."

For two weeks, Rood left the cabin only to find firewood and retrieve water. He worked hard nursing Bedard who regained enough strength to lift his head and shift about. But Bedard also developed a cough that kept him from sleeping and racked him in spasms. In his sleep, Bedard tossed about fitfully and often cried out.

One night he clutched Rood's arm and pulled him down to his wan face. "We go back in dat mine tomorrow, my friend," he rasped, his thin eyes burning bright. A few moments later he suddenly relaxed his grip and stopped breathing. Rood collected his friend in his arms and held him for hours before he moved to re-stoke the fire and then fall asleep. When he awoke, he picked a hole in the frozen ground into which he laid the body of his partner before stacking stones and boulders on top and fixing a crude crucifix of branches.

The following day, Rood trudged out to Dawson where he reported Bedard's death to an officer of the Northwest Mounted Police. A six-man detachment of police had traveled by dog-sled from Edmonton to Dawson in mid-winter and erected a crude outpost from which they were working to ensure the rule of law during the gold rush. The officer followed Rood back to his claim and went down into the mine to inspect the tunnel and record details of the cave-in. He also examined a small diary that Bedard had been keeping in his back-pack. He snapped the book shut and informed Rood that he was now the sole owner of the mining claim and Bedard's gold stake, as written out by Bedard. Then he turned and left Rood on his own.

For the next month, Rood did very little but tend to the cabin and walk in the forest. He never again went into the mine, but covered the opening to the mine shaft with some boughs. One day a voice yelled out for him and he opened the door to greet three strange men. They asked him if he was interested in selling his claim and offered him twenty thousand dollars. He agreed and relocated to Dawson within the week, to await the first boat out.

When he finally walked down the gangplank in San Francisco, Rood was carrying a bank-note for twenty thousand dollars and hauling twenty three thousand dollars in gold nuggets and flakes, won in the stifling darkness of the Yukon winter with his late partner.

By any banker's evaluation, Rood was a rich man. But as he lay in the soft comfort of his bedroom in the *Jade Pacific*, his mind flitted over the perplexing events of the past year. He had no plans or great ambitions though the hospitality he was receiving at the hotel was helping to soften his sharp memories.

A soft knock at the door garnered his attention. "Who's there?" he called out.

"It's Gina, sweetness. I've brought you some delicious things from the bakery."

"Uh huh, hang on a minute, while I stand myself up," Rood said, swinging his bare feet over the bed and wrapping the sheet around his midriff. He tread over the floor and unlocked the door and a delicate woman swept into the room holding a tray of food that she placed on a walnut dresser. In the next motion she turned and slid her arms around Rood's waist then pulled his face down to hers and employed her lips in a long hard kiss.

"Good afternoon, sugar," she said when their lips parted. "You must be starving."

"Yeah, I'm hungry," Rood said, continuing to clutch her body to his an extra few seconds. "Still tryin' to figure a few things out, too. Like what the hell I'm doin' in this hotel room."

"Why, you're thawin' out after that perishing cold winter you spent in the land of gold. You were so chilled your poor body didn't think it was ever going to warm up again."

"No, that's not quite what I been workin' over." He paused. "I was just remembering that when I was in that tunnel I thought I was going to end up working there forever, like some kind of animal that lives underground. And the look on those men's faces in Dawson, like they were already dead but hadn't laid down yet. I don't really understand that."

"Maybe there's nothing to understand, precious. Now you're a rich man, richer than most people imagine. And your hot roll is cooling down. Though I could always warm it back up for you," Gina teased.

"Hmmm," Rood moaned, hugging Gina closer and rubbing his head against hers. "I still can't believe that Andre died and I'm standing here in this hotel room. It's so unreal to me I'm thinking I'm living somebody else's life."

"Oh baby, you should just let it go. You can't change anything that happened." Gina reached up and kissed his lips, pulling him to the bed. "Come on now, sugar. Why don't we try some lovin' to warm you up. I bet this time you'll do just fine."

Phinius Grant and Windy Woolner walked from the train station in San Francisco under the stifling, late afternoon sun up Pine St. They each carried leather satchels, worn at the edges after numerous trips in trains, wagons, boats and by horseback. Their careers as mining men had brought them to San Francisco many times as well as other regions of the world that most people would shun. Grant and Woolner gauged much of the world according to its potential to produce wealth from mineral deposits. In their quest for gold, silver, copper, iron and other minerals they had probed sun-baked deserts, frigid mountaintops, swamps and thickly-forested wilderness, often employing their satchels in carrying clots of rock and soil for follow-up examination and assaying. Several times they had counted themselves extremely rich men as a result of mineral discoveries only to re-invest their fortunes in new ventures that lost money and swallowed their wealth. Such was the cycle of mining ventures. They were presently playing out a streak of luck in the Silver Calf mine in Nevada though the lure of the Klondike tugged at them as a thirsty man seeks water.

This day the well-traveled satchels of both men were not carrying rock samples, but overnight clothes and toiletry articles. The purpose of the trip was to investigate the opportunities by which the Olympia Mining Company might acquire a share of

Klondike fortune. On the train trip each man had read the previous day's newspaper stories which continued to portray the Klondike as a new-day Temple Mount where golden riches were heaped and accessible to any able body that was fit enough to complete a journey there.

Woolner had wired ahead of time and arranged a meeting with Ernst Gerhardt, a wealthy businessman who was buying California wheat and shipping it out of San Francisco Bay. He had other shipping interests as well as owning a significant interest in the Silver Calf that had paid him a handsome dividend for several years. Gerhardt would assuredly be carefully monitoring news of the Klondike strike with keen interest to gain a toehold in the action.

Woolner paused outside the offices of Gerhardt Shipping and Trading to wipe the sweat dripping from his forehead and survey the street from which most people had retreated in favor of cooler shelter. One delivery wagon complemented by a swayback chestnut horse remained immobile next to the sidewalk, the only sign of life a slowly swinging tail.

"I've been reading that these streets will soon be filling up with automobiles, Phinius. It's already happening in Chicago and New York. What do you think of that?"

"They'll never make it up the hills here, Windy. Chicago and New York are flat as piss on a plate. No, I think the horse and buggy will be around this town for a long time."

"Well, that may be true, but I've seen changes in my lifetime I never imagined I'd see. And I think I'd like to travel in an automobile someday."

"Well, maybe you'll just have to travel back east and try one out."

"If I never travel east again I'll die a lucky man. All those goddam immigrants make my flesh crawl. Maybe I won't try out an automobile after all. C'mon, let's find Gerhardt. He'll have a palpitation if we're late and then we'd lose one of our best investors."

Inside, they made their way along a hallway to an office where a man behind a large plate glass window was seated over a glistening redwood desk. Woolner rapped on the door and the man gestured for them to enter. A bulbous man with a scarlet face fumbled with a long string of paper that wound its way across the breadth of his desk. The three men shook hands and Gerhardt arranged seating on two highback chairs facing his desk.

"It's good to see you, Windy, Phinius. So much news. And this tickertape spitting numbers at me from all across Europe now. Imagine, the wheat crop in Europe is already considered in jeopardy because of two extra weeks of rain in July. For that good fortune, I can expect to make an extra five to ten thousand dollars shipping wheat from here at a premium. And the bank has already told me I can borrow money at excellent rates against crop returns for which I won't get paid for another six months."

"But I just read that California farmers say they can't afford to bring in their crop this summer because prices are too low," said Grant.

"Farmers are being squeezed," Gerhardt replied. "The bastard railroad has raised their freight rates again on wheat and hops. I wouldn't want to be a farmer, I can tell you that."

"I've said it before," Woolner cut in. "They ran out of room in Hell so the devil formed the railroad to take care of the overflow."

Gerhardt laughed and wiped a cloth over his glistening forehead. "You'll hear no protest from me Windy. There's far more competition in the shipping business which has been my saving grace. But I'm taking up your time. You've come to talk about the Klondike and I'd like to hear what you have to say."

"We only know what we've read in the papers, Ernst," Grant said. "What have you heard? How much of this story is bullcock?"

"Well, nobody is talking about anything else, I can tell you that. I was taking a beer two nights ago when I talked with Freemont Berryman. He wants in on the action. He has already paid a prospector who'd struck it rich two hundred dollars to meet and discuss the man's ideas on where to look for the real lode."

"The 'real' lode?" Woolner questioned.

"Well, the gold they've retrieved so far in such enormous quantities is loose, stored in the ancient creek gravels. It must have come from somewhere. This man figured he knew where it originated and hinted that the real lode would certainly contain much, much more gold than was mucked out last winter."

"It's plausible," Grant cut in. "Though any prospector worth a kick in the ass knows how to sniff out a lode. How come the source wasn't staked this spring?"

"You haven't heard?" Gerhardt inquired. "I understand the terrain is fairly flat with no outcropping. I can't believe I'm lecturing two seasoned miners like you but then every housewife within fifty miles knows all about this and is now an expert on the geography of the Klondike."

"And pecking their husbands to drop their tools and travel north, right?" Woolner said, sarcastically. "Every sodbuster and layabout between here and Paris, France, is suddenly a gold mining expert, thanks to those ridiculous stories run in the papers every day. Don't people realize it takes some experience to bring in a real mine?"

Gerhardt interjected with a nervous grin. "Well, I heard a story about a luckless prospector who staked a fraction in the Klondike just two hundred feet by fifty feet. Know how much gold he found in two months? About fifteen thousand dollars worth. Not bad for a fraction."

"That's shithouse luck, Ernst," Woolner insisted. "Are you saying knowledge and experience are worthless?"

"I'm not saying that at all. But it is apparent that the Klondike is an exceptional place where many of the prospectors met with extraordinary luck. That you can't deny."

"Well, that luck will end soon," Woolner said gruffly. "I've seen this cycle a dozen times before. Sniffing out the real lode will take know-how, experience."

"I agree, my friends," Gerhardt spoke affectionately. "So what are your plans?"

"We'd like to get someone up there right away. Simple as that."

"Well, there are several boats preparing to sail in the next few days and coming weeks. In anticipation of your enthusiasm I have secured passage on a vessel called the *Onyx*. It is departing Saturday.

I can't vouch for condition of the vessel, but at least it will be near the head of the pack."

"Good work, Ernst," Grant glowed. "You've got a miner's nose, after all."

"I like the smell of gold, if that's what you mean."

"That gives us only three days to find the right person for this job, Phinius. I can think of a half-dozen men I would send but I don't know how in hell I can round them up in three days."

"I was reading in the newspaper recently that one man who I believe was working the *Big Bluff* mine for you a few years back is languishing in one of our jails."

"Who is it?" Woolner demanded.

"His name slips my mind at this moment. But he was your foreman there or something and, as I recall, you praised his capacities."

"I wonder if it's Pat Parrot."

"That's his name, I remember it now."

"He was assistant mine manager. What sort of trouble is he in?"

"He beat up a bicycle salesman one night at the *Oasis*. The young man is still lying in hospital and charges against Parrot are pending the man's recovery."

"As I recall, Parrot's very good with machinery," Grant mused. "If something's broke, he can fix it, or invent something better. But he's unpredictable, hard-headed. That's why we let him go, Windy. I don't know if he's the man for this job."

"He may be the best man we can find by Saturday," Woolner said. "And hard-headed is just what this job calls for, Phinius."

"Look," Gerhardt interrupted, "why don't you join me for supper tomorrow night at the *Jade Pacific* and we'll discuss our venture further. I'm sorry but I really must get back to my tickertape now."

Woolner rose. "Excellent, Ernst. Thanks for your time today. We'll see you for dinner tomorrow at seven."

Gerhardt waved for a man passing by to enter the office.

"My typesetter will show you out, gentlemen. Until tomorrow then."

They shook hands and Woolner and Grant exited in single file.

"You can't be serious, Gina. Traveling halfway to the north pole just because you read some stories in a newspaper? You're not talking sensibly."

In a corner of the lounge at the *Oasis,* Gina sat upright in a wicker basket chair. Slumped on a chaise nearby, Aster and Madame Rosalba stared at her, fanning themselves to diminish the desultory afternoon heat.

"What on God's green earth do you know about looking for gold?" Aster continued.

"I don't plan on looking for gold, Aster," Gina replied.

"You don't? Then why are you thinking about traveling to the Klondike?"

"Because there are other ways to get rich in a gold camp than mucking out creeks and mine tunnels," Gina said emphatically.

Aster paused a couple of seconds to interpret this, before

continuing. "But there's nothing there now except for tents and a few rough-board shacks. Is that where you plan on selling your boodle?"

"With a little money, I can build an adequate shelter to meet my comforts and satisfy certain requirements. After talking to Mr. Rood I know I can do it."

"He's the man you've been cozying up with at the *Jade Pacific*?" Madame Rosalba asked.

"That's right, madame," Gina replied.

"Didn't you tell me that he thought the 'land of gold' more resembled the hubs of Hell, and that he suffered terrible deprivations up there," Aster admonished.

"It's true that his partner died a horrible death and the climate of the Klondike is very harsh. But Mr. Rood returned a very rich man even if he isn't much of a lover. But he assured me that with a few supplies a person could be adequately comfortable up there."

"Well, I admire your pluck, girl," Madame Rosalba spoke up. "And just how much money do you think you would need to help establish yourself up there?"

"You're not seriously thinking about such a venture, are you?" Aster asked, her eyes flicking from Gina to Madame Rosalba. "Why, I believe you are both afflicted. Gina, as a friend, won't you please stop thinking such foolish thoughts and get back in your right head."

"I am in my right head, Aster. I want to go to the Klondike and I believe I can do it. I think I can make enough money to do right as Madame Rosalba has done here in Manzanita Springs. I'm not afraid of working hard to get what I want, Aster. That's what it took you when you first landed here, isn't that right, Madame? It wasn't all set up. You had to work hard. I ain't no, that is, I am no fool, I know the Klondike is a land of hardships but I think I could gain an opportunity there. And I would pay you back, Madame, as soon as I can, which I fully expect would be within one year."

"If you live that long," Aster said reproachfully.

"That's enough, Aster, you've made your feelings quite clear," Madame said flatly. "If you're serious about this, Gina, I expect nothing less than a detailed accounting of the expenses you expect to incur, including the costs of your travel, set-up, and adequate supplies to get established. That way you acquaint yourself with the full costing of such a venture. When you present me with such an accounting, and only when, we will sit down and discuss the terms of any loan I might make available to you. And mind, don't you undercut expenses to make your accounting more favorable. I want to know the full expenses, inflated though they might be, given the highly exaggerated nature of the stories printed in those dreadful papers."

Gina's face beamed and she fawned beside Madame Rosalba. "Oh madame, I already have such an accounting nearly complete. I will present you with a finished list sometime tomorrow."

Aster shook her head and protested further. "I can't believe what I am hearing. I believe you have both taken too much heat."

Madame Rosalba rose, and placed her hand on Aster's arm. "That may be correct, Aster. So would you mind taking a long swim in the bay for both of us?"

Aster's face flushed deep crimson and she remained frozen as a stone.

"Mind you complete your chores before dinnertime, girls," Madame Rosalba said, gliding from the room.

Aster remained to stare vacantly at Gina who flitted about stacking a tea pot and several dirty cups onto an ornately carved tray. In her nervousness, she tipped over one of the cups that spilled some tea onto on a purple-plush carpet.

"Damn," she muttered under her breath and moved to mop up the tea with the hem of her dress.

Aster followed her friend's foible from her seat. "Gina," she said.

"What, Aster?" Gina replied sternly. "Can't you see I am trying to clean up a mess here."

"Aster, what about your man, Mr. Rood? I mean, if you went together he could set you up and ... "

"I am planning on traveling alone," Gina asserted. "As far as I know, Mr. Rood has made his fortune and he is not planning on returning to the Klondike. Lord knows he is a confused man, with a prick as limp as seaweed and cold as a clamshell."

"Oh," Aster said softly.

Word of boat departures for Alaska circulated rapidly throughout San Francisco. Animated conversations were held around kitchen tables, tavern counters, church pews, job sites, wagon benches, over fences and across pillows. All aspects of the imagined journey were discussed and analyzed, including perceived hardships, appropriate supplies and strategies to ensure success at journey's end.

The *Shield* egged readers on in a contest that offered a berth on the *Onyx* and $250 toward supplies for the best strategy for finding gold, as judged by three experienced prospectors who would review all entries received by noon the following Friday. The name of the winner would be announced by Mitchell Toffan outside the offices of the newspaper at 5:00 pm, Friday afternoon. Stores agreed to remain open until midnight so that the winner could acquire supplies in time for the *Onyx's* noon sailing on Saturday. The contest fixed the citizens inside the city limits like an incantation and by Thursday, people were pouring into San Francisco by rail, boat, horse, wagon and on foot.

Alongside the berth of the *Onyx* on the main wharf, men and wagons came and went as the ship was outfitted with supplies and refitted for the voyage. The *Onyx* was actually an aging tramp steamer that had spent much of her life plying the relatively calm waters of Puget Sound off northwestern Washington state, ferrying supplies between logging camps and salmon canneries. Each summer, the owner and captain of the *Onyx,* Barnum Ruckles, sailed south under sunny skies to San Francisco to acquire items that were unavailable in the northwest. It was happenstance that placed Ruckles and the *Onyx* in San Francisco when the *Excelsior* docked, and Ruckles astutely determined that he might turn a small fortune in voyaging north to Alaska. The *Onyx* was equipped to carry only 25 passengers, but Ruckles moved quickly to hire contractors who were now working to double capacity and improve the kitchen and dining facilities. Ruckles needed a hefty bank loan to finance the refit and new paint being applied to the *Onyx's* rusting carapace but by being one of the first ships to announce a sailing date to Alaska after the *Excelsior's* remarkable docking, seats and berths quickly sold out with barely a complaint raised that the captain had trebled the normal price of single passage to Juneau.

After Ruckles secured the bank loan and initiated ticket sales with the help of a newspaper ad, he immediately set out to locate a ship's engineer who would help rejuvinate the aging boiler affixed deep within the bowels of the ship. Most able, sober engineers garnered steady employment tending railway locomotives and the growing fleet of ships that sailed between continents. Ruckles was unsuccessful until he passed between the doors of a darkened pub in the middle of an afternoon. A bartender pointed out a negro slouched in a chair clutching an empty glass. "That's 'Rags' Sidley, from the colony of Barbados. If half his stories are true, he's been workin' on boats since the time of Francis Drake. He's cleaned out more bottles of rum in recent memory than steam engines, but I hear he knows his tools. Hey Rags! Wake up. This man wants to talk with you." The negro stirred. Ruckles walked over, introduced himself, and inquired if Sidley was fit enough to improve the workability of the *Onyx's* boiler. Sidley nodded and mumbled that he had worked on many similar vessels, but he wasn't convinced of the *Onyx's* seaworthiness.

"I seen dat boat in da water. It seen much better days. If da big weather hit, dey be no way dis ship stay floatin'. I know dat by lookin' at her."

"I've sailed the *Onyx* for 14 years," Ruckles insisted, "and she's sailed in the worst muck the northwest can throw up. There ain't no big weather in mid-summer in these parts. All you need to do is keep her greased and she'll make it at three-quarters throttle. That's what I'm paying you to do. If you're not interested, I'll find someone else."

"Rags be da only grease monkey you be findin' 'round here now, Cap'n. But I don't want to go on no ocean voyage. I be partly-retired and very happy to stay in port after I work her up for you."

"Those aren't my terms. I'll only work with an engineer that commits to round trip."

"Daoult is very smart, cap'n, but in truth I don't like boatin' long distances no more. All dat rollin' about makes me seasick now."

"I'll pay double wages for round trip, or I won't pay you at all."

"I like to get half pay before dis boat sail."

"One third pay the day before sailing, two thirds the day we arrive back in port. Take it or leave it."

Rags studied the bottom of his empty glass and pursed his lips. "Okay, I start for you tomorrow."

"The hell you do," Ruckles slapped him on the back. "You start today, before you fall down drunk on the floor. I need a workin' man who is sober, hear me? And if I find you drinkin' on this job, you'll be swimming with the seals before you can squeeze out a fart. Now let's get going."

Ruckles lifted Sidley out of his chair and directed him out the door.

Over the next few days Sidley commenced to renew the engine as best he could, declaring regularly that the best fate for the *Onyx* was immediate dispatch to the ocean bottom.

"Dem pistons gonna shoot right trew da main block and den where we be?" he asked Ruckles.

"Grease 'em and pack 'em tight as you can. She'll purr like a kitten," Ruckles insisted.

On Thursday morning, news of the *Onyx's* sailing was announced in the papers and, within hours, people congregated in the dockyards like corn-fed cattle to observe and discuss the activities on the ship. Young boys scuttled around workmen and caches of goods being hoisted aboard in great nets to be stowed in the main hold of the boat. In the afternoon, Sidley came up from his station below to rest on a grimy toolbox. He hadn't worked this hard in years and the sweat dripped from his brow as from a mountain spring.

"Hey, engineer! Is that ship gonna to make it to Alaska?" a newspaper reporter called out to him.

"It's best you be askin' da Lord above to answer dat question," Rags yelled back, toweling his forehead.

Just outside the main entrance to the wharf, people collected under the blistering afternoon sun to observe another spectacle. The outer ring of the crowd spoke in hushed tones, the inner watched in silence. Their attention focused on a large gray mass, an elephant, lying still on the dusty roadway. It was being led across town along with several other elephants when it suddenly stumbled to the ground. The only sign the elephant was alive was the cadenced flicker of its tail and the languid movement of its beetle-black eyes. Beside the elephant knelt a circus worker, a midget who was imploring the elephant to rise to its feet and continue. Someone broke through the crowd with a bucket of water and handed it to the midget. He poured half the bucket over the head of the elephant and then bent over to offer the beast a quantity of water cupped in his hand. The elephant ignored it. The midget lifted up the elephant's limp trunk and dropped it into the bucket. Still the elephant did not drink.

"That elephant's done for," one onlooker asserted. "It's dying."

"No, it's not," the midget retorted. "Will someone please go and get me some more water?" he implored.

Someone picked up the bucket and ran off with it.

"Get up!" the midget insisted, pulling on the ear of the elephant, which remained immobile.

"I'll bet its heart has stopped," another voice pronounced.

"Either that or it's got an infection," someone added. "I hear wild animals are very susceptible to sickness if you take them out of their own habitat. You should probably shoot it."

"She just needs a rest is all," the midget replied.

The elephant closed its eyes, even when the midget threw another bucket of water over its head. Several people moved in and hove on the elephant in an attempt to roll it. They failed to displace it one inch.

"That's a solid bulk," somebody commented.

"What did you expect, it's an elephant," a woman replied haughtily.

"I still think you'd better shoot it. You never know, it might be carrying some rare tropical disease that'll kill people quick as the pox," one man said in no hurry to move on.

"Kill it and we'll have enough dog food in this city for a week."

Suddenly another midget pushed excitedly through the crowd.

"The other elephants just stopped up the road," he announced. "They won't go on."

A woman suddenly shrieked.

"Here they come!" somebody yelled out.

The crowd around the prostrate mass rapidly retreated as three other elephants walked up to their companion lying on the ground. They stood in a circle around him and snorted up clouds of yellow-brown road dust. The midgets also withdrew, not knowing what to do.

The crowd remained at a distance, silently watching the elephants mill about.

"These animals are mad," a man yelled out. "We should shoot 'em all."

"They're not mad," one of the midgets yelled out. "They're as gentle as mice."

"Just the same, the police should be here. They'd know what to do."

Suddenly the prostrate elephant opened its eyes and flicked its ear like a giant blanket. Then it rocked its bulk to one side and heaved itself up to a kneeling position. An elephant standing beside it raised its trunk and trumpeted a great shriek through the air. A few seconds later, the fallen elephant again heaved its great bulk and this time raised itself to its feet.

One of the midgets walked up to the elephants and clapped his hands. The elephants slowly shuffled into a line and continued on their way through an opening that formed in the crowd.

Late Thursday afternoon Phinius Grant and Windy Woolner were in discussion with San Francisco magistrate Gareth Parsons in a spare, stifling office above Clay Street. Woolner remained seated, fanning himself with a wide-brimmed hat while Grant paced the floor. Parsons sat opposite the two men, fixed as a statue.

"I'll come to the point, magistrate," Grant said. "The man you're holding in confinement is valuable to us and we're willing to post his bail if it's a fair price."

"I have little jurisdiction in the matter, Mr. Grant," Parsons replied. "The man is being held pending charges which have yet to be determined with finality. For that reason I have not set bail."

Woolner drummed his fingers upon a tabletop. "You've been holding this man for several days without charging him and without providing him adequate representation. I dare say you are stretching the limits of the law, magistrate."

"I hardly need reminding of my duties, Mr. Woolner," Parsons snapped back. "A man lies in grave health. This man is responsible for beating him. He may soon be charged with murder."

"I think not. We have a letter from the attending doctor penned this afternoon, magistrate," Grant intervened, procuring a white sheet from a leather satchel he picked up from the tabletop. "The doctor says the patient Mr. Robinson is no longer in danger and, moreover, he is expected to make a full recovery."

"Let me see that," Parsons insisted. Grant handed him the letter that he read three times. He then looked at the two men across from him.

"I will release him, pending charges of assault and battery, for a bond of thirty five dollars."

"That's excessive," Woolner protested. "He was in a bar-room fight, nothing more. In fact, it will likely be proved that he acted in self-defense."

Parson's eyes glowed. "I have little faith in your speculation, Mr. Woolner. This man attacked and bludgeoned a man much smaller than himself. And I know for a fact he has been charged and convicted for assault in other jurisdictions of this state."

"Which should have no bearing on your court," Woolner said.

"We're prepared to offer twenty dollars," Grant replied.

"He'll not leave here for a penny less than thirty," Parsons countered.

Woolner looked across to Grant. "Thirty it is then providing you release him immediately into our custody."

Parsons pursed his lips and pondered the offer, glaring at Woolner, before he lifted and rang a bell resting on his office top. A clerk appeared a moment later.

"Release the prisoner in cell number eight." The clerk hurried away. In silence Woolner authorized a bank note that he slid across the table to Parsons.

A couple of minutes later the clerk opened the door and Pat Parrot shuffled into the room, looking dazed. Grant stood before him.

"Hello, Parrot," he said, examining him. "Mr. Woolner here has put up your bail. Let's go somewhere and talk, shall we?"

Parrot looked around the room. "Sure. Let's go and talk. That beats staring at four walls."

Woolner stood and turned to the magistrate. "Thank you for your assistance, Magistrate."

"Mind he shows up for hearing and trial, Woolner," Parsons admonished. "This court doesn't like bail jumpers."

"Rest assured we will take your sentiments into our fullest consideration," Grant said, as the three men exited the room.

Friday, the population of San Francisco was swept up in a palpable, giddy anticipation. From early morning into the burning heat of the afternoon people thronged in the streets. Many businesses closed by noon, though most stores and taverns accommodated crowds of people. When prospectors emerged with purchases from stores, crowds gathered outside parted to let them pass but not without bantering and trying to provoke conversation.

"Think you're going to strike it rich?" someone yelled out.

"I'm gonna try. Figure I got as much chance as the next sap."

"I hear supplies are mighty short up there. Whaddya think you'll miss the most?"

"That's easy. Beer and women."

"You bringin' lots of wooly underwear?!"

"He looks more like the 'lace-frillies' type."

Barnum Ruckles and Rags Sidley took the *Onyx* out of her slip for a test run around the harbor in the afternoon. Ruckles had hired several additional crew for the voyage including a ship's mate, two cooks, a couple of bus boys to help in the dining room and kitchen and swampers to help with odd jobs on board. Conditions on board the *Onyx* were expected to be crowded and primitive but functional.

"I'm not promising a cruise on a luxury ocean liner," Ruckles told a newspaper reporter nosing around. "My main function as captain of the ship is to complete a safe passage to Juneau. I don't expect real men to complain if the toilet paper runs out. In fact, I'd advise them to bring their own."

Out in the harbor, Sidley eased the *Onyx* up to about three quarters throttle with some trepidation. He had overseen some improvements to the boilers and he listened carefully to the cadenced rumbling of pistons and camshafts. In a single motion he wiped some grease oozing from a seal and transferred it unconsciously to his forehead where he dabbed at beads of sweat glistening in the glow of the pulsing firebox.

"It's runnin' mainly fine, Mistah Ruckles," Sidley yelled up through the communication horn to the bridge. "But I don't care for number tree piston and I suggest we pack an extra."

Sidley cupped the horn to one ear and stuck a filthy finger in the other to listen for a response.

"Ease back to half throttle and we'll turn her about. Once we're back you hustle over to the shipworks and pick up a handful of extra cams and cotter pins. We don't need no extra piston, this ship hasn't handled this well in ten years."

"Yessuh, but we ain't fully loaded down yet and we ain't runnin' open ocean," Sidley yelled back through the hose.

"The open ocean is smooth as a horse's ass through the summer along the coast. I know this boat and she's good for the trip."

Sidley hung up the horn, sighed and stared at the throbbing engine. "I hope you be right, cap'n," he said to himself. "I hope you be right." Then he reached over and took a long drink of water out of a tin wedged in beside the firebox.

Like angry bees, crowds of people swarmed through downtown streets in late afternoon. Extra editions of the papers were published, hawked on the streetcorners by screeching vendors, and passed from person to person. The *Daily Examiner* ran an exclusive interview with a seasoned prospector who listed the supplies he would pack with him to the Klondike and the strategies he would invoke to strike it rich, knowing that many of the richest placer claims in the creeks had long been staked. Speculation ran high as to the location of the mother lode, the hard-rock source of the loose gold found in the creeks and buried placer deposits. The gold rush of '49 had spawned many similar dilemmas, spread over a much wider area in the Sierra Nevada and Klamath Mountain ranges of eastern and northern California. It was commonly suggested that the hard-rock source of Klondike gold might lie many miles away based on many creative theories, spanning the scientific to the biblical, about how such a deposit might have formed in the first place.

Excitement rose for the anticipated announcement by Mitchell Toffan from the Shield's storefront office of the newspaper contest winner. By four o'clock several hundred people were milling about on Ferry street, jostling each other for closest position to the rough podium erected earlier in the late afternoon.

At twenty minutes after five, Toffan and several other people emerged from the offices of the *Shield*. Toffan stepped forward to a walnut dais mounted on the platform, gripped both sides of it with his hands and spoke to the audience that had grown silent.

"Good afternoon, ladies and gentlemen. My name is Mitchell Toffan, publisher of the *San Francisco Shield*. As you know, the *Shield* has endeavored to bring you enlightened news of the most important gold discovery in half a century, from the fabled new El Dorado of the north, the Klondike."

A heckler from the back of the crowd croaked, "your paper isn't fit to wrap fish, Toffan!"

Some chortling was heard and Toffan was momentarily distracted.

"Either my ears deceive me or I detect the dulcet tones of Clarence Grenville," Toffan responded. "Well, Grenville, I'd say if you could actually read the English language you might have an opinion I'd consider important, but I know that is not the case. Perhaps you'll consider entering our next literacy competition and, if you win, we'll sponsor you to start your schooling again. This time, however, you must promise to mind your lessons."

Many people chortled with laughter and the heckler retreated behind a post.

"Who won the contest?" someone else yelled out.

Toffan started again. "If I were a younger man, I would have booked passage myself and assembled an outfit to travel north for the adventure of a lifetime. The Klondike is the land of dreams where untold riches might be found by an enterprising man in a day's work."

"Or a woman!" someone in the crowd yelled out.

"Madam," Toffan cut back in, "I am not the kind of man to deny hardship to any person, male or female, or animal, who wishes to undertake such activity. And to all who wish to try their luck and deposit their sweat in the Klondike, I impart my heartfelt best wishes to you. Unfortunately, passage to the land of gold at this time is limited to those with booked passage, including those sailing on tomorrow's historic sailing of the *Onyx*, now completing final preparations in our dockyard. Evidently, this valiant ship represents the vanguard of a fleet of ships preparing to sail to Alaska.

"But let us turn our attention to the intrepid souls who have secured passage on the *Onyx*. Tomorrow's departure will take with it a group of courageous pioneers who carry provisions to endure their assured hardships and the dreams of those of us left behind. I count myself among those unfortunate persons remaining here, but I am pleased to tell you the *Shield* will be sending an emissary who will dutifully return dispatches for circulation in our newspaper. So that you, our faithful readers, may be kept fully apprised of the miraculous accounts from the gold fields. I can also tell you the reporter chosen for this task has not yet been informed of this important assignment but I will now make this known to him."

Toffan turned to address the staff of the *Shield* assembled behind him.

"At this time I would like to extend my congratulations, and best wishes, to *Shield* reporter Frank Bunty."

Bunty, standing a few feet behind and off to the side from Toffan, looked stunned as he absorbed the news. Toffan started to applaud and then motioned for Bunty to come forward, which he did. The crowd hooted and applauded as well.

"Congratulations, Bunty," Toffan said pumping his hand at first, and then slapping him on the back. "Now, Frank," Toffan began as the applause died down, "I want your word, declared before these witnesses, that you will faithfully report on the discoveries you encounter in the Klondike."

"I will, sir," Bunty affirmed, still looking perplexed.

"Excellent," Toffan continued. "And I want your pledge that, no matter how much gold you personally exhume in the course of your duties, you will continue in the employ of the *Shield* serving these people arraigned before you today, who expect nothing less than the highest quality journalism as can be provided."

Bunty nodded. "Yes, I will."

"Then I wish you Godspeed and fair winds, Frank," Toffan said, again shaking Bunty's hand.

The crowd cheered as Bunty returned to his place behind Toffan.

Toffan again gripped the edges of the dais and faced the crowd.

"Now ladies and gentlemen, I know you are as anxious as I to learn the identity of the lucky person selected to travel to the Klondike at the expense of the *Shield*. But let me assure you that in addition to luck, this person, the identity of whom I will reveal momentarily, is additionally blessed with uncanny intelligence. This much has been confirmed to me by the panel of astute judges who personally reviewed the hundreds of thoughtful entries in our competition.

"'Where do the best opportunities for finding gold lie in the Klondike, based on the information revealed in our newspaper' was the question we posed only a few days ago. You scurried for your pencils and tablets dormant since you retired from schooling to ponder this question, and then you told us your answers. Rarely, in my professional career, has it been my pleasure to solicit such insight from our faithful readers. And at this time I am pleased to tell you that the *Shield* will be publishing the winning instructions and other entries in select editions of the newspaper beginning tomorrow."

"Cut the blather, Toffan!" another heckler shouted from the crowd.

"I am approaching the climax, my good man, please be patient," Toffan retorted. "Now our panel of judges is ready to inform me of the most insightful response to our question." Toffan turned to his staff behind him. "May I have the name of the competition winner."

A man chuffing a pipe shuffled up to him and handed him a folded piece of paper. Toffan unfolded the paper and stood before the dais. For a moment the only noise heard was the rustling of the wind. Toffan surveyed the crowd.

"Ladies and gentlemen, the lucky winner of our competition, who will be travelling to the Klondike at the expense of the *Shield* is 'Mr. W. Kettle'. Will he kindly come forward at this time."

The crowd stirred to life with everyone looking around and inquiring about the winner.

"Mr. W. Kettle," Toffan repeated. "Come and claim your prize."

Suddenly someone approached the dais, and the crowd again grew quiet. That person was a diminutive woman. She walked up to Toffan. Toffan stared down, his mouth hanging open. The woman muttered something to Toffan, who swallowed hard and regained his composure.

"Ladies and gentleman, our prize is claimed. I guess a schoolteacher can find gold as well as the next person. Please join with me in congratulating Miss Winona Kettle."

For a moment the only sound again heard was the wind. Then someone began clapping and the crowd followed in wild applause. Toffan reached down and shook Kettle's hand who offered hers limply in return.

Thousands of gawkers and giddy or drunk revelers patrolled the sidewalks, taverns and streets during the duration of Friday evening. It was a spectacle unlike anything the young city had ever birthed before. Timid men and women peaked from behind lace curtains adorning windows, while children scurried from laneways to street corners and back again. Periodically, gunfire, firecrackers and Indian war whoops sounded above the general din, but no one took any real notice.

Near midnight in the *Redwood* room of the *Jade Pacific* hotel, Mitchell Toffan sat reading proofs of the early morning edition of the *Shield*. Every couple of minutes Toffan took a pen he clutched in his hand and scribbled notes onto the paper, then took a sip from a glass that was initially filled to the brim with whisky and a modest quantity of water. When he finished a page he held it up and a young boy seated nearby sprang up, snatched the paper from Toffan's hand and raced off back to the *Shield* offices.

Frank Bunty suddenly appeared and pulled out a chair across from Toffan.

"You wanted to speak with me, Mr. Toffan. I was getting a kit together for the trip and telling my wife about it all."

"Well, you needn't get too excited, Bunty," Toffan said without looking up.

"Oh I don't know about that, Mr. Toffan," Bunty stammered. "This is about the most exciting thing that's ever happened to me. You won't be sorry, sir. I'll do a good job, like you asked."

"I know you would do a good job, Bunty," Toffan said, putting his pen down and looking across the table. "But you're not going to the Klondike."

Bunty looked perplexed. "I don't understand, sir. You said I was leaving on the boat tomorrow."

"You're going away alright," Toffan countered. "But I'm not going to spring for a second passage at Barnum's prices. Instead, I'm transferring you to Sacramento. There you can file stories from the Klondike and the state legislature. Nobody'll know you're not in the Klondike and when you're filing from Sacremento, you'll use a sage pseudonym, say 'Brant Reeves'. I'll have to recall Lesem, who's filing for us from Sacramento now, but his liver's about to give out anyway, so it's all for the better. How does that sound to you?"

Bunty's face and jaw hung slack.

"You want me to write stories from the Klondike when I'm in Sacramento?"

Toffan stared at him. "You *will* write stories about the Klondike from Sacramento." He had a sip of whisky before continuing. "Good stories that our readers want to hear. Is that understood? And you'll get an extra seven dollars pay each week."

Bunty said nothing.

"Now," Toffan continued. "Disappear and do *not* show yourself at the sailing of the *Onyx* tomorrow. You're on board, remember. Take a couple of days off. But lay low, I don't want to read about this in any other paper. You can catch a train to Sacramento on Wednesday after meeting with me on Tuesday afternoon. Okay? Now buzz off. I've got to finish proofing. And mind, Bunty, this is our secret, right? Good. See you Tuesday."

Pondering these instructions, Bunty slowly rose from the table and ambled toward the door like a bear awaking from hibernation.

Daybreak on Saturday morning emerged out of the inky blackness accompanied by a slight breeze on San Francisco Bay. First light also brought renewed activity at the dockyards, much of it in the vicinity of the *Onyx*. Stevedores bustled along the planking, yelling out orders, pushing wheelbarrows and carts, loading crates. Dockside, huge draft horses clopped along bricks, tatooing the news of arriving freight. The air sang with orders like "Get on now!", "Haw!" and "Comin' through," as wagons cued up for unloading. The first warmth of the morning sun soon gave birth to the smell of working horses and humans. More people seemed to arrive with each passing quarter hour, most of whom gathered to gawk at the ship and the attending activities. Some of the voyeurs had stayed up through the night, plying streets that remained active and taverns that never shut their doors.

Barnum Ruckles hustled about on the deck of the *Onyx*, yelling orders to the men storing freight. He dispatched a boy to the port police office to request immediate assistance controlling the arriving throng. The first passengers also arrived with their gear and Barnum gave orders to a ship's hand about examining tickets and issuing receipts so he could accurately confirm passengers at sailing time. Most of the arriving passengers wished to stay topside on the ship after stowing their gear so Barnum had another dilemma to contend with, the likes of which he had never faced in his entire career. He conferred with the arriving police constable and enrolled him in pushing the gathering crowd back off the main dock so he could proceed with loading. More than one person was squeezed off the planking and into the harbor water, unable to retain footing in the force of the writhing crowd. Laughter roiled up with shrieking and shouts of "*Wahoo!*" and "*On to the Klondike!*" as the morning progressed.

"I been to Mardi Gras in New Orleans, and some other fine festivals, Mistah Ruckles, but I never seen nothin' like this," Rags Sidley said when he came out on to the main deck. "This be a special kinda circus happenin' here this morning. I just be hopin' most everybody don't try to climb on board when we be gettin' under way. No, I hope they not be thinkin' of tryin' that."

"I've asked for more police to help out," Barnum said, with a small measure of desperation in his voice. "I'm trying to run a business here and I've got a schedule to keep."

"There's probly rascals in that crowd who figure their business is keepin' you from any schedle," Sidley added facetiously.

Barnum turned to him in anger. "Why don't you ..." He shoved a rag into Sidley's chest. "Make sure we're ready for sailing," he added sternly, before turning and walking away.

"Oh dis ship is ready for sailin', Cap'n Ruckles," Sidley said as Barnum thumped away. "Ready as she ever be, I figure."

Among the first passengers to present his ticket and stride up the gangway of the *Onyx* pulling a small trunk was a tall, lanky man with a mustache. It was Isaac Fayne, looking very serious and seemingly little impressed with the condition of the *Onyx* or the events surrounding the departure. Fayne spent little time on the deck before humping his trunk through a doorway and disappearing inside.

Not long after Fayne boarded, a younger man, looking much more excited and nervous, dragged a duffle bag onto the ship. Liam Minney looked around the ship and then strained his eyes to try to observe someone in the distant crowd. He eventually raised his arm and waved out to the crowd uncertainly. His eyes detected nothing of familiarity, his ears heard only cacophony punctuated by a shrill whoop that rose momentarily above the general din.

On the street approaching the docks a bearded man in a wrinkled white shirt adorned with a lifeless black tie wiped sweat beading on his forehead and positioned a wooden crate on the sidewalk. People milling by narrowly missed bumping him as he tentatively stepped onto the crate and cleared his throat. He reached his arm into a tired black shoulderbag he toted and removed a thick, dusty-brown bible.

William Benning stepped onto the crate, raised the book to his chest in one hand, and began addressing the crowd swimming past.

"Friends," he bellowed, "Renounce your dreams of easy riches in the Klondike. The real rewards are in God's Kingdom to which you will gain entry by a life of penance and contrition. Gold is the stuff of false idols for which God punished our forbears."

Benning breathed deeply before continuing.

"Gold is a lifeless metal, nothing more," Benning roared to a few people who had now stopped to stare at him. "Gold will not nourish the soul but it will strip it clean of your duty to God and His glory." Benning held his bible over his head. "God's holy book is the true sustenance that will provide you with a path to eternal salvation. Do not forsake it for stories forged by Satan's agents. Do not cast your fate with demons who would lead you into Babylon."

"This is one sinner with a ticket for Babylon, preacher," answered one man passing close by and traveling toward the docks pulling a battered trunk. "Maybe you'll say a prayer for me."

A few people laughed aloud.

"Tear up your ticket, sir," Benning responded. "God has better plans for you. It's all in this book."

"Better'n finding a load of gold to send back to my family?" the man countered aggressively. "I don't think so."

"Maybe you should save your voice, preacher, and leave gold mining to real men," another shouted.

"I don't think so, my good fellow," Benning broke in. "I have heard that the region of the Klondike is bewitched, the devil's own playground."

"Then maybe you'd better have a word with the United States Geological Survey," said another man, holding up a newspaper and turning to face a crowd that had formed around the preacher. "Listen to this report written by geologist James Duncan and carried in the *Sacramento Bee*: 'The real mass of golden wealth in the Klondike remains untouched,'" Duncan says. "The original source of the gold lies in the virgin rocks and the veins in the hills. These must be of enormous value.' On to the Klondike, I say!"

"Amen!" another man yelled out.

The speech served to galvanize the throng. Benning was suddenly hit with a clot of dirt in his chest. He ducked while more debris was flung at his head and he received a dollop of muck on his hip.

More men closed around Benning and one shoved him from his perch.

"Your blather don't belong here today, preacher," he demanded. "Best you stick to comfortin' women and children."

Another man approached close and hissed at him. "Get outta here now, ya fool, before I heave ya' in the bay. Or worse."

Benning backed away, clutching his Bible and glowering back.

"Mammon has overtaken you but you are blind to see it," he hurled back.

The man stepped forward and kicked Benning full on in his leg, sending him sprawling across the dirty roadway.

"Get outta here, vermin!" he scolded.

A short distance from where Benning was picking himself up from the street, a horse-drawn wagon was being helped through the crowd, making its way slowly toward the docks where would-be prospectors were unloading their gear. A tall, black man gripped the reins and shouted to people ahead to clear the way. It was slow going as the crowd thickened.

Four men sat on benches in the wagon and a load of equipment protruded from the back. The men were Windy Woolner, Phinius Grant, Ernst Gerhardt and Pat Parrot, talking loudly to be heard over the din.

"Of course I told her I was only expecting to get a haircut," Grant said to the others.

"You dog!" Parrot shouted out, excitedly. "She was a young filly. You were old enough to be her grandfather."

Grant scowled at Parrot. "Keep it down, man. I don't want people to get the wrong idea about me."

"It's a little late for that," Parrot shot back, grinning.

"Hold your tongue, Parrot," Woolner snapped. "God, man, you do roar. Use some discretion when there's people around."

Parrot's jaw tightened and he moped like a boy who'd been caned.

Gerhardt shook his head and turned his gaze toward the waterfront. "Well, this is some spectacle, I tell you. There must be two thousand people here."

"I've never seen anything like it before," Grant agreed, standing up to look around.

Woolner remained severe and focused on Parrot. "Now, you've

got everything straight in your mind, Parrot."

Parrot perked up. "The next time you see me, I'll be ridin' a grizzly bear and flingin' gold nuggets like popcorn!"

Woolner scowled. "You do try me, Parrot."

Parrot remonstrated. "Oh, lighten up, Windy. This'll be like takin' candy from a baby."

"Remember, Parrot," Grant spoke up. "It's other people's money you're dealing with. A pig in a poke won't do."

"I told you fellas, 'I'm your man'. You want gold and I'm gonna find it for you."

"You have the proper maps and other authorizing papers, Mr. Parrot?" Gerhardt asked.

Parrot nodded. "I do, but those maps don't tell me much."

"They're the best maps the Geological Survey has produced on the region, fresh from the press."

"That may be, but they still ain't showin' many details."

"Try not to be so belligerent and you may learn something from your fellow passengers, Parrot. Remember that," Grant told him.

Parrot fixed him with a cold eye. "You got your way of workin', I got mine. I expect the minute I step foot on that sloop it's every dog for himself."

"I think we be about as close to that boat as we gonna get, mistah," the man leading the horse shouted back. "The crowd is all jammed up and I don't think this wagon is gonna get much further 'long."

Woolner stood up, surveyed the crowd and shook his head.

"Look at these parasites. I'll bet half of them never worked an honest day in their lives," he announced. "Damn, but I wish I was getting on that boat."

"The nigger can help me hump my kit the rest of the way," Parrot spoke up loudly. Several people turned to look at him.

"C'mon back here, boy," Parrot yelled ahead, "Gimme a hand and we'll carry my outfit to the boat."

The wagon-man turned and walked slowly back behind the wagon, watching Parrot with simmering eyes. Parrot jumped down and began lifting gear out of the back. He was strong enough to lift a hundred- pound trunk and another duffle bag without stooping.

"You grab that crate and haul it along," Parrot ordered, turning and entering the crowd. "Outta my way!" he bellowed, pushing people aside.

The black man struggled to lift the crate. Grant jumped down. "Just a minute," he said. "I'll give you a hand." Grant helped raise the crate onto the back of the wagon-man, who gripped it with both hands and struggled into the crowd. Grant jumped back into the wagon.

"You've got a live wire there, Windy," Gerhardt remarked, watching Parrot disappear in the crowd.

Grant looked severe and shook his head.

"I think he'll do the job we need him to do," Woolner said, tugging nervously on his beard.

"Hey, Windy!" a voice yelled out in the crowd. A man in a brown suit presented himself at the edge of the wagon. "I should have known I'd see you here," the man said, extending his arm.

Woolner shook the man's hand. "Hello to you. Phinius, Ernst, this is Caleb Bergson, of Bergson Metalworks, the foundry on the east Bay."

"Biggest foundry in the Bay area now, Windy," Bergson said admiringly. "We just expanded our main shop area by thirty per cent."

"Congratulations," Woolner said.

"Yes," Bergson continued, "and business is picking up with this news, though I wish I were in on this Klondike play. What about you? I guess your sitting there means you aren't headed north."

"We've got a man on the *Onyx*," Grant said. "Just dropping him off, in fact."

"Are you really?" Bergson asked. He reached out and squeezed Woolner's arm. "How much will it cost me to get in on your action, Windy?"

Woolner puckered his lips. "Klondike Enterprises is tight up, Caleb. Our partnership has been established."

"Gentlemen, "Bergson said looking around. "Are you telling me there's no chance of a share for five thousand dollars?"

Woolner looked around at his partners and slowly nodded his head with the others. "I'm sure we can accommodate your request, Caleb. We'll need to talk among ourselves, of course."

"Look, why don't you come around to the foundry tomorrow," Bergson said handing out business cards.

Woolner fingered the card and looked up. "Here's our man, now," he said as Parrot emerged from the crowd and appeared at the wagon.

"Shit," Parrot swore. "I ain't seen a crowd like this since I went to a hangin' picnic in Laramie." He muscled another bag out of the wagon.

The negro reappeared and moved to adjust the hames on his horse and stroke its snout. "I tell you gentamen," he called out over his shoulder. "We ain't goin' nowhere 'til these people move along."

"Did you get your kit stowed?" Woolner asked Parrot.

"They don't have it all figured out on that boat, I can tell you that," Parrot said. "But I know how to look after Pat Parrot, which is all that matters, ain't it?"

"Well, good luck to you, Parrot," Grant announced.

"Luck don't got nothin' to do with it, Mister," Parrot scolded him. "I got a job to do. I'm gonna get to it." With that he turned, picked up his bag, and pushed his way back into the crowd.

Bergson watched Parrot wade into the crowd then turned to the other men in the wagon.

"He's your man, is he?"

"Yes," Grant replied. "Why, do you know him?"

"I saw him not long ago in the *Oasis*," Bergson said. "He's quite excitable."

Woolner glanced at Grant and Gerhardt with glassy eyes but said nothing.

"Of course, he might be just the kind of fellow you need for this job," Bergson opined.

Despite the efforts of a phalanx of security guards and police that had been called out, the crowd of onlookers pressed tighter around the *Onyx*, making it increasingly difficult for passengers with gear to pass through to the gangway as the planned departure time drew nearer. People gawked and a few chortled aloud as a diminutive body pushed through the crowd and struggled toward the boat. It was Winona Kettle, winner of the contest sponsored by the *Shield*. Mitchell Toffan suddenly emerged from the crowd to help Kettle with her luggage, which was three times as bulky as she.

"Hey, Toffan!" someone yelled out. "Why don't you get on the boat and let that gal run your newspaper? Might be a big improvement!"

"I offered to change places," Toffan yelled back. "She didn't want my job!"

At the bottom of the gangway, a man in a striped, greasy shirt stepped forward and stopped the pair.

"Who's travelin' here?" he asked. Kettle presented him with a ticket and he waved for her to pass by. Toffan tapped her on the arm. She turned and looked up at him with a face flush as an apple.

"Best wishes to you, Miss Kettle," he said, doffing a felted bowler, and leaning closer to be heard. "And may your pack be laden with gold on your return."

"I'm not going to the Klondike to find gold, Mr. Toffan," she said, smiling broadly at him.

Toffan looked puzzled. "Then why on earth would you throw yourself in with this scrofulous lot?" Toffan probed.

Kettle met his eyes with certainty. "My fate is in the Lord's hands, Mr. Toffan. I am certain He has special plans for me."

Toffan's eyes opened wide and he stood erect, his smile continuing to curl his lips.

"Of that I have no doubt, Miss Kettle," he replied, "though maybe your heavenly father would be interested in a Klondike stake. A poke of gold can help save a lot of orphans, you know."

Kettle turned and struggled up the narrow walkway. The passengers lining the deck of the ship studied her carefully. Nobody moved to help her until another woman on deck suddenly appeared and reached down the gangway to help hoist Kettle's pack.

"Let me help you," she said, grabbing hold of the luggage and dragging it on board. "Lord amighty," she exclaimed, tugging hard. "I believe you're packin' gold back to the Klondike."

The crowd parted as they boarded, and another woman came forward to help.

"Hello, "she said, reaching to help pull on the bag. "Welcome aboard. My name is Gina."

The other woman smiled at Kettle, as well. "And I'm Aster. Perhaps you'd consider bunking in with us, the captain has consigned us to our own berth."

Fifteen minutes after one o'clock in the afternoon, the man in the greasy shirt pulled up the gangway and waved toward the wheelhouse. A few seconds later the ship's whistle blew a sonorous, percussive note and belched a thick cloud of black smoke. The man jumped down to the dock and scurried along the planking, releasing the ropes tethering the *Onyx* to the dock staves. He then jumped back on board and waved again toward the bow. The whistle blew three times and the ship lurched ahead, jarring the passengers on deck. A second later, the crowd of onlookers and on-deck passengers exploded into raucous cheers, yelling and pumping the air with outstretched arms and fists.

"Yahhhooo!" " Klondike or bust!" people bellowed at the top of their lungs, with several people jumping into the water and stirring it into a froth with flailing arms.

Under a pellucid blue sky etched with a filigree of high, white cloud, the *Onyx* slowly made her way out into San Francisco Bay, underway at last for Alaska.

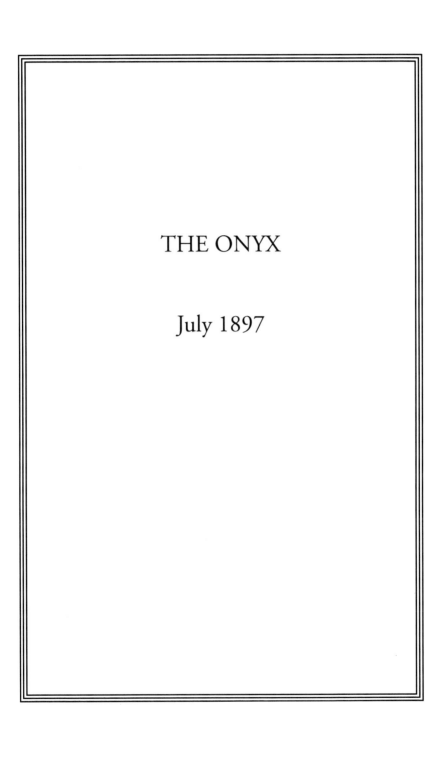

THE ONYX

July 1897

On board the *Onyx*, passengers lined the rails along the deck as the boat plied past the entrance to San Francisco Bay and rotated her bow northward. The boat's swollen load encumbered navigation and required ample space to complete the slow turn. Along the shore, herds of sunning seals slid off rocks into the surf and flocks of shore birds rose into the air as the steamer slowly chuffed by.

In the wheelhouse, Ruckles angled the boat into deeper water, wary of rocky shoals. He was familiar with this part of the journey but sweat collected on his brow, nonetheless, as he gripped the wheel and carefully espied his course. By the math Ruckles had worked out in his mind, after he cleared expenses, he stood to reap a small profit from this voyage. More important to him, Ruckles gauged this would only be the start. More gold discoveries in the north, he calculated, would mean many future round-trip voyages. If he squeezed in two or three more trips this year before stormy weather curtailed sailing in October, he might even be able to bankroll another ship next year, and after that, who knows. He might gain his way within a couple of years to overseeing a new Pacific Northwest shipping line. That would certainly provide him a stake on which to retire within ten years.

Ruckles had worked on boats since he was 11 years old, and he'd had some fine adventures and paydays. Now, at 47, however, he had begun to believe his glory days were behind him. The corporations were always working to squeeze out lone-horse operators like him. He'd had chances to work for some of the bigger fish, run newer boats, but all for wages. Long ago, he vowed he'd rather drink piss than work for wages.

In getting an early jump on a Klondike run, Ruckles saw a future for himself that he hadn't seen in years. The bigger companies would catch up soon enough but right now he was running at the front of the pack.

Ruckles wanted his maiden voyage to Juneau to run smooth. He wanted this so much, he was more nervous than he'd been in years. On this first afternoon, Ruckles was recounting the past few days in his mind, reassessing the preparations he had made. He took a certain satisfaction in what he had accomplished. He had worked hard, thinking aloud through many nights, licking a stubby pencil and scribbling notes on dirty scraps of paper that he stuffed in the bib of his overalls. He had negotiated a bank loan, improved and refurbished the *Onyx*, sold out all the berths and hired a crew. There were plenty of details to fuss over yet, but with each passing mile, he felt more confident and more resolved to concentrate on navigating the overloaded, aging boat through what should be relatively calm waters and disgorging his passengers in the shadow of the towering St. Elias mountains.

The steady throbbing pulse of the engines' pistons provided a primordial cadence that also comforted Ruckles. Years ago someone had told him it was a similar pulse to that a baby hears in its mother's womb from her beating heart. He didn't know about that but he did know he was deeply connected to the sound. He could be asleep but if the rhythm of the engine changed he awoke in a moment and listened for what he could learn. From the pistons' tatoo he could tell if the ship was laboring against the current or picking up slack water, and he could tell the health of the engine, when the pistons were firing smoothly or when one or more was firing out-of-turn. He set about mentally diagnosing any unusual sounds and moved quickly to gauge its severity and repair worn parts that placed excessive stress on the rest of the mechanical system. He prided himself on getting extra life from aging engines that should have been replaced by making sure any engine problems did not become acute. On the docks and in the pubs he listened carefully to stories about engine performance, mentally filing away details for future reference when he shopped for second-hand deals or dealt with ship-board problems.

Ruckles had waged many an argument with engineers over the years, and rarely backed down when it came to troubleshooting problems, no matter how perilous the situation. Earlier in the summer he had nearly come to ruin in the Tacoma narrows when he insisted on shutting down and replacing a worn engine cam during slack-tide. His engineer at the time disagreed with the diagnosis and work order so Ruckles pushed him aside and completed the job himself. When he returned to the wheelhouse a little over an hour later, the boat was being dragged on the outgoing tide between two gravel shoals, however Ruckles luckily maneuvered it back into open water. He parted company with the engineer in Port Townsend and completed the voyage to San Francisco with his first mate and eight passengers making their way out from a logging camp.

Ruckles reached up and gave two quick tugs on the ship's bell cord, signaling for the ship's mate to report to the wheelhouse. The young man newly hired on, Brent Cameron, was more of an apprentice under Ruckles than a seasoned mate. Seasoned hands were scarce as hen's teeth in the port in mid-summer, so Ruckles sized up Cameron when he interviewed him and decided the 21-year old was worth the risk, trusting he would be a quick study and could carry out Ruckles' commands earnestly and punctually, though he had logged less than three years' experience on water. Ruckles had taken more than his share of chances hiring novice crew and now he felt he had pretty good instincts about who would turn into an able hand. He expected them to work hard, in return for which he parsed out his knowledge, lesson by lesson, depending on what the task at hand called for. "You got a lot to learn, laddie," he told Cameron in their first meeting, "but if you stick close to me, you're bound to pick up something of what I know, the way one dog picks up fleas from another!"

Cameron, a tall, lanky young man with a ruddy skin condition, stooped his head as he entered the wheelhouse. "You rang, Mr. Ruckles?"

"I did," Ruckles replied. "What's happening below? Anything to report?"

"The passengers are settling for the most part, sir, with a few exceptions," Cameron told him.

"Coffee's on in the galley?" Ruckles asked.

"Yessir, and tea as well."

"That's good. I told you I want that coffee on around the clock. It quells a lot of grumbling and takes the edge off seasickness," Ruckles asserted. "We got ourselves a jumpy group, here Cameron. Greenhorns and women and potato farmers. And a midget. Wouldn't know a nugget of gold from donkey snot."

"And Indians," Cameron added.

"Indians?" Ruckles said, surprised. "I didn't see any."

"There's at least one on board that I've seen," Cameron said. "He was burning some kind of grass a few minutes ago and a few passengers complained."

"What! I'll lock the bugger in the brig if he does it again. Where is he?"

"He's in the main room. You can't miss him, wearin' a fringe buckskin and a sombrero with a couple of feathers stickin' out of it."

"You hold course while I drop below and have a word with our Indian friend and check in with Sidley," Ruckles said, wiping his face with a rag and stepping back from the ship's wheel for Cameron.

"Yes sir."

Ruckles ducked out of the wheelhouse and observed the main deck and smokestack that billowed black smoke into an azure blue sky. The cool sea wind felt refreshing on his face as he trod down the wheelhouse stairs and made his way along the slowly rocking ship. A handful of passengers gathered beside the railing and nodded to him as he pulled open a door to the main galley.

Inside, a pungent, acrid smell lingered in the air. Ruckles surveyed the passengers seated at the benches and tables until he spotted a man fitting Cameron's description seated across from another passenger at a table on the other side of the room.

Ruckles slowly wound his way over to the man occupying the buckskin jacket and gripped him by the shoulder.

"Hey, Geronimo."

A long, gentle, nut-brown face adorned with a drooping mustache and two braids looked up at Ruckles through chestnut-dark eyes.

"I'm here to tell you that I'm chief of this boat and if you burn any more of that loco weed, you're going to be swimming for shore. Got that?"

"I burned a little sweetgrass to bless this boat and protect it," the Indian replied, slowly.

Ruckles ignored the Indian's comment and began to move away from the table.

"A little smoke helps cure white man's seasickness," the Indian said after him.

"What's that?" Ruckles said, turning back.

"Burning sage helps cure the sickness white men get in their bellies when they ride on boats," the Indian replied.

Ruckles again put his arm on the Indian's shoulder. "Listen to me, Crazy Horse. I got a pot of coffee boilin' around the clock on that table over there. That's the best cure for seasickness I know of, and I been ridin' on boats since you was a little baby grubbin' in the dirt. So I'm tellin' you for the last time, you aren't gonna be burnin' no more weed on this boat. You do and I'll pitch you over. Now that's the last word on this."

Staring hard at the Indian, Ruckles' face turned plum red. No one said anything else, so Ruckles turned and walked away. The other passengers had stopped talking and observed Ruckles closely.

"Ain't nothin' to worry about," Ruckles spoke up. "Just me and him reaching an agreement."

"Why don't you pitch the mutt overboard?" a voice spoke up. "I didn't know we'd be travelin' with any stinkin' Injuns." It was Pat Parrot, sitting at a table in the middle of the room and gripping a cup of coffee.

"This here Indian is 'Raindog', a famous medicine man," the other man seated across from the Indian spoke out.

Ruckles glanced back but continued his way out of the galley without responding.

Parrot stared hard across the room then yelled out, "He's worse'n a nigger and he should be shot!"

Nobody said a word in the tense silence that followed. The Indian slowly got up from the table and exited the galley by the opposite door from which Ruckles had departed.

A steep ladderwork of stairs separated the main deck from the engine room. Ruckles carefully backed down, gripping the rail. With each step the temperature rose and the air grew more sultry. The pulsing throb of the engine doubled in sound as well. In the flickering light of the boiler fire a nimble shape was seen moving about.

"Well, engineer," Ruckles bellowed above the engine. "This

bucket sounds like it's runnin' fine to me."

Sidley emerged from the darkness, wiping his forehead.

"She heats up in a mos' peculiar way, mistah Ruckles," Sidley said.

"That's because the governor isn't worn true," Ruckles responded. "It's lopsided."

"Yes it is, sir. I noted that. I'm wishing I had a replacement for it."

"Just pack up the third bushing, Sidley, and throttle back when you need to. You engineers always want new parts. But I ain't no money tree, so we make do with what we got to get the job done."

"I know what you be talkin', mistah Ruckles," Sidley acknowledged. "I was only dreamin' out loud."

Ruckles turned away toward the stairs. "I'll check on you in a few hours and I'll get the mate to bring you down some more water."

"And a bite of food, too," Sidley yelled up to Ruckles, waddling back up the stairs. "I be hungry as an alligator."

The first night and day on board the *Onyx* passed without incident. Many passengers stuck to themselves while others formed small social groups. Though a couple of passengers had traveled north previously, the main party of argonauts were uninformed and had to rely on second or third-hand bits of knowledge they circulated among each other to expand their knowledge of the land and the tasks that lay ahead. As eager ears absorbed story after story, the eyes of each traveler served as the crucible in which each particle of information was gauged for its accuracy. It was in the process of consuming such information and choosing that which would be most useful to store and press into practice when they docked in Juneau that could well determine who survived, who thrived, and who might be wiped out or even die. In this filtering of information, raw greenhorns chattered endlessly while seasoned prospectors remained mute and appeared at a clear advantage. Occasionally, someone would pipe up to dispel the most outrageous exaggerations.

"I heard that you feel a strange tingle in your hands and feet when you're nearby a vein of gold," said one novice, who was trading his knowledge with several men around a table in the galley.

"Not a word of that's true," said a weathered-looking drifter, sitting nearby with his boots up on the table. "It's pure hokum."

Three men abruptly turned to look at him intently.

"And I suppose you've worked with gold, have you?" the novice challenged him.

"I worked six years up the Scott River, mainly for the *Diablo* mine but a few other gippo outfits, too. I washed gravel and worked hard-rock. I know gold. And you don't get no tingle from a handful of nuggets or if you're carryin' round bricks of the stuff. It's mighty pretty to look at, though," he added with a narrow smile.

The other men slowly digested the information but were eager to learn as much as they could from a veteran gold miner.

"Say, mister," one of them said, shifting his weight and leaning toward the man, "I hear tell that some people just have a knack for turnin' up gold. What do you know about that?"

The miner pursed his lips and pondered the question. Then he slowly nodded his head. "That's part true. Some fellas I worked with did seem to turn it up more'n others. But most of them knew the best places to look. See, gold is real particular about where it forms in rock or where it settles out in a creek. Like it's got its own mind."

The other men soaked this up attentively, trying to decide whether they had learned something special or they were being set up as the brunt of a joke.

"Gold is where you find it," a loud voice spoke out from another table. The men shifted around to locate its source. Pat Parrot sat alone at a nearby table, thumbing a deck of cards. "I know gold, too," he continued. "I worked all through the Nevada, California, Dakota, and Mexico some."

"Whaddya mean, 'gold is where you find it'?" asked one of the men across from him.

Parrot shuffled the deck. "You get the right technology you can find gold just about anywhere. Nowadays, you can pull it out of places where you couldn't before.

"How so?"

"I just said it, 'technology'," Parrot shot back. "I was assistant mine manager at the *Big Bluff* in Grass Valley. For a bunch of years we was dumpin' rock that was loaded with gold, only we didn't know how to extract it properly. Before I moved on we figured it out. Reprocessed the dump rock and got a bunch more gold."

The novices again didn't know how to respond, but only stared at Parrot, hoping he would continue.

The other prospector spoke up. "That fella's right, too. There's been lots of new discoveries about how to get more gold, silver and copper outta mine rocks." Then the prospector swung his boots to the floor, pursed his lips and leaned toward the men. "And I heard tell that pretty soon we're gonna be able to get pure gold out of horse shit."

The other men looked stunned. Then the prospector's face broke into a wide smile and he rocked back on chair in raucous laughter.

"Ha! I can see the newspaper headlines now: 'Gold discovered up horse's ass!" He doubled up with laughter, having a good joke at the expense of the greenhorns. A few other men in the room chuckled, as well, at the joke.

Parrot smiled weakly but didn't join in laughing. "He's having you on. But, mark my words, one day somebody's gonna figure out how to get gold out of dirt."

"Dirt? What do you mean, dirt," asked the prospector, who had stopped laughing but was still grinning.

"Dirt's made up of rock particles, including gold," Parrot said. "Just need the right technology to pluck it out. Same's true for sand on the beach."

"Well, amen to that," said the prospector, chuckling again. "I'd like to spend my day workin' at the beach, with a few ladies standing around wearin' them fancy bathing outfits. That'd be alright with me!"

Parrot rose from the table, irritated that he wasn't being taken seriously. "You laugh too much, mister. I'm beginning to think you don't know a dam thing about finding gold."

With that, Parrot tucked his card deck into a saddlebag he carried under his arm and strode from the room. Watching Parrot, the prospector continued to smile weakly before rocking back in his chair. "Gold is where you find it," he said slowly, glancing at the novices who continued to sit in silence. "That's a good one."

Barging out of the galley, Parrot swung the door with pent-up anger. The door smashed into a passenger, Aster, who was sent sprawling to the deck with the force of the blow. She yelled out in shock and pain and clutched her wrist. Parrot took a couple of steps onto the deck and looked at Aster but made no move to help her up. Gina stared at Parrot, gasped in shock and took several steps back. Winona Kettle stood her ground and glared at Parrot. Parrot glanced at all three before a deep, furrowed sneer grew on his lips and his eyes widened. "Whores!" he rasped. "Stay out of my way." He tightened his clutch on his saddlebag and strode away.

When Parrot moved on, Gina and Winona rushed to comfort Aster who continued to whimper. Gina was white as alabaster and though she dropped to her knees, she was too shaken to be of much help.

Winona felt Aster's wrist and began to wrap a hair net around it. "You've probably just sprained it." She offered up a hankie that wrapped around a pinch of lavender to quell nausea and instructed Aster to inhale its vapors. Looking down the deck and then glancing at Gina, she said, "My God, who was that oaf? What a bull."

"He's not a bull," said Gina, shaking her head. "He's a despicable brute," she sobbed into a handkerchief.

By afternoon of the fourth day on the water, the *Onyx* had chugged past the northern tip of Vancouver Island, the voyage more than half complete. Off the port side of the boat lay the vast tableau of the Pacific Ocean that bisected the horizon evenly with the sky. As typified summer maritime conditions, the surface of the great ocean stirred with large, gentle swells that rolled the boat but didn't impair its travel.

On board, many of the passengers were feeling nauseous from the rolling ride. Those who were feeling poorly divided their time between the main deck, where they could enjoy the benefit of fresh air, and the sleeping quarters which offered some seclusion but, packed tight four men to a room, were cursed as cramped and stifling.

Later in the day, the setting sun burned less intensely and the heat of the day gave way to a cooling breeze that offered relief. After dinner had been served and eaten in the main galley, most of the passengers exited to enjoy the cooler evening air on the main deck.

Along the rail near the bow, two men shared stories and discussed various strategies for achieving their goals in the Klondike.

"I don't' know much about history 'cept for what I heard," one man said, "but I figure something like the Klondike comes along every few hundred years. When I heard about it I felt I had to try my hand. I told my wife I didn't want to be no pig farmer forever."

"Where'd you turn up money for passage and supplies?" asked Liam Minney, standing alongside.

"My sisters loaned me some, and I borrowed the rest from an uncle who owns a slaughterhouse," the man replied. "I made a deal to cut them in for a share of my profits. How about you, what's your line of work?"

"I been working as a human pack mule for about as long as I remember, humpin' freight for slave wages. Wherever I worked, it was the same conditions. At home I got three screaming kids and a wife naggin' me to get ahead. I just couldn't stand it any more, so I talked my boss into sponsoring me a grubstake to get up to the Klondike and get in on some action. He didn't offer me much, but if I get in on a strike, I just might find my way to doin' something else before I work myself to death."

"Do you know much about lookin' for gold?" asked the potato farmer.

"About what you could stick in a hummingbird's ear, partner. And you?" Minney asked.

"About the same. But the way I read it, there ain't that much to it. I mean, I got a brain, I'm willing to work hard and I'll learn as I go. If all them yahoos that came down a few days ago can get lucky, I can, too."

Minney kept gripping the rail and staring out at the ocean. Then he sighed deeply. "I never appreciated dry land as much as I do now, and I sure wish there was another route to the Klondike than travelin' on this scow."

"I agree with you there, friend. I can't swim any more'n a pig can fly. Hey, by the way, name's Henry Jacobs," he said, extending his hand. "What's yours?"

"Liam Minney. Glad to know you, Jacobs." He shook Jacobs' hand then turned back to looking out over the sea.

"Did you leave family behind?"

"Yup. Wife and child. Daughter's not yet ten. I love her to pieces, and I'd surely love to earn enough money to send her off to school in Santa Rosa."

"Yeah, it's a nice dream, that one," Minney responded.

For a few minutes neither man said anything else. Then another tall, serious man with a trim suit and thin mustache walked close to them. Jacobs glanced at the man, studying him closely.

"'Scuse me, partner," Jacobs said to the stranger. "Don't I know you from somewhere?"

The tall man stopped and confronted Jacobs, looking puzzled. "I don't think so."

Jacobs continued. "I remember now. You're the fella that helped me with that chinaman in the bar last week." He stuck out his hand.

Isaac Fayne tentatively returned the offer. "Hmmm. That's correct. You're a farmer."

"That's me," Jacobs said. "Name's Henry Jacobs. Excuse me, I forget yours."

"Isaac Fayne."

"Well, Fayne, this here is Liam Minney," Jacobs said.

"Pleased, I'm sure," Fayne said, glancing at Minney.

Minney nodded slightly in Fayne's direction. "You don't look like a prospector, Mr. Fayne."

"No, gold mining is not my concern, Mr. Minney," Fayne said dryly.

"I remember now," Jacobs broke in. "You're some kind of doctor.

No, wait, that's not it, you're a scientist. What kind of things are you gonna be doin' up north again, Mr. Fayne?" Jacobs asked.

"Well, my plans have recently changed. I have now been retained to travel to the Klondike and complete a report on all manner of culture and geography."

"Well, that sounds real important," Jacobs fawned. "I wish you a lot of luck."

"On the contrary, I would suggest it is the gold seekers who are in need of luck, Mr. Jacobs," Fayne replied.

"How do you figure that?" Jacobs inquired.

"I am skeptical by nature. In this case, little is known about the geology of the northern region. Based on probability, the chance of locating a 'pay streak' of gold is extremely small."

"So I take it you don't figure we got much chance, then?" Jacobs asked.

"Based on scientific fact, the probability of winning a fortune is very remote, though, unfortunately, it has been highly exaggerated by the scurrilous newspapers," Fayne replied.

"Well, most people on this boat figure they got a pretty good chance of findin' gold, Mr. Fayne, and that's a fact, too," Minney added.

"To my observation," Fayne corrected him, "most people booked passage on this boat because they want to believe there is ample gold there. That's quite different from scientific reasoning."

"Is that such a bad thing, Mr. Fayne," Minney responded, "if people believe the gold is there and are willing to bust their ass to find it?"

"I don't know about that. I would attribute that response to a general weakness of human nature."

Minney gripped the rail and stared hard at the sea. "You sure seem to have it all figured out, Mr. Fayne," he said. "If it's all the same to you, I figure I can't do much worse than what I left behind, so I'll take my chances in the Klondike."

"That is clearly your prerogative," conceded Fayne. "And to you gentlemen I wish the same luck I offer to the others on board, including the women."

"That's much appreciated," Jacobs replied, much less effusive than before.

"And now I'll bid you good evening," Fayne said, preparing to depart the conversation. "I sense a chill in the air and I think I'll step inside to take some tea."

Inside the galley, gas lanterns were lit and several groups of men sat huddled around tables, talking, smoking cigarettes and cigarillos, and sipping coffee or tea. At one table a trio had begun a game of poker, swiping cards and small coins across the table. Snatches of conversation punctuated with laughter and swearing rose and ebbed in concert with the steady pulsing of the ship's engine.

Pat Parrot approached the table where the card game was in progress.

"Mind if I join in?" he asked, setting himself down on the bench.

"I don't care none," one of the men said.

"Howdy, Parrot," one of the players, Horace Geery, replied.

"Sure, why don't you join in. We could use a fourth, long as your money's green."

"Green like this fella here," Parrot said, gazing at the other card player, seated across from him, who looked uncomfortable.

"Oh, that's my cousin, Jeb Smithers," Geery said. "Play's a mean fiddle but he's been puking his guts out the last day."

Parrot tipped his Montana hat toward Jeb. "That's rough news."

"And this fella's Mason Barlip," Geery said, pointing to the other player, who nodded toward Parrot.

"Pleased to meet you, Barlip," Parrot said, fingering a few coins from a musty leather pouch onto the tabletop. "I hope you got a lucky deck and everybody's got a lot of change, 'cuz I aim to win a few games."

"Just so you know, Parrot," Geery said, "we already agreed to penny ante, three-cent limit on bets and the game winner contributes two cents for the next pot."

"Three cents a bet?" Parrot said, incredulously. "Shit. I'll never be able to retire at this rate," he said, facetiously.

"Hold on to your pistol, mister," Smithers advised Parrot, dropping a couple of pennies into the pot. "Two cent raise."

"Nah, it's yours," Barlip said, dropping his cards onto the table. "I don't have nothin' here."

"Okay," Smithers said, sweeping up the small pile of coins that comprised the winning pot. "It's my deal this game and I'm playing stud. One down, four up. Everybody ante?"

Grubby fingers pushed coins into a pile into the center of the table.

"I'm in," Parrot said. "Stud's my game."

Smithers dealt the first round of cards face down, followed by a round of cards facing up. Ten-high held the bet. A bet was called and another round of cards followed.

The game continued at a brisk pace over the next hour with Smithers raking in the most winning hands. Parrot was the most competitive, often jibing the losers, but the other players did not overly concern themselves with his banter nor did they take the game too seriously. Win or lose, they were playing poker to help pass the time and relieve tension, and as an opportunity to discuss finding gold.

"My grandad used to tell me there's two kinds of luck in the world," Mason Barlip opined, after folding another hand of cards onto the table. "Bad luck and no luck at all."

"I sure hope you find better luck in the Klondike," said Smithers, tossing a couple of coins into the pot.

"Me, too," said Barlip.

"Weren't you telling me your grandad could find gold with a dowsin' stick?" asked Clarence Geery.

"He's the one," Barlip chuckled. "Old man tramped around, worked a bunch of mines. Showed me a thing or two about sniffin' out gold but I never worked the stick like him."

"I got a pair of knaves," said Smithers, unfolding a hand of cards.

"Take it, you rascal," said Geery.

Smithers reached out and palmed a small handful of coins toward himself.

"You seemed to have recovered your health there, partner," Parrot chimed in.

"He sure has," added Barlip. "But you're not doing too bad, yourself."

"Well, I play to win," Parrot said. "Learned that from my daddy. Before I bashed his head in with a shovel."

Eyes glanced in Parrot's direction while Barlip gathered up the cards and began to shuffle them.

"I don't think my father would've taken it too kindly if I had whacked him with a shovel," Geery said. "Probably would've evened the score real quick with a walnut stick he kept around for me and my brother."

"Follow the Queens is the game," said Barlip, who began dealing the cards.

"My old man was whippin' me good with a strap of leather he'd wrap around his fist," said Parrot who waved his arm in the air. "Cuz I didn't want to work as a farmer's helper or waste my time in school. Used to beat on me all the time. Only one time I grabbed a shovel leanin' against the wall and creamed him a few times. He never knew what hit him," Parrot said, "and he never woke up."

"Ya killed him?" Geery asked.

"That's what they said," Parrot said, who began studying his cards.

"Your mother have somethin' to say about that?" asked Barlip.

"Never had no mother. Just a son-of-a-bitch old man who said I killed his wife and called me a bastard every day he was alive. Now I am startin' to like the way this is shaping up. I'll throw a couple of cents in to sweeten that flower pot."

"I'm in, too," Geery said. "So what happened to you after ya killed yer old man?"

"Got sent to a god-dammed prison for kids. Worse'n rats in a cage. Brawlin' from dawn 'til midnight. Then I got shipped out to work in an iron ore mine and I been workin' in mines ever since. Came to like minin' work. Hell, I don't know why I'm tellin' a bunch of strangers my life story. Christ, gimme another card."

"I'm folding up this game, gents," Smithers said, dropping his cards onto the table.

"I'll pay to see another," said Barlip, who turned to glance over his shoulder where Isaac Fayne was standing a few feet back, watching the game.

"Hey mister, you gonna stand there or would you like to join in?" Smithers asked.

"I'm content to observe the game from here," Fayne said.

"Suit yourself. Last round down," Barlip said. "Queens and sevens are lucky."

"It'll cost ya' to see that last card," Geery said, tossing a coin into the pot.

"I'm out," Barlip added, folding his cards.

Parrot moved some coins into the center of the table and shook his head. "This is child's play." He looked up from his cards and glanced up at Fayne for a moment. "Now, mister," he said, chuckling, "don't take no offence, but you're kind of gussied up to go snufflin' for gold."

"I am not interested in prospecting," Fayne replied. "I am, in fact, a scientist."

"Well," Parrot drawled. "I ain't no scientist, but I do believe I got a winning hand here and I'll bet a couple of cents to prove it."

The other men snickered and Geery studied his cards.

"I see your bet, Parrot," said Geery, laying down his cards. "Three tens."

"Dam!" Parrot cursed. "I only had a lousy pair of nines."

"That's a bluff in my books, Parrot," said Smithers, collecting the cards and shuffling them.

"So what if it is?" Parrot countered. "I told you I play to win. Course, maybe our scientist friend could tell ya' if I'm bull goose loony. Well, what about it, scientist?"

Fayne looked stern. "I don't have any opinion. I'm not a gambling man."

"I guess you ain't," said Geery. "But maybe you got a name."

"My name is Isaac Fayne."

"That a fact," Parrot said, sarcastically. "Any relation to 'Iron-jaw' Fayne, commander of union troops at Gettysburg'?"

"I'm impressed. As a matter of fact, he was a distant relation," Fayne said.

"My grandaddy served under Iron-jaw," Parrot said. "Before he got buttshot and spent the rest of the war in hospital. I never saw him walk a step in his life."

"Let's play another round of stud, five high," said Smithers, dealing the cards.

"Sounds good to me," Parrot said. "So tell me, Mr. Fayne, what kind of 'science' are you interested in way up north?"

"I am to complete a report for the Swan Institute of Washington

DC on the geography of the Klondike region."

"Hmm," said Parrot, again studying his cards, then glancing again at Fayne. "Well, that sounds real fancy."

The other men chuckled again.

"I'll bet a couple of cents on my king," said Geery. The other men added their coins to the pot.

"Pardon my ignorance, Mr. Fayne," Barlip said, "but what exactly will you be studying?"

"I will examine the land forms and the various native groups of the region."

"Native groups?" Parrot said. "You mean Injuns?"

"That's right, Mr. Parrot," Fayne said, carefully. "I will be studying the customs of the Indian tribes that live there."

"Study their customs?" Parrot continued. "Well, I hope you're packin' plenty of lye soap. Specially if you plan on sleepin' with any of them squaws."

The other men laughed again.

"I can assure you, Mr. Parrot," Fayne responded, adamantly, "I am not planning on sleeping with any Indian women."

"No?" Parrot said. "Well, if you're not gonna sleep with 'em, maybe you plan on picklin' some of them," he said.

Geery chuckled at the suggestion.

"No, Mr. Parrot, I can assure you I am not planning to 'pickle' any of the Indians I will be studying, either," Fayne responded, becoming more agitated. "It seems you have a rather disparaging view of science."

"Well, I don't know about that," Parrot said, "but I know you scientists like to get your hands into just about everything."

"Hey, are we gonna play cards or yak?" Smithers asked. "I don't know nothin' about this 'science' stuff."

"This is my last hand," Geery said. "I'm ready to turn in."

"Me, too," said Barlip.

"And I will bid you good night, as well," Fayne said, turning and walking away from the table.

"Sorry gents, I didn't mean to cut the game short. I just got kind of riled by our fancy pants friend there. Hell, if this is the last round, I'm gonna bet three cents on my winning hand right now. Who's in? Let's see your turkey."

Outside the main galley, few passengers remained on the deck of the *Onyx*. A blanket of summer sea fog had enshrouded the vessel as the sun faded. The fog was accompanied by a brittle chill and inky darkness, obscuring the panoply of stars that had glittered overhead on previous nights. The steady pulse of the engine and the rolling motion of the ship produced a mysterious, hypnotic effect. What had been magnificent and awe-inspiring beneath a shimmering tableau of the cosmos had been replaced by something inorganic and constricting.

After entering the fog, Ruckles had left Cameron in control of the ship's wheel so he could go below to the engine room and confer with Ridley. The fog had descended above a gently rocking sea so they had agreed to maintain their daylight speed, led on by a compass bearing pointing north.

When the poker game wound down, Geery, Barlip and Smithers

vacated the galley to return to their berths and retire for the night. Parrot remained a few minutes extra, swilling a last cup of coffee before exiting. He pulled up his collar and tugged down his hat, but decided he would circle the deck. Mid-ship, he leaned over the railing to stare into the fog and down to the waterline where the wake slapped against the hull. He remained lost in thought for several minutes and didn't hear approaching footsteps.

"Quite a change in the weather," a voice spoke out.

Parrot whirled about in surprise and gripped the rail with both hands. "Whoa! Don't go sneaking up on me like that!" he yelled out, as if in anguish. "Who's there?"

Isaac Fayne emerged from the darkness and came to within two yards of Parrot.

"It's me, Isaac Fayne. I didn't mean to startle you," he said.

"Fayne! Well, what the hell are you doin'?"

"I am reconnoitering the deck. This fog is certainly a surprise."

"Yeah," Parrot agreed, regaining his composure but still looking startled. "I thought for a minute there I was back in the mines. Blacker'n half a yard up a horse's ass."

"It appears very dense in nature," Fayne posited.

Parrot looked around. "Yeah, that's a fact, mister."

Fayne stood alongside Parrot next to the rail. "So you've worked in underground mines, have you?"

"I sure did. Until I got caught in a cave-in. Whole shift of men died except for me. They dug me out three days later."

"That must have been a terrible hardship," Fayne said.

"Well, they got better technology now. But I'm spooked about workin' underground, I tell you that. I used to like the darkness of the mine, but after the cave-in I didn't trust it. Cut off my breath. It's why I took to prospecting."

Parrot started showing signs of becoming more agitated. Fayne said nothing but continued to watch him. Parrot tugged at his collar.

"I don't like this ocean much, neither. Too dam big."

"Well, we'll be there soon enough. The captain says we might even arrive a day early, " Fayne said, trying to soothe Parrot.

"What the hell does that captain know," Parrot asked, shaking his head.

"What do you mean?" Fayne asked.

"I'll bet that captain is more used to barging ladies up a river. 'Why captain, it's a little rough, could you slow down please, captain'."

"I'm sorry, I don't follow you," Fayne said.

Parrot looked at him fiercely. "I didn't think you would. You see, Fayne, everybody's happy doin' something for a while. Then along comes a gold rush and everything changes. There ain't no rules in a gold rush, amigo, and no one to be trusted. Why, that captain probably wants to find gold even more'n me. And I want it bad."

"I would speculate that you and I have that much in common," Fayne added. "We both hope to find success in the new land."

"So you got the fever, too," Parrot said with conviction.

"If you're implying that I am as crazed as these vagabonds, you're mistaken. The pursuit of science is rather more respectable than scrambling for gold."

"Bullcrap!" Parrot spat back. "Just because you give some critter a fancy Latin name don't mean you know any more than the average buck."

"Mr. Parrot," Fayne asserted. "You are a mining man. Even you must recognize the great debt that is owed to science."

"If it helps me get rich I'll be real grateful," Parrot said, chuckling. "I'm all for new technology and progress."

"Then we have that in common, too."

"I'm just more honest about my business."

"In your eyes, Mr. Parrot," Fayne countered. "To me your business seems very brutal."

"Brutal is just what a gold rush is, Mr. Scientist. Make your own breaks or starve. Or worse. And don't trust no one," he said emphatically.

The still night air was suddenly rent by a huge 'Crack' that sounded like a cannon shot and the boat lurched violently to one side. Fayne and Parrot clung to the railing as the boat heeled over, and gear stowed above suddenly broke free and sailed through the air. A large trunk pinioned along the inclined deck before smashing into them and trapping them against the railing. Parrot clutched his knee and yelled out. Then the boat lurched again and the two men released their hold on the rail and catapulted away from the deck out into the gaping darkness.

CAPE BEULAH

BRITISH COLUMBIA COAST

Late July 1897

The coastline hugging the Pacific Ocean adjacent to British Columbia is rough-formed, a work in progress. Sharpened spires of sandstone and granite jut from the tidewater like broken teeth, enameled with barnacles, mussels and rockweed. Twenty-foot waves powered by currents originating far to the north or incubated in Pacific storms pound the rocky shore, sending great spumes of water cannonading into the sky. Tireless winds hurl spindrift and sand across the foreshore with menacing force, re-sculpting bedrock and battering the living.

Life is established here, but consists only of those organisms that co-evolved with the land since the time the great ice-sheets abandoned the terrain fifteen thousand years earlier.

Twice each day, the pounding waves draw back, revealing foaming tidepools and stretches of cobblestones and sand where the richest array of life in North America clashes to eat or be eaten. For several hours, bears, cougars, wolves, otters, mink, eagles, ravens and myriad sea birds sojourn here to consume a seemingly bottomless smorgasbord. Oysters, clams, mussels, crabs, primitive organisms and fish marooned in tidepools exist in such quantities here that their numbers can't be counted in a squared acre of coastline.

As regularly as it opens, the inter tidal zone closes up and the animals retreat on worn pathways across a silent, redoubtable margin marking the verge of earth's most astounding forest. Its edges guarded by near-impenetrable salal vines and biting brambles, the coastal forests of British Columbia are a humbling testament to Creation. Towering cedar, hemlock and fir trees soar to three hundred feet in height, where branches adorned with beards of spectral moss conjoin to prevent direct sunlight from infiltrating beyond the uppermost canopy. Life here is cast in hues of brown, grey and luminescent green, eternally damp and softened by velveteen quilts of spongy moss that blanket the forest floor.

Save for a dawn chorus of birdsong and the croaking of ravens, the air of the coastal forests is quiet as a cemetery. Occasionally this silence is seasonally punctuated by the sound of flowing water as it makes its way through the great forests in arterial tributaries moving rain and melting snow. Deceptively gentle in dry weather, the tributaries and creeks swell to raging torrents during autumn, winter and spring rains, capable of callously grinding boulders into sand and uprooting staunch, thousand-year old trees with impunity.

On a warm summer afternoon, the wind from the ocean rustled the pale grasses that crept tenaciously from the forest toward the beach. Squalls of sand swirled up, abrading the vegetation and the bleached, twisted drift logs that lay on the upper tidal flats. Overhead, gulls looped lazily, squawking and hounding each other in a relentless chase for food, sporadically banding together to drive away ravens and eagles and smaller mammals that foraged on the beach when the ocean retreated.

By the water's edge, hundreds of plovers, oystercatchers,

sanderlings and other shorebirds skittered along, hunting down sand fleas in the effervescent foam. Tidewater tongues licked across the sand, endlessly rearranging the flotsam that washed in with the tide.

Along the beach a pair of children, a boy and a girl ran barefoot, occasionally chasing the tidewater tongues, squealing and splashing in the shallows. The children's arms and legs had been tanned auburn under the summer sun though they otherwise looked quite pale. Their hair was long and unkempt like the fabled *enfants sauvages*, children of the forest.

Enjoying the delights of the beach was not the main goal of the children, however. In their hands they each dragged a sack of netting in which they placed any recently-deceased rockfish, cod or salmon they located on the exposed sands that birds or animals had not yet discovered. In the absence of fish, they would dig for clams and cockles in the sand or collect oysters from among the cobblestones at tidewater.

Racing along the beach, the children suddenly stopped in their tracks to look down on the bodies of two men that lay prostrate upon the sand, next to a large piece of planking. The boy reached down to probe one of the bodies on the arm. The flesh radiated a white-blue sheen and was gelid to the touch. The boy jumped back as the fingers on the man's hand flinched and reached out to paw the sand. He lifted his head a few inches and attempted to focus his eyes. His eyes rolled back a few seconds later, though, and his head flopped back down onto the sand in exhaustion.

The children looked at each other, their eyes round as sand dollars, before they turned and raced off down the beach.

CAPE BEULAH

BRITISH COLUMBIA COAST

Autumn 1897

Pat Parrot lay with his legs pulled up toward his chest, a thin blanket shrouding his scrawny body. His eyes were closed though his jaw moved involuntarily and his arms twitched. A scraggly beard grew on his face that was otherwise defined by red blotches and chalk-white skin.

Parrot's body shivered and he kicked out a bony bare foot from beneath the blanket.

"My maps," he blurted out. "They're ruined." His eyes flashed open then shut again. He moaned and clawed at the side of the bed.

A woman sitting nearby leaned over and daubed at his face with a damp cloth. "Rest easy, mister," she said, with a thick British accent, attempting to comfort him. She turned to a child standing nearby and instructed him. "Run and fetch Cyrus. Tell him the man is waking up."

The child ran from the room. Parrot continued to thrash about in the bed for several minutes before resting again. Then his eyes flicked open and he struggled to focus his vision. He slowly rotated his head and looked about the room.

The woman reached over to wipe at his forehead and Parrot drew back nervously.

He groaned loudly and retracted.

"You have nothing to fear," the woman said.

At that moment a door opened and three men with long beards and farmer's clothing entered the room and approached the bed where Parrot lay. Again Parrot drew back in his bed and stared at the faces gazing at him.

"Who the hell are you?" Parrot rasped. "Where am I?"

An older man whose beard was streaked with gray answered him.

"Welcome to Cape Beulah, my friend," he said. "You washed up on our shore almost four weeks ago after a most unfortunate shipwreck. My name is Cyrus," he continued. "This is Edmond, this is Anton, and the woman is Lucy, my wife. She has taken care of you, nursed you, and so have several others."

Parrot remained silent. Another skinny man entered the room and joined those gathered around the bed.

"So, Parrot," the newcomer said. "You've woken up."

Parrot stared back, quizzically.

"You don't recognize me," the skinny man said, shaking his head. He tried again. "I'm Isaac Fayne. We were together on the deck of the *Onyx* when it struck god-knows-what and sank like a stone. We survived and washed up here."

Parrot swallowed hard and his adam's apple expanded and contracted like a bullfrog's. "Well, that's a story and a half," he said slowly. "When the hell is the next boat stopping by?"

The men exchanged glances.

"Boats do not stop by here, my friend," Cyrus told him. "Our village is isolated far beyond shipping traffic."

Again Parrot stared back, incredulous. "I don't understand. How do you get supplies?"

"We don't need anything," Cyrus replied. "We are self-sufficient. We grow and find our own food, make our own clothing. We are quite well-established."

Parrot remained still, pondering this, before blinking his eyes slowly.

Lucy reached over and wiped his face. "Enough talking for now, he is still very, very weak," she announced. "Don't worry, Mr. Parrot. We will continue to take care of you. Now close your eyes and go back to sleep."

Parrot looked over at her before his eyes fluttered shut.

"The poor man," she said. "He's been terribly shaken and needs more rest."

"Oh, he'll bounce back," Fayne pronounced. "He's a regular firecracker, you watch."

Two days later Parrot was feeling strong enough to arise from his bed. Lucy had left him with a crooked stick for support and he tottered toward a rough-hewn but properly fitted door. He leaned heavily on his crook as he took his first steps. His legs barely supported him as he fumbled with the wooden latch and tugged the door open. His eyes were unaccustomed to the brightness outside and he leaned against a wall, struggling to keep his balance and adjust to the sunlight. With much effort he slumped onto a crude bench fashioned from a cedar log next to the door.

Parrot regained his breath and gazed at his surroundings.

Squinting, he saw a gravel wagon road winding past towering hemlock and cedar trees and other cabins in the distance. The air carried the sound of children squealing and a moment later two young boys ran into view. They ran a few steps toward Parrot's cabin before they saw him and stopped dead in their tracks. They stared at him in silence until Parrot spoke up.

"What's the matter with you scugs?" Parrot called out. The boys clutched each other's hand in fright. "Ain't you ever seen a ghost before!" he yelled. "Here, I'll give you a taste what a real ghost sounds like," Parrot announced, tilting his head back. "Owwwwoooooooo!" he yowled out, tapering off into a choking growl before collapsing in a fit of coughing and sputtering.

The boys turned and ran quickly toward an older woman who had appeared on the gravel roadway. She glared at Parrot who wheezed and fought for breath. Several dogs picked up Parrot's cue and howled nearby. The woman muttered something to the boys who turned and ran off. She hurried along the wagon trail, turning once to look back at Parrot before disappearing from sight.

Parrot slowly regained his breath and clung tentatively to his bench. "Whatsa matter with people around here?" he spoke out to no one in particular, pausing to listen to the dogs yelping in the distance. "I guess you ain't never seen anyone as fearsome as Pat Parrot," he continued, chucking quietly to himself. "Just wait'll I get my leather back. Then you'll have something to think about." Parrot sat outside another minute before lifting himself from the bench and hobbling back inside.

With each passing day, Parrot regained strength little by little and was soon able to straggle beyond the cabin to explore the pathways and wagon roads nearby. He watched the comings and goings of the villagers who, for the most part, were preoccupied with farming activities and constructing new buildings. Some of the families exchanged greetings with him and asked him how he was feeling or commented on the weather while others spoke in foreign languages amongst themselves. Some nodded at him while others gave him a wide berth. He tried to engage Lucy when she brought him his meals but she was shy and avoided much conversation.

Parrot was sitting outside on his bench one afternoon when Fayne crunched along the roadway and turned toward the cabin for a visit.

"Hello, Parrot," he said enthusiastically, waving his hand as he approached. "Are you recovering your health?"

"Well, I guess I'm doing okay for a dead man," Parrot replied.

"I heard from the villagers you were starting to move about," Fayne said, "so I guess you've got some life left in you. I can tell you, though, we didn't hold out much hope a couple of weeks ago."

"Well, I'm not hoping to repeat the experience anytime soon. But it'll take more than a dunk in the ocean to kill Pat Parrot."

"You're tough enough, I'll grant you that, Parrot. But you're not much of a swimmer."

"I draw pretty much a blank on what happened out on that ship. If you saved my life, I'm grateful to you."

"I think these people deserve most of the credit for saving your life and mine."

"That may be so, but I'm still feeling kind of spooked in the head."

"You squawked and yelled out when you were lying in that bed, Parrot," Fayne said. "You shook these villagers up plenty, I can tell you that. You sure ranted on about your gold."

"That so?" Parrot said, staring up into the trees. "I hope I didn't give away any secrets. What I remember most is dreaming of some woman comin' at me with a candle."

"Really?" Fayne cocked his head at him.

"Yeah, she had long hair and funny-looking eyes and she kept muttering something."

Fayne's eyes sparkled in recognition. "That wasn't a dream you were having. That was Hilda. She lives by herself, a kind of wild child. Part Indian. That's where she got her gray-green eyes."

Parrot spit something onto the ground.

"She says she escaped from some place before joining up with this lot traveling west."

"Just where are these owly folks from," Parrot asked, disparagingly.

"They're a mixed lot, actually. Cyrus and a few others are American but most of them are from Europe, mainly England," Fayne replied. "They didn't want to stay in Europe or America."

"Why the hell not?"

"They say they wanted more freedom to live as they wish."

"Well, I don't understand that," Parrot said, shaking his head. "But if they came here there must be a way out."

"None that I know of, my friend," Fayne replied. "Apparently they sailed here but their boat has long since deteriorated."

Parrot glared hard at Fayne. "Now that just don't make sense to me. I've had a look around and there ain't a goddamm thing here 'cept for this godforsaken forest and some mean-lookin' geogerphy."

"I think I've found some evidence of Indian life here," Fayne said, fidgeting and rising to his feet. "I intend to explore the region for artifacts. You might want to help out the villagers get ready for winter, to help you regain your strength and get to know them a little. Perhaps you'll learn something. I don't know, you might come to enjoy helping them out in their farming work or you might learn if there is an overland route that they know about."

Parrot shook his head. "I ain't no farmer, but I sure as hell can't get into no trouble around here," he said, resolutely.

"I'm living down the beach a mile or so," Fayne said, waving an arm in the direction of the ocean. "I fashioned a comfortable dwelling from drift logs and am content there for now though I note the nights are getting cooler. You can come and visit me sometime."

Parrot looked up at him. "I'll do that, partner. When I'm up to the hike."

"Right, then," Fayne said, backing away, and tipping the corner of a floppy hat perched upon his head. "Good health to you, Parrot."

"G'day to you," Parrot said, bobbing his head and watching Fayne disappear along the roadway in the direction of the beach.

Two days later, Parrot was stirring about his cabin in the morning when someone knocked on the door.

"Come on in, I gave the butler the day off," he called out, wiping his hands through his hair.

A woman's voice called out. "My name is Hilda and I am just inquiring after your health."

Parrot tugged open the door and was startled to see the woman from his dreams. He backed up a few steps where he looked at her face and curly, flowing hair. She thrust out her arm to shake his hand.

"Hello, Mr. Parrot. I am glad to see you up and about. You are obviously feeling much better."

Parrot ignored her hand and spoke slowly. "Well, I ain't dead but I ain't quite fully alive, neither."

She lowered her hand. "Of course, that is to be expected. You are recovering, though. I am happy for you."

"I remember seein' your eyes when I was laid up. You're prettier than I recollect."

Hilda blushed. "Oh, thank you. I visited you a few times. And I said some prayers over you."

"That so? Well you wouldn't be the first. But I'm grateful for your help."

"Oh, it was nothing." Hilda's face darkened and she brushed a ringlet of hair from the front of her face. "I was wondering if you have met all the villagers yet. I could show you around if you feel strong enough."

"I hobbled about some, but I ain't seen too much. I suppose I wouldn't mind learning what the hell's going on around here."

Hilda lowered her eyes and plunged her arm into a woven string bag she was clutching. "I have brought you something, a shirt to wear."

Parrot accepted the offering and held it up. "It looks good enough. I'll just try it on." He pulled the shirt over his dungarees and swung his arms. "This is what I call a workin' shirt. I was tellin' Fayne I ain't no farmer but I might sweat some to get the cobwebs out."

"It looks good on you," Hilda admired. "Come, I'll show you around. I think the villagers are a little scared of you. If you got to know them it would be better."

Hilda and two older brothers had been raised by mixed-blood Indians that traced their lineage back to the first boatload of European settlers that came ashore at Virginia. The first settlers at Roanoke were befriended by Indians and eventually moved in with them in order to survive. This situation horrified British officials who ordered troops to hunt the Indians down and imprison or murder their leaders. The surviving members of the tribe, including the settlers and their mixed-blood children fled south into the swamps of the Carolinas, before heading west. One group of Indian refugees struggled for more than 250 years before being ambushed by civic troops in Louisiana. The children, including Hilda and her older brothers, were separated from their parents and marched to a reformatory work-farm in Oklahoma. Enduring prison-like conditions for nearly two years and an epidemic of smallpox that killed her two brothers, Hilda escaped the reformatory after some children started a fire. She managed to survive by living in a cave and eating berries and wild plants.

One day she spied on a rag-tag group of travelers camping beside a wagon road. They were held up because one of them was lying near death from a rattlesnake bite. The group was startled when Hilda emerged from the bushes and approached them, fitting a description of wild savages they had been warned against. They cautiously peered about, expecting a sudden ambush from an attacking tribe and were doubly startled when Hilda greeted them in English. Hilda had knowledge of plant medicine she learned from the Indians and offered to help. Her offer accepted, Hilda prepared special herbal poultices which she applied to the bite and the soles of the man's bare feet over the next three days, after which it was determined his life was saved and the danger of gangrene had passed.

The settlers were grateful and invited Hilda to join them. They explained that they were journeying until they could find a tract of land as far from the clutches of modern civilization as possible. Some of them had been persecuted, they said, for certain ideas they held. They wanted to create a village according to the 'Natural Laws of Harmony', which they explained involved not creating harmful materials or willfully hurting other living beings, excepting animals killed for food. Unlike many other settler groups and farmers, this group was eager to learn about, and from the Indians that had lived on the land.

Hilda agreed to join them on their journey, winding through

the mountains of Colorado, across the barren Basin and Range lands of Utah, over the Cascade mountains and then along the Columbia River valley toward the Pacific.

The group stayed more than a year on the outskirts of Portland, working at odd farm jobs and trades, eventually pooling enough money to buy a sailing ship the following summer. After repairing leaks, mending rigging and buying foodstuffs, tools, animals and other supplies, the group, including Hilda, launched the last leg of their journey in early summer. Sailing past the trading post of Fort Astoria, built where the Columbia River empties into the Pacific Ocean, they pointed the prow north. After several days sailing they began probing the fiords on the coast of British Columbia in search of the land they desired. Eventually, they waded ashore to explore a spit of coastline that held some promise for farming, though the mountains behind were formidable and impenetrable, an apt location for people wishing to live beyond detection. They named their new home Cape Beulah.

While establishing their wilderness outpost, Hilda taught many of the villagers how to gather wild plants for foods and make special medicines. Eventually, she built a small shelter in which she lived by herself. She spent much of her time exploring the mossy, cavernous forests and the wild, stormy coastline, where she felt an abiding sense of peace. She was self-reliant and sometimes disappeared for several days then returned to tell the villagers about a new plant she had discovered or about an animal she had observed. Hilda was pleased the villagers were content to work in peace with the land in contrast to the settlers that had burned and dug up enormous tracts of land across America in service of farming or settlement. She believed that the land around which they had settled was specially formed by the Creator and that the features of the surrounding land - the towering trees, the cavorting pods of whales, the jutting granite precipices and the restless sea – were imbued with a vital spirit that she had been summoned by the Creator to witness and sanctify. She created rituals of worship, including chanting and burning special herbs for the passage of seasons. Some of the villagers thought Hilda a little queer but she was well tolerated and welcome in every home.

In her mind, Hilda thought of Parrot and Fayne as mysterious interlopers who offered some excitement in the remote village. From the moment Parrot and Fayne were discovered in the tidal wash, some of the villagers were extremely wary that the two posed a threat to the villagers' relatively simple lifestyle. The kind of threat was not detailed, but the suspicion harbored by some was manifest in shaking heads and pursed lips. Others merely shrugged, and some of the villagers were mildly excited by the arrival of the strangers who suddenly entered the lives of the villagers without warning, bearing no identity save for the stories they told.

Hilda felt quite certain that she had helped save Parrot in some way while his life hung in the balance. Almost daily, she had observed some improvement in his health as she massaged his body, rubbed his chest with special tinctures and recited prayers. She was excited to see Parrot walking around, believing now that his full recovery was imminent if he could be persuaded to join a work detail.

After Parrot and Hilda departed his cabin, she led him through the village to a large field cultivated for cropping. There, a couple of men were employed in threshing golden wheat while another trio guided a horse and harrowing disc turning under stubble. In a far corner, another group of men was working to remove an enormous stump and expand the cropping field.

Parrot and Hilda walked toward the duo threshing wheat. The men stopped working and stared at them as they approached.

"Hello, Hilda," one of the men called out in a Scottish brogue as Parrot and Hilda approached.

"Hello, Edmond," she replied.

"You've brought a friend."

"This is Mr. Parrot. Parrot, this is Edmond."

"We've met. Hello, Parrot," the man said dryly.

"Howdy," Parrot replied.

Edmond wiped his brow with a piece of broadcloth he pulled from a pocket. "Excuse me. This isn't difficult work but it makes one very sweaty."

"No problem. I've done some sweating in my time. But mining's my kind of work, not farming."

"I'm sorry we don't have any mines around here," Edmond said.

"Maybe nobody's gone lookin' in the right place yet."

Edmond looked at him quizzically. "That might be true. Of course, we don't have much reason to go looking for mines."

Hilda spoke up, directing Parrot to the other man. "Parrot, this is Einar."

The other man nodded and extended his hand to shake Parrot's.

His head glistened with beaded sweat.

"Pleased to meet you," Parrot said, guardedly.

"Einar is soon expecting a child," Hilda spoke up. "That is, his wife is expecting a child. Their first."

"Not for some time yet, Hilda," Einar said in English congealed with a Norweigan accent.

"Still, children are very special in the village," Hilda responded, justifying her enthusiasm.

"That so," Parrot said. "Well, being a kid wasn't special for me."

"No?" Edmond asked. "I'm sorry to hear that. Anyway, we have work to do here and we should get back to it. Do you feel you could swing a scythe, Mr. Parrot? We could use your help."

Parrot took a moment to look at the field and ponder the offer.

"There's an excellent crop in the field this year," Einar said, "and we are enjoying good weather. But rain will be coming soon. So we work hard now."

Parrot slowly nodded his head. "I reckon I could show you farmers a thing or two about hard work. Course, I'd rather be mining."

"So you said," Edmond replied, extending a scythe toward Parrot. "In the meantime, this will have to substitute for a sledge or pick."

"I guess it will," Parrot said, lifting the scythe and testing its heft. He turned to Hilda. "Thank you, darlin'. A couple of days of this and I'll be fit as a fiddle. Alligator tough."

"I'm so glad," Hilda said, smiling. "Your help will be appreciated." She turned to Edmond. "Don't work him too hard."

"A man should earn his way, Hilda," Edmond said, trudging toward the field.

In the next couple of weeks, Parrot helped the villagers in the field, working with Edmond, Einar and others gathering wheat, discing stubble and digging out potatoes and other root crops. October sunlight extended the growing season and enabled the villagers, united in their toil, to work long hours bringing in the summer harvest and sowing seeds for late winter vegetables. On the edges of the field the men burned the slash from the giant trees they had felled to expand their crop lands, and they spread ashes over the soil they had sown. Children and women hauled bagfuls of sandy kelp up from the shores and this, too, was added to the fields along with heaps of yellow and crimson leaves that drifted down from the trees. The villagers were very knowledgeable about farming but, coming from different backgrounds, they often had differing opinions and engaged in spirited arguments, the details of which spilled over into strategic lectures for Parrot's benefit.

Excepting one rest interval per week, each workday began in the early morning and continued until early afternoon when the villagers broke for a large dinner meal that many ate together in a common hall. If people didn't wish to interrupt their work to attend the dinner meal, food was brought to them at their work site, and people also ate by themselves or in their family cabins. An hour after dinner, work continued until early evening when people concluded the workday with a light supper.

Parrot preferred eating alone but the spartan routine agreed with him and helped him to regain his stamina and strengthen muscles that had weakened while he was bed-ridden. He had long ago learned the value of hard work and he knew how to set his mind to labor even if he had never worked at farming. For the time being he was content and he pushed thoughts of his isolation to the back of his mind.

On various jobs he also fashioned a camaraderie with his co-workers, though Parrot's sensibilities and gruff humor, especially, contrasted with their more taciturn manner.

One day, working to repair the wall of a supply shed with Einar and a Dutchman named Anton, Parrot turned to the men and began talking.

"The last time I done this kind of work was when I passed through St. Louis."

Anton groaned. "Not another tale, Parrot."

Parrot embedded his hatchet into a stump and continued his story. "Now listen to me Dutchey, you ever been to St. Louis?"

"I vaguely remember passing through it. It wasn't special to me."

"It wasn't special!" Parrot bellowed. "Did you ever visit the 'Lucky Dollar'?"

"I don't think so. I don't know what you mean."

Parrot scoffed. "The Lucky Dollar is just the most famous cathouse west of New York city."

"Cathouse?" Einar asked. "I don't understand. What is a 'cathouse'?"

Parrot looked at Anton who looked puzzled.

Parrot was incredulous. "You guys never been to a cathouse?"

Anton and Einar both shook their heads.

"I don't believe it. You guys musta grown up inside a cave or something. A cathouse is for whores."

They continued to look perplexed.

"Whores. You don't know whores! Oh man, you don't know shit! Whores are sluts that you rent for a couple of hours to screw. You understand that, don't you?"

"I know what you mean," said Anton. "Cathouses are known as brothels in England."

"That's the truth. I heard 'em called brothels. Same thing. You keeping up with us, Einar?"

"I'm not really sure what you are talking about."

"Oh sweet Christ. Listen, you had to screw your wife to get her pregnant, right? Well, it costs you about 3 bucks to screw a whore, 5 bucks in the Lucky Dollar cuz it's a classy joint, and they even throw in a few drinks. One night I spent 20 bucks in there, my month's pay. Oh man but they had some young girls there that wasn't older than 14 and soft as goose down."

Einar started to fidget. "Please, can we keep working."

Parrot laughed. "What's eatin' you friend? I was just going to tell you about one young filly named Honey at the Lucky Dollar who would fill up a bathtub with hot water and soap suds and take a bath on stage. Oowweeee, she would scrub herself up and ..."

"Anton," Einar suddenly called out, standing up. "Give me a hand moving this trunk."

Anton looked from Parrot to Einar and back at Parrot again.

Einar leaned over an old trunk pushed up against a wall and began to heave it forward.

As soon as he began to push on it, the lid of the trunk ripped free and Einar went sprawling onto the floor. Anton got up quickly to help Einar.

"Man, what are you doing?" Parrot said, retrieving the lid and moving to refit it to the trunk. "You coulda let me finish my story, Einar. Hey," he suddenly called out, leaning over the trunk, "What the hell is this!"

Einar and Anton looked at each other and then walked to the trunk and joined Parrot in studying the contents. Parrot smiled, then reached down and pulled out a full-length musket. He looked down the barrel, examined the trigger and flintlock and pronounced judgment.

"Well, well. I'd say this'd do the job, even if it is a few years old. Cut down a few Indians, for sure."

"I didn't know they were being stored here," Anton said.

"I remember now," Einar said. "They are for scaring off coyotes and wolves and other emergencies but I haven't seen them in a long time, maybe a couple of years. We don't really need them."

"Indians," Parrot said, "you got guns to protect you from Indians. Somebody was thinking."

"But the Indians here are friendly," Anton replied.

"I don't believe it," Parrot said, replacing the musket back in the trunk. "I'd sooner trust a wharf rat than an Indian. Or a chinaman. They're the lowest life on this earth. Worse'n maggots."

South of the village a couple of miles, Isaac Fayne was adjusting to a solitary life. He had fashioned a shelter for himself from driftlogs and large scabs of Douglas fir bark chinked with shags of sphagnum moss. Inside the shelter he lay moss and dried grass on the sand and he shaped a fireplace from sandstone slabs that adequately reflected the heat of his fire and warmed the chill night air. The villagers loaned Fayne a flint and he learned to spark a curl of cedar shavings into a tiny flame. The villagers also loaned him two blankets and a knife but he said he was content to supply himself with all other essentials. Fayne was a knowledgeable botanist who recognized many varieties of native edible plants, among them cattails, wild carrot, nodding onion and others. Hilda pointed out several other edibles to him, like salal berries that still clung to their vines like peas even late in the fall, and beautiful fluted Chanterelle mushrooms that sprouted like golden vases from the nearby forest floor. Steps from his shelter, on the beach, Fayne gathered a bounty of clams, cockles, oysters and fish washed up on the tide. These he roasted, sometimes with mushrooms and ferns, over his fire.

Fayne gauged that he would suffer no problems gathering food throughout the winter and that comforted him sufficiently to allow him to begin exploring and investigating the region into which he had been so abruptly introduced.

Fayne's voyage north was to have been an important stepping stone in his professional career. For the past eight years, since he had been awarded his Doctorate of Letters in Studies of Natural History from Harvard University, he had worked on various research projects. On behalf of the university, he had reported on rock and fossil formations in the Appalachian mountains, classified soils and vegetation in Massachusetts, and he had assisted in a study of Indian settlement patterns in New England prior to the time of contact with the first settlers.

Fayne was well suited to life as a scientist. He was goal-directed and he had a keen intellect. Since childhood he had been inquisitive and eagerly reduced the world around him into manageable chunks of information. His father was a well-connected lawyer and political advisor in Boston and he regularly brought home dinner guests from various occupations including adventurers, inventors and scientists. On one occasion the young Fayne was enthralled by Harvard scientist Grayson Ball, recently returned from an expedition to South America, describing his encounters exploring the jungle and meeting tribes of primitive Indians, some of whom he observed to be cannibals.

In the months that followed, Fayne regularly ducked out of grade school to visit the venerable Ball at his Harvard office and help him catalog artifacts from his expedition. The young Fayne proved indefatigable in his labor of detail for which Ball rewarded him with instruction in practical scientific protocol. At Harvard, Fayne met other scientists and listened to them argue theories and discuss discoveries. He proved a quick study, gifted in scientific reasoning and logical deduction.

One day Ball appeared unexpectedly at the Fayne home and asked to meet in private with Mr. Fayne in his study. When Fayne's father emerged some time later he asked Isaac to join them. Isaac's father explained that professor Ball had offered to sponsor Isaac, then 16 years old, in a new program to train young scientists at Harvard, and Fayne's father consented for Isaac to begin at the school the coming fall. In return for paying a sizeable tuition, he explained, he expected Isaac would apply himself to his studies in a way that would make his parents proud and reflect well on the Fayne family. Dizzy with excitement, Isaac could barely mumble a response before he did something he had not done in years – he hugged his father. His father blushed and pushed him away, assuring him such emotion wasn't necessary. He directed Isaac to go and inform his mother of the decision. His mother turned away from him and sobbed quietly when he told her the news.

Fayne excelled in his studies at Harvard and earned a scholarship in his third and fourth years. As arduous as his undergraduate studies were, the pressures intensified when he began to prepare for a career as a research scientist. Young aspiring scientists like Fayne were expected to keep abreast of new scientific developments, which seemed to be emerging at a dizzying pace, as well as complete whatever tasks were required of them by departmental professors who often piled assignment on top of assignment, many of which served capricious whim and self-interest. Throughout this ordeal of masked indenture, Fayne and his peers were expected to remain mute. If students failed in this, they risked abandonment or expulsion. On the other hand, if a student survived this highly competitive and ruthless apprenticeship through to graduation, he could rightfully claim the right to practice science, a highly-desirable profession in societal schema. This achievement did not mean the completion of apprenticeship, however. After graduation, as pointed out in a convocation speech by a senior professor, it was now assumed that young scientists would undertake their own research projects and begin to apply themselves socially, to take wives, begin families, and contribute to the needs of the institutions that nurtured them.

Graduate studies proved too onerous for many of his colleagues though Fayne survived and received his doctorate at age 29. In the heated fray of academic studies, Fayne abandoned the manners his mother had assiduously bestowed upon him as a child and, at his convocation, felt most akin to a mercenary soldier returning after years of warfare abroad, not at all ready, or prepared, to occupy his newly prescribed social role. He felt raw and primitive, with little self-confidence except for the saving graces of his own ego, which now guided him in social situations. Accordingly, Fayne emerged as stark and arrogant, alienating most people around him.

As a professional scientist Fayne prefered solitary work, eschewing the social circuits now plied by many of his peers, and he was eager for an opportunity to escape.

Answering an advertisement, Fayne was rewarded with a contract by the Swan Institute of Washington DC to travel to southern Alaska and complete a survey on the fauna, flora, geography and Indian tribes along the coast from St. Michael to Skagway, a region hitherto unexplored. Acquiring knowledge about previously undiscovered tribal cultures currently topped the list of valued pursuits in academic circles. Nothing, it seemed, attracted attention and financial donations for research, as much as a public lecture series on the discovery of a heathen native tribe. Inevitably, researchers were contacted by church groups for private meetings where religious officials offered to help fund scientific expeditions in return for information about how they might additionally make contact with the Indians and provide Christian salvation.

As part of his contract Fayne was encouraged to procure as many Indian artifacts as possible for which he would receive a bonus after shipping them back east. Fayne well understood the value of this practice to his employers who were engaged in a fierce competition with rival institutes to collect native treasure that they leased or sold to exhibitions and museums in the east or in Europe. In 1894, Fayne had spent much of the year under contract to work with a rival collector, the esteemed Franz Boas, preparing a massive exhibit featuring an entire Pacific northwest Indian village, including 18 native villagers, for the astounding Chicago World's Fair. Upon hiring Fayne for his present assignment, Douglas H. Swan, the founder of the Institute that bore his name, spent an entire day pumping Fayne for information about Boas and his practice, determined to outmanouever Boas along the southern Alaskan coast in the rush for Indian booty.

Fayne estimated he would need two years to complete the study before returning, after which he expected to travel for another year to lecture and present his findings to various universities and other interested groups. He was excited that this experience would help to establish his career and provide him with the leverage to undertake additional studies he desired. Yet when news of the Klondike gold strike reached Swan in Washington he quickly sent Fayne a telegraph instructing him to travel instead to the Klondike region, explore it thoroughly, and submit a report back to them within 3-5 months.

Fayne expected that it would be at least until spring before he might escape beyond Cape Beulah. As isolated as he was, he took some solace in recollecting the stories told by Harvard professors who had been likewise stranded in outposts during their field studies and collecting trips. Grayson Ball had told the tale many times whenever an audience gathered of how he been lost in the Yucatan jungle for several months after his assistant had been bitten by a venomous adder and died writhing in Ball's arms minutes later. On his own in unforgiving territory, Ball survived adequately for several weeks, subsisting on plants and bugs that he knew to be safe to consume, though he contracted a fever from drinking foul water and took very ill.

Ball recounted how he was eventually rescued after a tribal shaman had an hallucinogenic vision about a 'blanco' – a white man, all the more remarkable as no member of the tribe had ever heard of such a being. The shaman instructed hunters to go in search of the specter of his vision and they soon discovered Ball several miles away, lost and feverish and ranting to himself on a gravel river bed. The tribe nursed him back to health and later paddled him downriver to an outpost from where he inveigled passage north and eventually back to the United States.

Marooned as he was at Cape Beulah, Fayne was confident that this region of the Pacific northwest was poorly understood and he set out to reconnoiter the landscape and fashion a simplified scientific investigation of the region from his primitive beach outpost. Behind his cabin he had arranged great rinds of cedar bark into storage racks on which he began to display artifacts he collected. Initially, Fayne gathered shells and tests of marine creatures from beaches and tide pools and grouped them on the bark according to scientific characteristics. Though he lacked a notebook, Fayne was nonetheless anxious to record his observations so he devised strategies to memorize important details of specimens that could not be preserved and plants that quickly withered and decayed.

Roaming further abroad to observe birds and animals, Fayne made an exciting discovery in a clearing where he brushed up a scattering of bleached bones. Examining them carefully, he determined that the animal, likely a small deer, had not been killed by a predator, for the bones lacked the telltale signs of tooth punctures or splintering. He then surmised that the deer must have been killed by an Indian and cooked nearby, for he believed any villager who had killed it would have carried the carcass home. Sure enough, several feet away, Fayne found several rocks drawn into a circle and streaked with charcoal smudging from a fire.

Fayne recalled Hilda telling him that the villagers had been in contact with Indians on two or three occasions since they had colonized the cape but the Indians were skittish and the villagers hadn't developed a strong relationship with them.

This discovery of the fire pit kindled Fayne's interest in learning about any Indians in the present region on his own. With the diligence of a Pinkerton detective, he set out to discover more evidence of Indian culture in the area. He began by scouring the beaches, the verges just beyond the high-water mark, and the stream channels that incised the redoubtable forest. He was rewarded for his study with the slenderest of clues including several other fire-stone piles, a chipped log, and a pile of flint shavings that included several imperfect spearheads. He hoped that he would discover more.

At the end of October, the skies hugging the coast turned indistinguishable from the restless ocean. Comprised of roiling clouds cast in shades of gray and swollen with moisture as they buffeted against the coast mountains, the skies threw off the vestiges of Indian summer and flayed the coast with the first storms of winter. Fierce winds whipped ocean waves up to thirty feet and pelted the earth relentlessly with rain. During the storms' fiercest gales, sand and water blasted the foreshore with a force equivalent to the greatest cannonades of war. Animals retreated from the beach and the sky to the shelter of the forests. There, rain dripping from the forest canopy soaked silently from branch to branch into thick moss where it pooled and eventually drained into streambeds surging with power.

During storms and on rainy days the villagers took refuge in their cabins or gathered in the common hall. Like the Indians that occupied the cape before them, most were habituated to the inclement weather and spent the stormy weather working at chores. Women concentrated on spinning cloth, sewing clothes and preparing or cooking food while the men spent the time fashioning house wares and furniture, tools and boots.

Children attended classes held in the hall where they were

taught arithmetic and literacy skills for a few hours each morning. At noon, they helped the women prepare dinner. In the afternoon, children joined with their parents or other adults to help out with the chores for a couple of hours, after which they were permitted to read the books, including several Bibles that the villagers had brought along with them, or continue playing. By the time they were in their early teens, most children had mastered the skills required of them in the village.

Everyone, including Parrot, was encouraged to attend a monthly meeting at the common hall in which the villagers raised issues of concern and discussed new ideas. At a meeting held in early November, the villagers shuffled in and arranged themselves on stumps and on the floor in a large circle around Cyrus. Parrot attended the meeting and kept watch from the back wall where he remained standing. Sweat and wood smoke mingled in the air with conversation. Cyrus, speaking slowly, called the meeting to order and talked first about procuring more firewood for the hall and gathering more pitch for repairing roof leaks in village cabins. Anton stood up next and delivered a report on food storage for the coming winter, which was followed by a summary of late fall planting by another Briton named Samuel. Next, another man speaking in a thick European accent said that he had sampled a mushroom growing in abundance on dead trees in the forest and had found it be quite tasty when roasted. He believed the mushroom was related to a variety that was a popular foodstuff in the village where he had been raised. Hilda spoke up to warn the man to be careful about sampling strange plants, especially mushrooms. Several people nodded their heads in agreement. Cyrus said that he thought that sounded like good advice and that he would like to know more about any kind of food that could add to the village's food supply.

Lucy raised her arm and Cyrus nodded to her. She stood up and said that she wanted to raise an issue of concern. She had recently seen people deliberately jumping off a path to hide in the bush and avoid interacting with another person approaching. She said she didn't want to disclose the identity of the people involved but she didn't like this behavior and hoped it could be resolved. Cyrus nodded his head and asserted to the group that social exchange was considered a virtue by Piotor Illich, and that the villagers would be wise to heed this advice, by which they would come to better know each other and strengthen the bonds between them. Many of the elder villagers nodded their heads in agreement.

After Lucy spoke, another man with a long red beard, Robert, stood to address the group. "As you know, I have been teaching morning classes to the children, an endeavor with which I would like some additional assistance. Some of the children are struggling with lessons and I think the adults here have much to contribute. I would like to remind you that when we began this experiment we agreed that we would all pitch in with teaching and learning chores, and that it wouldn't only fall to one or two individuals to carry this out."

He paused and looked about the room where he saw several nodding heads.

"As I did last year, and the year before, I would like to bring forward a motion that each adult over the age of 14 years assist me for one morning each week until the present school year is adjourned."

A moment's silence the hall as people contemplated the motion.

"I agree to it," said one young woman.

"So do I," said another.

"I think it's too much", said a young man. "There's too many chores to do," he reasoned. "I agree to one morning a month."

"How many people would assist Robert for one morning each week?" asked Cyrus.

About half of the villagers raised their hands.

"Do the rest of you agree to contribute one morning per month?" Cyrus continued. He observed many nodding heads, then addressed Robert.

"Well, Robert, is that sufficient to meet your needs?"

Robert nodded his head affirmatively. "I'll prepare a daily schedule and affix it to my skill board. If people would match their name to a work day, I would be most grateful."

"It is agreed then," Cyrus continued. "People will assist Robert beginning tomorrow."

Cyrus then turned to address Parrot, who was leaning against the wall at the back of the hall.

"I would now like to recognize a guest among us at tonight's meeting. Mr. Parrot." All the villagers suddenly shifted to turn and look at Parrot.

Parrot's back stiffened and his eyes flashed. "I ain't done nothin'," he growled.

Cyrus smiled at him. "I'm not accusing you of anything, Mr.

Parrot. On the contrary, I would like to thank you for your efforts in the last few weeks. You have regained your strength and made a notable contribution."

Parrot didn't know what to say. His eyes darted around before he stared at Cyrus and bobbed his head. "That's okay," he stammered.

Edmond spoke up from the floor. "We have fed and clothed the man, Cyrus. It isn't asking too much for him to work with us in bringing in our harvest and helping with chores."

Cyrus shifted his body to confront Edmond, who stayed seated. "Your comments are not necessary, Edmond. Mr. Parrot remains a guest in our village."

"Only 'til I can figure out how to get the hell out of here," Parrot said determinedly, glaring at Edmond, who stared back.

There was a moment of uncomfortable silence before Cyrus said, "let's move on. Einar, your wife is not with us tonight. Is she not feeling well? The baby is due soon, is it not?"

People shifted their gaze to Einar. Before he could speak, the sound of a slamming door echoed in the hall as Parrot exited the meeting.

The villagers turned back to Cyrus, whose eyes narrowed as he stared sternly at the door. Then he released a deep breath, softened his countenance and turned back to Einar.

"What were you saying, Einar?"

Einar shifted nervously, "Well", he began slowly, but was interrupted by the sound of the door opening and closing a second time as Hilda left the hall.

Cyrus pulled on his beard a moment before he motioned for Einar to continue.

"She is not feeling well this evening," he said. "Actually, she has not been feeling well all week, as some of you know."

"She will be fine, Einar," an older woman spoke out. "It's your first child. Do not worry."

"I was sick for many weeks before I went into labor with Nicholas," said another woman."

"She should rest now to build up her strength," the first woman advised.

Einar nodded his head shyly. Then the sound of the door was heard again as Hilda re-entered the hall. She returned to the place where she had been seated.

Cyrus stared at her a few seconds before changing the topic.

"If there are no more items for discussion, I suggest we conclude tonight's meeting."

A younger man raised his hand and spoke with a German accent. "I have something I wish to talk about. I think it is time we started discussing our trip to the outside. We have put it off for a long while and I think the time has come to begin planning."

Cyrus raised his hand. "Heinrich, I suggest we carry this topic over to our next meeting. I feel it is late tonight to begin this idea."

Heinrich remained firm. "I would like to discuss it."

Some muttering was heard among the audience, and one person said aloud, "not tonight."

Cyrus rocked on his feet and sighed deeply. "Heinrich, I agree it is an important topic for deliberation. But I move that we agree to discuss it at the next meeting. Tonight is too much."

Heinrich pointed his finger around the room. "Next meeting we discuss this. It is agreed?"

People nodded their heads. "It is agreed," said Cyrus. "Tonight's meeting is concluded. Thank you all for coming."

As people rose and began filing out of the meeting, one of the elder women approached Cyrus and spoke coldly. "I don't know what it is, Cyrus. But something is not right here."

In the days following the meeting, Parrot avoided contact with the villagers excepting for mealtimes when he appeared briefly at the hall to fill up his plate. Some people nodded cordially to him while others gave him a wide berth as he passed by. Usually he mumbled a few words before retreating to the solitude of his cabin and his own thoughts.

One morning, Parrot walked through the village to the woodshed where he grabbed an axe and started chopping some stacked logs into firewood. He found this work satisfying and when the supply of logs ran out he hiked into the forest to find more dead trees for chopping. Before another week had passed, Parrot had chopped enough wood to fill the shed that served as the village's supply depot. Some of the villagers recognized his efforts and thanked him when they encountered him while others still avoided contact.

Cyrus approached Parrot one morning while he was chopping his way through a large hemlock log that he had dragged and rolled out of the forest. At first Cyrus stood off to the side and spoke to

Parrot, admiring the quantity of wood that Parrot had added to the shed. Parrot took no notice of Cyrus.

Cyrus stopped talking to watch Parrot carefully for a few seconds before he went up to him and squeezed his arm.

"Parrot," Cyrus said again. Parrot turned to see Cyrus and suddenly lifted his axe to defend himself.

"Relax, my friend," Cyrus urged him.

"What do you want?" Parrot retorted.

"I wanted to talk with you, to ask if you are alright."

"I'm fine," Parrot replied, dropping the axe to his side but continuing to stare intently. "I'm just chopping up some wood. I like chopping wood."

Cyrus shook his head. "You have done an admirable job and, again, we appreciate your efforts."

"Well," Parrot said, spitting on his hands and turning back to the woodpile. "I'd like to keep on working if you don't mind."

"You seem very busy with your own thoughts, Parrot."

"That's true enough, amigo," Parrot confirmed, again swinging and driving the axe into a log.

"I'm wondering if you will eat with us at the hall for dinner."

"I prefer to eat by myself. I can get more work done."

"Well, when your work is done today, will you come to my cabin and join Lucy and I for supper? We have discussed it and we would enjoy your company for a meal."

"I don't really fit in here," Parrot said, slamming a log into the ground, and then staring at Cyrus with hard eyes. "Damn, didn't you know wood chopping is a lot easier with a wedge. What were you owly folks thinking about, setting up in the wilderness without the right tools? You know, I've got all kinds of ideas on how to make things more efficient around here, starting with building a sawmill. But it seems to me that most people around here just want to stay slow as mud."

Cyrus returned Parrot's stare for several seconds. "We eat in the late afternoon just before sundown," he said, before turning and starting to walk away.

"I'll think on that," Parrot called after him, as he worked to wrench his axe out of the log.

At the end of the workday, as a cream-cool sky faded into shadow, Cyrus busied himself inside his cabin coaxing a fire in a rounded stone fireplace while Lucy worked at preparing a pot of soup from vegetables and staples. When she was finished she added water to the pot and then affixed it with help from Cyrus to a peg protruding from the wall just above the nascent fire. Cyrus bent over and blew several times to encourage the flames. When the fire caught he placed several more split pieces of wood on top before shuffling back from the dancing flames. Lucy approached and leaned over Cyrus to stir the contents of the iron pot with a wooden spoon carved from yellow cedar. Cyrus waited until she retreated before fanning the fire with a curved slab of Douglas fir bark he gripped with both hands.

"I think we'll see frost tonight," he said aloud. "The sky is clearing."

"Well, we are ready for that," Lucy replied. "The winter crops are covered with straw, and a frost will help kill off the slugs. Believe me, the slugs are too many this year. It has kept the children busy pulling them off of the seedlings."

"Everything has its place in nature, my dear," Cyrus said. "Even slugs. I regret I cannot say the same about all the people I know. People are surely the strangest works of creation."

Lucy said nothing, but began kneading a large ball of dough on a wooden table set close to the fire.

"There are so many slugs because the weather has been so unusual this year," Cyrus continued. "Warm and rainy, that is what slugs like best. I expected a frost weeks ago but it never came. Young Lyman told me that he spied some snowdrops beside a trail yesterday. Can you imagine? Whatever are snowdrops doing growing in the middle of November?"

"I don't know, my love, the weather seems very strange. But it has been an excellent season for growing sunroot and we even got an extra bounty of potatoes from those that weren't dug up," Lucy said.

Cyrus again fanned the flames. "Hilda said she saw tremendous shooting stars the night before last. She believes it has important meaning."

Cyrus studied the fire carefully. "Of course, I don't believe in any of that business."

Darkness settled in around the village, bringing with it the coolest temperatures of the year. Inside the cabin, Cyrus let down some mats of cedar fiber that had been affixed against the north wall to afford greater insulation against cooling breezes. Outside, a neighbor's dog began barking, triggering other dogs scattered through the village to respond in kind. Lucy reached in beside the fire with a stout branch fashioned with a notch to grip the pot, which she lifted and placed on a rough-hewn table nearby. She adjusted an oil lamp to throw more light over the table then accidentally knocked a spoon to the floor. She stooped to retrieve it at the moment there was an abrupt knock on their door.

Lucy and Cyrus both turned toward the door and waited for it to open, or for someone to call out. In the village it was customary for someone to knock on a door before opening it to peer inside, or to call out a greeting to the inhabitants. In this case the door remained closed and silence prevailed.

"I wonder who that is," Lucy said, pushing herself to her feet.

Cyrus stood up, approached the door, and opened it.

"Parrot," he called out in surprise. "I'm sorry, I completely forgot I invited you to dinner. Please come in and join us." Cyrus turned to Lucy. "I invited Mr. Parrot to eat with us tonight, my dear, though I did not know if he would accept the offer. Actually, I thought the chance was remote. But here he is."

"Well, there's ample food for you Mr. Parrot," she said. "But please, come in and close the door behind you."

"Yes, come inside, Parrot," Cyrus said, stepping to the side and gesturing. "We are not trying to heat the village but only the inside of our cabin. Come in and welcome."

Parrot entered the cabin tentatively and peered around. In the flickering firelight his face looked strained and gaunt, though his eyes shone bright as stars. He stood in the center of the room before Cyrus guided him toward the fire.

"Warm yourself here, Parrot. Tonight is chilly. Are you comfortable in your cabin?"

Parrot didn't answer but stuck out his hands close to the fire. After a few seconds, he knelt down and added several pieces of wood from the woodpile to the flames. He stared straight ahead until the new wood caught fire then he rocked back on his heels and stood up.

Cyrus, standing to the side, glanced from the fire to Lucy who was seated at the table and then back at Parrot. "Please join us at the table for some stew, Parrot."

Parrot slowly turned and studied the table, Lucy and Cyrus.

"Here," said Cyrus, gesturing, "you may have my seat."

Parrot remained stolid.

"Sit down, Mr. Parrot," Lucy said to him.

At the sound of her voice, Parrot bobbed his head and exhaled. "Don't mind if I do," he muttered, while Cyrus guided him into a chair fashioned from branches. Cyrus rolled a stump close to the table and seated himself upon it.

Lucy ladled some stew into a bowl that she pushed toward Parrot. Cyrus handed him a spoon and a piece of bread that Parrot immediately bit into and briefly chewed before swallowing. He then dug his spoon into the bowl and raised a spoonful of stew to his mouth.

Lucy raised a hand in warning. "Be careful, Mr. Parrot, the stew is scalding hot! I've only just removed it from the fire."

Parrot slurped the contents into his mouth. His eyes stared

straight ahead as he chewed and swallowed. "I like it hot," he said, wiping his mouth on his sleeve but registering no sign of distress.

In minutes, Parrot methodically and efficiently ate his way through the bowl of stew, while Lucy and Cyrus glanced at him and periodically blew on the contents of their bowls.

"It's delicious stew, my love," Cyrus spoke, renting the silence.

Parrot noisily tracked down the last food in the bottom of his bowl with his spoon before looking up.

"You'd like some more food," Lucy said.

Parrot nodded, thrusting his bowl down the table toward her. "Yes, I would."

When she returned another helping of stew to him, Parrot swirled his spoon in the bowl and stared into its contents. The muscles in his face relaxed and he exhaled slowly.

"Is everything alright, Parrot?" Cyrus asked.

Parrot looked up but said nothing.

Lucy tried. "Are you okay, Mr. Parrot?"

Parrot cocked his head toward Cyrus. "I still don't understand what you folks are runnin' away from," he said.

Cyrus looked at Lucy and then back at Parrot.

"We're not running away from anything. We just wanted to find a place where we could live in peace, away from the tumult of modern cities and all the ... ideas that go with them."

Parrot didn't reply but lifted a spoon of stew to his mouth.

"In coming here," Lucy said, "we made a choice. We wished..."

Parrot cut her off. "What kind of ideas are you talking about?"

Cyrus put his spoon down. "Well, we didn't agree with some

of the laws passed by government and the emphasis all the time on building bigger machines and ships and cannons and ..."

"You don't like machines!" Parrot said, incredulously.

"I didn't say that," Cyrus responded. "Machines are neither good nor bad, it depends on how they are used. But the governments of Europe and America, and the businessmen seem only to want to build bigger machines which all the time seem to spew out more smoke into the air and poison into the waters."

"But that's progress. Modern technology."

"Progress to some. But sometimes, many people are hurt by machines or the products of such machines. I saw this in Chicago where I grew up. My father made a lot of money in business, but you know he grew sick and died from eating poisoned fish. I also saw this in the cities of Europe and England, where I met Lucy."

Parrot stared at Cyrus as he ripped off another piece of bread.

"Have you ever heard of Piotor Illich?" Cyrus asked.

"Nope."

"Well, Illich was a Russian fellow who spent a number of years in England. He wrote several books and his ideas were quite popular. He discussed how people might incorporate technology but continue to do the things they wanted to do. Without being forced to do things they didn't want to."

"Many of the people of the village believe in his ideas," Lucy said.

"Did he think everyone should be farmers?" Parrot asked.

"No," Lucy and Cyrus responded simultaneously. They looked at each other before Cyrus continued. "Illich talked about how people could come together and cooperate in a community to share ideas and skills and lead a good life."

"Without hurting the nature," Lucy added.

"Yes, without hurting nature," Cyrus added. "Like the way we farm here. We have learned, for example, to grow certain crops together so that they might produce a better harvest than if they were grown on their own. It is quite remarkable and doesn't require additional chemicals and fertilizers to be added each farming season."

"Sounds like something you could patent," Parrot said. "Make a lot of money."

Cyrus sounded surprised. "But we have no interest in 'patenting' this method, or making money from it."

"Why not," Parrot asked. "You went to the trouble of thinking it up, didn't you?"

"Yes, but I don't believe we are the first people to discover this."

"That don't matter if you got a good lawyer."

"But we have no interest in ..." Cyrus paused before continuing. "We would rather pass the knowledge on to our children, who might also improve on our techniques."

"Now that just don't make sense to me," Parrot responded, wiping his mouth on his shirt sleeve. "Where I come from ..."

Suddenly there was another knock on the cabin door.

"Now who can that be?" Lucy inquired before getting up from the table.

The door opened a crack. "Hello, are you there?" a voice called out. "It's Hilda."

Lucy approached the door. "Come right in, Hilda. What a

pleasant surprise. Come in and have some dinner with us."

Hilda entered the main room and swerved to the fire. As she began unwrapping a large scarf that was entwined around her neck she glanced over at Cyrus.

"Hello Cyrus, it's a very cool night out there and I …Oh, I didn't know somebody was with you." Hilda looked startled when she saw Parrot seated at the table. "Perhaps I should not stay."

"Nonsense, Hilda," Cyrus intoned. "We are grateful for Mr. Parrot's company and yours as well. Please sit down," he said, offering Lucy's chair for Hilda to sit upon. "Parrot, did you know that Hilda once saved my life after I had been bitten by a snake? She is like a daughter to me."

Parrot remained seated, his eyes fixed on Hilda.

Hilda smiled nervously at Parrot. "Hello to you, Parrot," she said.

His head bobbed slightly in greeting to her but he said nothing.

"Will you have some stew, Hilda?" Lucy asked, raising a bowl.

"No thank you, Lucy. I ate a short time ago. I only wanted to visit with you."

"Well, there will be tea ready in a minute," Cyrus said. "And I wanted to tell you that new plant you discovered imparts a very pleasant flavor to tea, as you described."

"I also believe it is helping to improve my circulation," Lucy said. "I've noticed my hands and feet do not seem to be quite as cold and deprived of blood as before."

"I think I am sleeping better for drinking it," Cyrus said.

"I am so glad," Hilda said. "The Indians of the Oregon territory told me about this plant when we passed through."

"Hell, you don't need no concoction to fall asleep," Parrot spoke. "Just a good work day is all. I'm sleeping before I finish lying down on my bed at night."

"Yes, you have been working hard lately, Parrot," Hilda said. "You must be very tired."

"I ain't. I'm just getting some spring back in my arms is all," he said, stretching out his arm and clenching and unclenching his fist. "I'm starting to feel like my old self."

A moment's silence hung in the air before Cyrus spoke up. "We were just talking with Parrot before you arrived about the intentions of our village."

"Oh it is a lovely place, don't you think so Parrot?" Hilda asked.

"I think you folks are bedrock crazy," Parrot replied.

"But you can't mean that, Parrot," Hilda pleaded.

"I sure do. There's a whole world out there goin' by, not to mention a gold rush, and you folks are pretending you're stuck on the moon. You don't even use any money. I just don't understand that."

"What use do we have for money?" Cyrus asked. "We share everything here."

"But that just ain't the way things are. From my side of the fence."

"I see it as a matter of attitude," Cyrus continued.

"Things are different here in the village, Parrot," Hilda added. "You can see with your own eyes that people here cooperate and are very peaceable."

"Well it didn't seem like that to me at that last meeting you had. I know when someone's trying to stir me up."

"That was Edmond," Cyrus said. "He can be quite objectionable at times."

"Well, he better watch out. I'm mean as an alligator when I get crossed. I got a friend in Anton, though. He's startin' to come around to my way of thinking. Got a good head on his shoulders."

Another pulse of silence rippled around the table before Lucy reached for another pot. "I believe the tea is ready. Will everyone have some?"

"I'll be going back to my cabin," Parrot said suddenly, rising from the table. "I think I'll go and visit that scientist tomorrow. He lives down the beach, don't he?"

"I know where he lives," Hilda said. "I'm happy to show you the way. If you like I can call on you in the morning."

Parrot thought a moment then nodded his head. "That'd be all right, I guess. You can find me chopping wood." He nodded his head toward Lucy and Cyrus. "I appreciate the food," he said before turning and quickly exiting through the door.

A moment later the neighbor's dog began barking, followed by a similar chorus throughout the village.

The next day dawned clear and bright as bone. The stormy weather of recent weeks temporarily yielded to blue skies and brisk winds and the tops of the surrounding mountains glistened with fresh snow, reinforcing a sense of enclosure and forbidding wilderness.

By mid-morning, Parrot had chopped down a hemlock tree that ran 150 feet in length but was by no means a large tree in comparison to its towering neighbors. It would take several days just to buck and chop the tree in lengths and drag it from the forest to the shed, a task for which he would need use of a pair of horses. After he had nicked off the top branches, he chopped and humped a length of the crown from the forest to the shed. Soaking wet from sweat, Parrot stripped off his shirt, wiped his face and arms, then hung the shirt on the branch of a small birch tree so that it might dry in the breeze. He began to chop the crown into smaller lengths when Hilda appeared on a trail and approached him.

"Good morning, Parrot!" she called out.

He noticed her and then turned his head back to complete a downswing of his axe.

"Are you not worried about catching a chill, working without your shirt in this weather?"

"I ain't worried about a thing, sweetheart," he replied, setting a log section on its side and splitting it with another swing. "There's nothing healthier than working hard, though that ain't the game with these here sodbusters."

"Oh, you have seen them work very hard," Hilda said to him. "But at this time of the year, after the harvest is brought in and the fields are prepared for winter, the villagers take a break. The same way nature does. At this time of year, many animals are asleep and few things are growing."

"Is that right?" Parrot asked facetiously. "Well this here wood don't seem to chop itself up without some help from me." He picked up several lengths of wood he had chopped and flung them into the shed onto a growing pile of firewood.

"Would you still like to walk down the beach to visit with the scientist?" Hilda asked.

"Yeah, I was planning on doing that," Parrot replied, putting down his axe and turning to face Hilda. He stared at her for several seconds before he shifted around and walked over to where his shirt was hanging. He took it down from the branch and pulled it over his head. He then brushed his fingers through his beard before gesturing toward the beach.

"Show me the way, darlin'. I'm ready when you are."

Together, they followed a path that wound through some low-growing cedar trees, past a swampy grove of alder and willow and out to the foreshore where sinusoidal waves crashed onto a sandy beach. Beyond the rolling waves, the Pacific ocean stretched to the horizon in three directions without interruption.

Parrot and Hilda began hiking determinedly in the soft sand, picking their way through piles of kelp and bladderweed heaped lifelessly on the tidal plain. With each step they scattered crabs and offended dozens of scavenging shorebirds that retreated from their approach. After a half-mile, the sand yielded to a beach of slick rockweed and barnacle-encrusted cobble-stones that slowed their progress. Near a bend in the beach they observed a flock of scavenging birds, including several eagles worrying something lying on the ground. Parrot threw several large stones into the flock and turned to investigate. Reluctantly, the birds lifted off from the sand to hover in the air and shriek complaints at Parrot and Hilda as they approached. Among the cobbles, they discovered the decomposing carcass of a small sea lion. Parrot poked the body with a long stick causing a fragment of yellowing flesh to spall away. Wriggling maggots and decaying tissue sloughed off, emitting a cloud of noxious gas that rose into the air.

"Lord Thunderin' Jesus!" Parrot blurted, dropping his stick and backing up into Hilda, who was sent sprawling.

"Sorry, Darlin'," he called out, lifting her up from the beach. She had stumbled on the slippery boulders and gouged one hand and arm quite severely on barnacles. In a moment, blood began to seep from several lacerations on her arm.

"Rinse that off in the water," Parrot advised, directing her toward a tidepool. Silently, she dipped her arm into the water and watched the blood dissipate.

"That'll be okay," Parrot said. "Now wipe it on your skirt."

Hilda looked at Parrot for several seconds and smiled, then she looked down at her feet and stooped to gather up some sea lettuce. She carefully draped it over her cut arm.

"What the hell are you doin'?" Parrot asked.

"This will help to disinfect the cuts and speed the healing."

"I ain't never seen that," Parrot said, shaking his head.

"Indians are expert healers," she said.

"That right? Well, let's move on, quick. That stink is following us over here."

They trudged further down the beach, skirting close to a sandy cliff that offered some respite from the wind. Offshore, a large flock of goldeneye ducks and surf scoters bobbed up and down in the waves. Several ducks lifted off from the water and, in a moment, the entire flock rose up and filled the air with a whirring sound that momentarily overwhelmed the sound of the surf. Parrot and Hilda stopped to study the flock flying overhead.

"I often come here to sit on the bluff," she said. "Don't you think it is a beautiful place?"

Parrot shrugged. "It's a wild place. Like the mountains and the desert. Hard to tame a place like this."

"I like wild places," Hilda said.

For several moments they stood in silence observing the landscape. Then Hilda moved in close to Parrot and slipped her arm in his. She looked up at him.

"Do you think you could stay in the village with us, Parrot?

He looked at her quizzically. "What are you talkin'?"

"Well, when you first came here you were very sick and I helped nurse you back to health. Now you are better and I am wondering if you think you would like to remain in the village with us. With me." Her cheeks blushed hot and scarlet. She continued in a halting voice. "You know, there is a shortage of men in the village. I could cook for you."

Parrot continued to look at her and then his face broke into a smile.

"You'd cook for me?"

"Yes. Why, is that funny?"

"Oh, I'm starting to understand this," he laughed.

Hilda stared back at him and cocked her head. "I don't think I understand you."

He put an arm around her shoulder and grinned widely. "Well, truth be told, I ain't yet got around to thanking you properly for saving my life."

Hilda looked startled and started to withdraw but Parrot tightened his grip on her arm.

"Parrot, you are hurting me."

"Oh come on darlin', let's have a little fun."

Hilda struggled harder but was helpless to move in Parrot's clasp. He pulled her over toward the sandbank and pinned her to the ground with one arm. She continued to struggle while he positioned himself on top of her.

"Let me up, Parrot. What are you doing? Stop!"

"You're a frisky filly," he laughed, reaching his hand up between her legs. "I like that in a girl. Now, let's get down to business. How about you start with a kiss."

Further along the beach, a short time later, a body jumped nimbly over rocks sticking up like turtles in the tidewater. Hands gripped a crude wooden spear and the body crouched, poised, beside a tidepool. The spear handle vibrated slightly as it slowly rose higher in the air. Suddenly it plunged down and was thrust into the water. A few seconds later a pair of hands reached into the water, churning red and white froth, to grip the spear handle and lift it out. Impaled on the spear tip was a large reddish-orange fish that wriggled desperately to escape.

"That's a good catch!" a voice yelled from a distance.

Isaac Fayne, still crouched on the rock, turned around and observed Parrot and Hilda standing close by. Parrot was grinning. Hilda looked pale and strained.

"Hello," Fayne yelled back. "I'll be right there."

Fayne jumped back over the rocks toward his visitors and walked toward them through shallow water, crunching dozens of black mussels under his boot with every step.

"You've got quite a knack with that pike pole," Parrot said to him.

"Yes, some Indians once showed me how to fashion and throw a spear," Fayne said, holding his catch out toward his visitors. "I made this only a few days ago and I finally caught my first fish."

"Congratulations. So, you livin' 'round here?" Parrot asked.

Fayne pointed with his speared fish. "Come, I'll show you. It's not far."

Parrot gripped Hilda's arm and steered her in the direction Fayne was walking. "We'll follow right behind."

They had only walked a few steps when Fayne quickly turned around and held up the fish excitedly. "Wait, I forgot to clean my catch," he said, brushing past them back to the water. Reaching down, he held the writhing fish on its side against a boulder. Then he palmed another rock lying in the sand and pounded it into the fish's head until the fish ceased wriggling. Fayne dipped the limp fish into the water to wipe the blood and mucus away, then he reached into a twine bag slung about his neck and procured a short knife. Kneeling down in the water, he jammed the knife blade into the fish just behind its head. With an effort he twisted the blade back and forth through the tough skin and cartilage and finally the head dropped free and slapped against a rock. Fayne grimaced as he next worked to insert the knife blade into the fish's soft belly and push the blade away from him. As he did so the viscera within slid out and hung from the body. Exhaling, he leaned over and severed the intestinal umbilicus against the toe of his boot. He twirled the remains of the fish, still impaled on the spear, in the water to rinse the blood one last time.

Fayne stood up and raised the fish up for inspection. "That'll do, I guess." The he looked toward his visitors. "Perhaps you'll join me for dinner."

Hilda wriggled her arm and shoulder to get away. She looked pale and strained. "I would like to go."

Parrot held her firm in his grip, looking at Fayne and grinning. "We can't go now, darlin'. We've been invited for lunch. Wouldn't be polite."

Fayne looked at Hilda struggling and then at Parrot before he slowly turned and resumed walking through the sand.

After a short hike past a scattering of driftlogs piled on the beach, Fayne trudged up toward a squat structure comprised of odd shaped beach logs and bark slabs, banked with sand on the side. He jammed his spear into the sand before he approached a large shag of bark standing vertically against the structure and lifted it aside with both hands. He wiped the sand clean from his hands and turned again to Parrot and Hilda. "Welcome to my home. Watch your head as you duck inside."

Inside, Fayne had banked additional sand and arranged more bark slabs against the wall. In the center he had created a fire pit from flat rocks and rolled a couple of logs nearby to sit upon. Cedar boughs arranged on the ground served as his sleeping area.

Fayne knelt down beside the fire pit and reached for a handful of shredded cedar bark that he placed on the rocks. Gripping a flint-rock and cobble-stone in his hands, he leaned over and began banging them together and shooting off sparks. "It won't take me long to start a fire," he said without looking up. "Please sit down."

He continued to chip away and intermittently wave his hand just above the tinder. All at once he leaned low and began to blow gently on the fluff and fan the air with a piece of bark. A few seconds later a glowing coal the size of a pea emitted a thin tail of smoke.

Fayne delicately piled more bark shreds on top of the coal, blowing gently until a small flame erupted. He reached over and added a small handful of twigs and small branches to the top of the fire. In a few seconds the twigs and branches began burning and he added a few larger branches. He then picked up his spear and slid the fish off the end, skewering it onto another slim stick lying nearby. He placed this stick in the crook of two branches sticking up from the ground on the perimeter of the fire pit. The fish was now positioned above the dancing flames. Fayne added a couple more branches to the fire then sighed and stretched his back before shuffling back several steps and studying the smoke that disappeared through a slight space in his roof. He smiled faintly and looked over at his guests watching him from a nearby log. The whole procedure had taken less than five minutes.

"Well ain't you a busy beaver," Parrot commented.

Fayne shrugged. "The key is making sure that you have dry tinder and dry branches. There is excellent natural flint rock found around here, so I know the Indians had no problem making fires."

"What do you think, darlin'," Parrot nudged Hilda who was seated beside him on a log and staring intently at the fire. She said nothing but stared at the ground.

Fayne looked from Hilda to Parrot.

"So, Parrot, you seem to have regained your health."

"Me? I never felt better. Thanks to this sweet little filly!" He had his arm around Hilda and gave her a squeeze.

Hilda tried to wriggle free from Parrot's grasp. "I want to get away from you, Parrot."

Parrot shook his head. "Honestly, sugar, you act like you've been bitten by a rattlesnake." He retracted took his arm. "There you go."

In one motion Hilda pushed away from the log and hustled out the door.

"Hey, get back here!" Parrot yelled at her, without rising from the log.

"You are rough on her," Fayne commented. He leaned over and pulled a bark slab aside from the wall. "Come back some time and we'll gather more plants," he yelled after Hilda who was running down the beach.

"Leave her be," Parrot said. "I can't figure out those dumb-ass villagers, and she's no different."

"Well, Parrot," Fayne said, sitting back down to tend the fire and adjust the spit. "I dare say the villagers have no interest in the modern world as you and I know it."

"Ain't that the truth! They don't got no common sense livin' the way they do."

"Certainly different than you or I might choose."

"I mean, here we are, living in a new era of technology and banks and money and these squirrel brains don't seem to care a nut for it. Hell, in my line of work, I seen men who had nothing, not a shirt on their back, start scratching out a mine with their fingers. And next time I see them they own two or three mines and they can't get their gold fast enough. Is that such a goddammed shame? That's progress."

"I suppose that's one way of looking at it, though I am dedicated to science, not riches. But tell me, Parrot, do you think there will be any gold left in the Klondike by the time you get there?"

"Damn right I do. We got a theory on how to get the gold other folks'd skip over. Has to do with new technology I used on my last job. We figure a thousand men'll be working for us inside of five years."

Fayne reached under a bark slab and brought out a rusted metal pan that he held under the fish to catch some of the drippings. "You know all this and you haven't set a foot in the Klondike yet? That's quite remarkable. I would think even in your business …"

Parrot suddenly cut him off.

"Hey, where'd you get that pan?" he asked eagerly, reaching out to pinch it and rub his fingers over its pitted surface.

Fayne furrowed his brow and studied the pan. "This pan? I found it on the beach a couple of week's ago. I occasionally find things just washed up. That's probably from our ship wreck."

"That's a prospecting pan," Parrot said excitedly. "Now ain't that interesting."

Fayne pulled down a few bits of cooked fish and dropped them into the pan. "I'm sorry to disappoint you but I don't think the rocks here are suitable for finding gold."

Parrot was still excited, his face grinning. "Gold is dam peculiar, my friend. The minute you think you've figured out all the rules for finding it a new one comes along." He waved his arms. "We could be sitting on the biggest mother lode of all time and you'd never know it 'til you stubbed your big toe on a nugget. It's happened before, plenty of times."

Fayne offered some of the fish in the pan to Parrot. "Please, start eating."

Parrot looked at the pan but not the fish, before standing up from the log and withdrawing from the fire. "Excuse me, partner, but I'm not too hungry after all. I think I'll take a walk and catch a meal at the hotel later." Parrot snickered and exited out the doorway.

From inside the cabin Fayne heard Parrot singing a song and laughing as he walked up the beach. Pulling aside the bark covering on his wall, Fayne studied Parrot retreating into the distance as he chewed on a piece of fish and licked his fingers.

One week later, the region was blanketed in three inches of snow that fell during the night. Few of the villagers ventured far from their cabins or beyond the community hall where many gathered for meals and social exchange. Children ran in and out, opening the door and letting in gusts of chilling wind. At one of the tables, a group of women sat carding and spinning wool while several men seated at an adjacent table, including Cyrus and Robert, the teacher, were deep in discussion. Conversation ranged from speculating about the effects of the snow on winter crops to weather forecasting to discussing the health of the animals. Several men were concerned that a rheumatic infection in one of the sheep might spread to the other animals in the flock, though the animal was quarantined in a shed. Isolated as they were, the villagers were fearful about any potentially contagious illness that could kill their animals. The men agreed that on their next trip to the outside they would purchase additional animals to increase cross-breeding and build up the health of their stock.

While they were conversing, Isaac Fayne slid in to join them at the table with a bowl of hot food. Fayne was wrapped in a long tattered scarf that wound about his neck and a long scraggly beard poked out beneath his gaunt face. Several of the men stopped to stare at him. He nodded nervously to them before ducking his head and beginning to eat.

Cyrus found his voice. "Mr. Fayne, this is a surprise. It's been several weeks since we've seen you. We were wondering how you've been faring."

Fayne swallowed hard and worked his tongue round his teeth. "I'm doing fine," he said, glancing briefly at each of the men. "Very well in fact," he added, spooning more food into his mouth.

The other men studied Fayne intently as he rapidly devoured the bowl of food, glancing occasionally to Cyrus who also studied him.

After a couple of minutes Cyrus spoke again. "You must not be used to such inclement conditions."

"I come from New England," Fayne asserted, swallowing again. "Winter is much harsher there. This is mild." He scooped bare fingers around his bowl and licked each one. "I'm grateful for the food, however. Foraging is much more difficult with snow on the ground and ice on the rocks."

"Might I suggest you consider moving into the village for a while," Cyrus replied. "You could ..."

"No," Fayne said gruffly, his eyes darting around the table. "Thank you, I appreciate the offer but I prefer living in solitude to complete my research."

"What is it exactly that you are studying?" Robert asked Fayne.

"I'm completing an inventory of plants and animals in the region." The men continued to stare at him. "And the geology. The rocks."

"That is commendable, I'm sure," said Cyrus.

"I would also like to know more about the Indians living around here."

"So would we," Robert said. "The Indians are a source of knowledge about how to survive in this area. They have helped us on several occasions."

Fayne fixed Robert. "How do I contact these Indians?"

"I can't answer that, we don't know where they're living. They arrive without warning."

"They communicated through Hilda," Cyrus added.

"Why do you want to contact the Indians?" Robert asked.

"I'd like to know as much about them as possible. It is quite profitable to study indigenous tribes."

Cyrus shook his head. "I'm sorry, I don't understand. What do you mean by that?"

"I mean I would like to describe their practices and customs and report back to my research institute on my discoveries."

"Is that all?" Robert pressed.

"I would bring back Indian artifacts as well."

"And that is profitable for you?" Robert probed.

"Yes. It is," Fayne confirmed. "I can sell them to museums."

"And how would the Indians gain from this exchange?" Cyrus asked.

"I can offer to provide some recompense to them. At a later date of course."

"It seems to me the Indians of this region are content to live as nature intended them," Robert said. "Or as they have fit into nature. I'm not sure they have need of money."

Fayne stared fiercely at Robert and clenched one of his hands into a fist. "Listen to me, teacher. I'm not sure you have a mote of understanding about science. Pure science. It is dedicated to expanding knowledge, which is the task to which I am dedicated."

The men listening stared intently before Cyrus attempted to soften the tension. "I think your dedication is commendable, Mr. Fayne, especially under the present circumstances in which you find yourself."

"I do know a little about science, Mr. Fayne, having apprenticed for two years in a laboratory on the outskirts of London," Robert cut in. "And it seems to me that science is more problematic and rather less precise than many scientists assert."

"What are you talking about?" Fayne asked harshly.

"Well, I was an unwitting participant in several procedures that turned out considerably different than predicted. Several of my colleagues, in fact, were injured, one of them killed, in a poorly designed experiment that went awry. That resulted in the termination of my apprenticeship."

Fayne fixed Robert with his fierce gaze before shaking his head. "In other words, but for the clumsiness of your employer you are willing to impugn my profession and the great practice of science. I might consider that a base insult but I doubt your grasp of scientific principles would withstand rigorous examination." Fayne's voice rose and others in the room turned to observe him. He addressed the larger group. "Do you not understand that were it not for science, first articulated by the great Greek philosophers, then we would likely still be dwelling in caves, eating maggots and carrion and suffering the ravages of disease. Are all of you ignorant of the great debt that is owed to science? Or would you prefer to live like heathen Indians?"

"The heathen Indians that you are so interested in," Robert rebutted.

Fayne glowered at Robert.

"Yes. Those Indians. They offer clues and insights about human development from our lowliest roots."

"Tell me, Mr. Fayne," Cyrus said, "what happens if these heathen Indians don't want you studying them?"

Fayne glared at Cyrus for several seconds, his breath coming in shallow bursts, before he arose and stomped out of the community hall.

In the days that followed her encounter with Parrot on the beach, Hilda withdrew from social contact among the villagers, remaining in her shelter. For two days she bundled herself in a blanket and sat mute against the wall. On the third day, she nibbled on a little dried fish but spat it out and began to sniffle. She cried quietly for much of the day, at the end of which she lit a fire and heated some water in a pot. When the water was hot, she drew out several dried plants from a string bag nearby and crumbled the leaves into the water. She took a large black feather with a white tip from a shelf and knelt beside her fire. She waved the feather back and forth above the tea and inhaled the vapors. After several minutes, she dipped into the pot and lifted out a cup of liquid. She held the hot cup between her two hands and slowly rocked on her knees, eyes closed.

After drinking the healing tea for a day, Hilda left her shelter in early morning and padded silently along a snowy trail to the beach. There she stripped off her clothes and draped them over a beach log before she walked, naked, across a sandy flat and into the frigid surf. She tread water for several minutes, bobbing up and down in white-tipped waves, before she emerged and walked back across the beach to dress. She returned to her shelter and drank tea for much of the remainder of the day, occasionally lighting clumps of dried, pungent herbs and fanning the smoke with her feather. She ate some dried fish that night that helped to renew her energy and allowed her to sleep.

Long before the first European sailors explored the coast of British

Columbia, the region formed part of the home territory of the Kwakiutl Indian nation that established several villages along the coast. The Kwakiutl were known as fierce warriors who alternately traded and competed with other Indian tribes of the region – the Haida to the north, the Salish to the south and the Nootkah to the west. The Kwakiutl built enormous seafaring canoes from giant cedar trees that they hollowed-out and carved. They developed great skill at fishing for salmon, halibut and rockfish with nets woven from cedar roots and by hand-lines fashioned with hand-carved hooks of bone and wood. Each year they would also take to the water in their canoes to lance one or more gray whales for a supply of meat and blubber that the Indians would render into oil for cooking and as fuel for lamps.

On land, the Kwakiutl hunted deer, bear, marten, mink and otter for fur and they harvested numerous wild plants for food, medicine and clothing. Their villages were comprised of various shelters built from cedar, spruce, hemlock and alder kept warm in the autumn and winter by fire. Shelters included family dwellings, store-houses, smoke-rooms, where the flanks of thousands of fish were cured at any one time to supply the village with food through winter, and one or more communal long-houses. During times of celebration or mourning, Indians would gather inside the village long-house to beat drums, raise their voice in song and dance in the shadow of fire-light. In this fashion the Indians communed with the spirits of the animals, plants and rocks with whom they shared the land. As a further expression of this communion, the Indians also erected massive totem poles adorned with the delicate carvings of their spirit world nearby to their long-houses and burial grounds.

The arrival of European sailors dramatically interrupted the culture of the Indians of the Pacific northwest coast, including the Kwakiutl. While some trade was initially established the Europeans also initiated conflict and helped to incite warfare by pitting tribe against tribe. They also deliberately introduced diseases that decimated Indian populations.

Following contact, the Kwakiutl of the mid-coast avoided direct warfare with the sailors, who expressed no real challenge to the Indians for their lands. But in the wake of an epidemic of scarlet fever against which the Indians had no natural immunity the remaining Kwakiutl of the north coast abandoned their coastal villages and retreated to the shelter of deeper, inland fiords where they hoped to safeguard their surviving members.

The villages left behind suffered the ravages of rain and wind and the biology of decay that worked to convert the edifices and traces of occupation into mud and debris. Village structures withered and were overwhelmed by other vegetation, totems grew moss and toppled or leaned precipitously, and the bones of the dead, though laid to rest on ceremonial platforms, often slipped from their perch and merged into the earth.

One afternoon, while picking his way through a shintangle of brambles and scrub cedar, Fayne trapped his ankle beneath a root, stumbled and fell heavily to one side. Fighting to clear the scrub, his hand closed around a solitary, yellowing skull lodged in the moss. He drew back in horror initially, then gradually yielded to a scientific instinct that urged him to investigate. Probing in the underbrush he found additional bones and several skulls, leading him to surmise that he had discovered an abandoned burial ground.

In the following days, Fayne carefully extended his reconnaissance of the area and discovered several raised platforms on which rested intact skeletons and artifacts of their long-deceased occupants, and several well-weathered totems that had fallen to the ground. Sifting the soil beneath the platforms with bare hands, he also discovered arrow and lance tips fashioned from flint, and the remains of shell and bone jewelry that were obviously meant to accompany the deceased on their final journey to the spirit world.

Fayne was exceedingly pleased, giddy even, with his discovery and he yearned to share the news of his discovery with a colleague or an interested audience. Certain that his discovery would be met with reward and great interest by others, Fayne vowed to expand his exploration and study.

In successive days, Hilda left her shelter to hike in the forest. The temperature warmed up, melting the snow and enabling Hilda to successfully forage for plants. Some of the plants she ate raw, others she placed in the string bag slung over her shoulder. With a pointed stick she often dug in the ground and pried up the roots and shoots of shrubs and young trees, which she also added to her bag. As before, she would sometimes sit and contemplate a vista or an arrangement of rocks and trees, absorbing details.

She was walking along a stony trail close to the village one afternoon when a voice yelled out, "hello." Hilda stopped and retreated a few steps, watching nervously as the bushes rustled nearby. Fayne emerged and stepped toward her.

"Hello," she replied, timidly. "You surprised me."

"I didn't mean to." Fayne cocked his head and looked at the bag upon her shoulder. "You've been gathering plants?"

"Some roots and medicines, is all. I have not been feeling too well."

"I am hoping you can tell me more about the Indians that used to live here."

"I know very little about this. After all, the Indians don't live here any more."

"But you have met Indians who visited the village. What did you learn from them?"

Hilda turned and began walking away. "I will tell you another time, when I am feeling stronger. I am just returning to my cabin."

Fayne seemed not to hear her. "Would you like to see what I have found?" he asked hurriedly, not waiting for an answer before he took out an object wrapped in a rag that he had been holding within his shirt. He quickly unwound the rag and held up a human jawbone that he thrust toward her.

Hilda jumped back. "Unhhh, where did you get that?" she asked, horror-stricken.

"I recently discovered an Indian graveyard on a hike near the beach. I suspect this specimen belonged to an ancient chief. I also found a number of other interesting artifacts." He reached into his pocket and pulled out a beaded necklace. "He was probably buried in a splendid ceremony."

Hilda scowled. "But you shouldn't ... take these things."

Fayne looked puzzled. "Why shouldn't I? These artifacts will help my research."

"But they are not yours to take."

"Nonsense. The Indians have abandoned them. They will serve the advancement of science."

Hilda, unnerved, withdrew and began backing away along the trail. "I'm sorry. That is not right. I must go now."

Suddenly, on the trail behind them, came the sound of a wagon clopping along. In a moment, the wagon appeared, one horse pulling a cart containing Cyrus, Parrot and Anton, holding the reins and guiding the horse.

Hilda stood without moving in the middle of the trail. Anton pulled up hard on the reins to stop the wagon or the horse would have bowled Hilda over.

"Whoah," Anton yelled out, steadying the horse. Hilda looked beyond Anton to Parrot, seated in the back of the cart. Parrot looked disheveled but was grinning widely.

"Hey, sweetness," Parrot yelled out. "You got to watch out for traffic on this road. Anton here's a mean driver."

Hilda remained immobile in the middle of the trail.

"Hello, Hilda," Cyrus said. "We haven't seen you in several days."

"I haven't been feeling well," she said quietly.

"Hey there, perfesser, " Parrot yelled out to Fayne. "Don't you get any ideas about that girl. Touch her and I'll stuff you like an

African lion in one of your mu-seeums!"

Fayne glared at Parrot but didn't say a word.

"Are you going back to the village?" Hilda asked Anton.

"Yes, you can ride with us," he replied, maneuvering the wagon alongside her.

"Shift over Parrot to make room for Hilda," Cyrus urged.

"That purty thing! She can sit right here on my lap," he said, reaching down and sweeping her with one arm up from the trail and onto his lap. "There, the 'wild rose of the island' is safely aboard."

"I'm sorry there isn't room for you, Mr. Fayne," Cyrus said.

"That's alright," Fayne replied. "I prefer to walk."

"Just remember the next stage won't be around anytime soon, partner," Parrot yelled out. "Hey Cyrus, it is all right for the perfesser to join us for dinner tonight?"

Cyrus hesitated but forced out an answer. "Yes. That would be fine. Would you join my wife and I and Mr. Parrot for supper tonight, Mr. Fayne? Just before sundown."

Before Fayne could reply, Anton shook the reins and the wagon jolted off along the trail. As it jostled along, Parrot began improvising a song. "Don't leave the lights on tonight, cuz I'm on my way to the great Klondike, But I'll soon be ridin' high, coming back in style, in a little while. Hey, What do you think of my singing, sweet lips? Bet you ain't heard nothin' prettier 'round here in years. Yeehaw!"

Hilda looked frozen in space as she bounced in the wagon with Parrot's large arm cinched tight around her waist.

In the late afternoon, when the workday was complete, Fayne, Parrot and Hilda gathered at Cyrus and Lucy's cabin for supper. Lucy had baked a fresh loaf of bread and stewed a large squash with some beets for the main supper dish. She spooned food onto several dishes and into a hollowed out burl. She handed a portion of food and a large slice of bread to each person seated at the table and awaited Cyrus who added a log to the fire before sitting down.

"Please, enjoy your food," Cyrus urged them. With that, each person dipped their head and began eating, with little conversation. In less than ten minutes, most had consumed the contents from their dish.

Parrot burped loudly and nodded his head. "That was right fine food. Much appreciated after a day's work."

"I'm glad you enjoyed it, Mr. Parrot," Lucy responded. "Would you like another slice of bread?"

"I sure would."

Lucy cut Parrot another slice of bread and handed it to him. Cyrus watched Parrot closely as he wiped his mouth.

"You seem to be feeling much perkier these days, Mr. Parrot."

"That's the truth, partner. 'Loaded for bear' is the term that best describes me, near as I can tell. 'N I got him to thank for my improved character," Parrot said, nodding toward Fayne.

"Me?" Fayne asked. "What do I have to do with you?"

"Well, it was that prospecting pan of yours that got me to thinking that I might coax a little gold from the creeks around here. Get off on a prospecting trip while the weather warms a little."

"But it's still winter time," Cyrus said. "What will you do

for shelter? Or food?"

Parrot chewed his remaining knob of bread while he answered. "The elements don't bother me none when I'm lookin' for gold. And I get along right well in the woods." Parrot grinned widely at Hilda. "Fact, I'm thinking I might be part Indian!" He next cocked his head toward Fayne. "Speakin' of Indians, what should I do if I run into one of those chiefs like the one you dug up?"

Fayne clenched his teeth. "I didn't dig anybody up."

"No, then where'd you find that set of dentures you were holding onto?"

"Not in the ground if that's what you mean. The body had been left on a burial platform."

Parrot shook his head. "I can't figure out how anybody can get so excited about something that's already dead."

"The artifacts from here will make a remarkable addition to the collection at the institute," Fayne replied sternly.

"Whatever are you talking about?" Cyrus asked.

"I intend to ship the entire skeleton back to Washington. Perhaps even the whole burial ground including several totem poles, though their decay is advancing rapidly."

Hilda gasped. "You can't do that."

"I think that is a crazy idea," said Cyrus.

"It's been done before, I reckon," Parrot added.

"But it is sacred to the Indians," Cyrus said.

"Look, there's nothing to discuss, really," Fayne replied. "I also hope to persuade one of the natives to return with me."

"I've heard you talk about this before," Cyrus said, growing angrier.

"How could you possibly do that?" asked Hilda.

"I could arrange for him to be paid by a fundraising committee. And I'm sure the institute would treat any volunteer with special care."

"Maybe even pickle em," Parrot added, laughing.

Fayne glared at him. "Your humor is tasteless, Parrot."

"I still think it is crazy," Cyrus said, incredulous.

Fayne continued. "I'm certain the institute will be very interested in my findings from this region. My discoveries will really help to put this area on the map."

Cyrus gripped the edge of the table. "Our community doesn't want to be on any 'map', thank you, Mr. Fayne. And I'm sure if you asked the Indians, they wouldn't care much for the idea either."

"I'm sorry, but the advancement of science is more important than the sentiments of this arcane village. You can't stand in the way."

Cyrus rose from his seat and leaned toward Fayne. "Oh, can't I? If it means destroying what we have built up here I want nothing to do with your ideas of so-called science."

Fayne glared back at Cyrus and then at Parrot. Parrot rolled his eyes. "I'm on your side, partner. But these folks get riled up if you mention stuff like 'science' or 'new technology.'"

Cyrus slammed his hand down onto the table and glowered at both men. "No! We don't need any of your 'science' or 'new technology' here. We are content with what we have."

"Is your religion against all progress then?" Fayne asked harshly.

"What religion? We are not zealots here. We come from various backgrounds, wishing only to live in harmony. It seems we can do that without too much 'progress'."

Lucy came around the table to comfort her husband. "Please stop this," she implored him and the others. "Stop the arguing."

Fayne and Parrot remained silent. Cyrus stared at them, his chest heaving rapidly.

After a few moments Fayne pushed back the stump on which he was seated and rose up. "I think I'll be leaving," he said, nodding toward Lucy. "Thank you for the food." He walked quickly toward the door.

Parrot called out after him. "I'd be obliged for the use of your prospecting pan for a few days."

"Stop by to pick it up," Fayne said opening the door and exiting the cabin.

The next morning, Parrot rose after daybreak and was soon thumping around his cabin. He gathered a few items of clothing together and stuffed them into a gray pack sack. Then he sat down on the edge of his bed, carefully threaded a large needle with some coarse thread, and began to darn a large hole in one of his socks. He was brimming with enthusiasm, singing and muttering to himself.

"'Yes, I'm off to the Klondike, but I might be awhile, leave the lights on honey, cuz I'm comin' back in style'." He held up his sock and examined his repair work. "There, can't have my feet sticking out in the mud when I go dancing in town with fine ladies, can I?"

He looked up when he heard a shuffling noise outside, followed by a gentle knocking on his door.

"If that's Lucifer, I ain't home. And I won't be a-working in that mudhole you call a field today, neither. That's niggers' work, and I ain't no nigger."

"It is Hilda," a voice called from outside his door.

Parrot grinned and stretched over from the edge of the bed to open the door, before sitting down again. Hilda stood in the doorway before timidly passing through the threshold.

"Mornin', sweetness," Parrot said.

"Hello," she said flatly. She looked at the pack on the bed beside Parrot. "You are going away?"

"It's the early worm that catches the bird." He again tested out his darning and glanced at her. "I'm sorry to disappoint you but there's gold to be found."

"I don't think you are sorry."

"No? Well, a man in my position can't afford to be sorry for long. Gotta' be a rollin' stone."

"Don't you remember what you said to me. On the beach." Her voice trembled. "Don't I mean anything to you?"

Parrot stuffed the repaired sock into his pack and jumped up from the bed to leave the needle and thread on a nearby table. He smiled quickly at her, then knelt on the floor to examine under the bed.

"Of course you do, sweetness. You're as soft as buttermilk and that comforts a man." He stood up and cocked a finger at her. "And I know I'm the first real man to come along in your life, ain't that right?" he asked, grinning at her.

Hilda retreated a step and gripped the doorframe. Her breathing was shallow and rapid.

"Now here's what I plan on doing, sugar plum. I plan on finding gold and gettin' rich. But I won't be the only one to find gold around here. No sir, there'll be plenty to go around. Gold's like that. Then everybody in this village will be rich beyond their wildest dreams."

"But don't you see? People here don't want that kind of rich."

Parrot cinched up the backpack and hoisted it onto his shoulder. He shrugged. "That means there'll just be more for me and those who do want it." He approached Hilda and reached out with one hand to draw her face toward his. "Now, how about a little smooch for luck?"

Hilda flung up her arm to ward Parrot off and scrunched up her face. "No, get away. You hurt me!"

Parrot gripped her arm solidly and stared into her face. "You're wild today. I like that! Now give me that kiss and I'm on my way." He yanked her off her feet and kissed her roughly on her lips for several seconds while she struggled to get away. Then he released her and she stumbled backwards against the wall of the cabin.

"So long, honey pot," Parrot said, before he walked through the door and down the path.

Hilda continued to stare at Parrot as he hiked and cackled along the trail in the direction of the beach. The color had drained from her face and she held her arms tightly together, shaking involuntarily.

On the day after Parrot departed to explore for gold, the villagers gathered in the community hall for their monthly meeting. They arranged themselves on chairs and stumps and blankets in a semicircle around Cyrus, who noted the items people wished to discuss and then called the meeting to order.

The discussion began with Cyrus requesting that each of the villagers in attendance "check in" or describe any special news or concerns they wanted to relate. At the invitation, Anton raised his hand, stood up and removed his hat from his head, and haltingly addressed the other villagers. He was very happy, he said, that Greta had consented earlier in the day to marry him. He smiled and blushed deeply as the villagers clapped and voiced their approval. Greta, a young woman seated on a blanket nearby, was encouraged to stand up, which she did so in great embarrassment, holding a hand up to shield the lower half of her face. Anton reached across and clutched her hand as they received more applause.

"That's wonderful news!" exclaimed Cyrus, as the clapping died down. "When have you planned your wedding day?" he asked.

Anton looked at Greta and then replied, "we are hoping for a ceremony in one month's time, if that is not too early."

The villagers murmured approval and Anton and Greta sat back down.

"More news?" asked Cyrus, looking around. Another arm raised up. "Yes Einar?" Einar half-raised himself from a stump to address the group. He gestured to a woman seated beside him. "We feel our baby is ready to come soon. Maybe in the next week or two." Again, the audience voiced its approval. "That, too, is excellent news. And may I ask how you are feeling, Inge?" The woman beside Einar, who looked very pale, glanced quickly at the group. "I am very tired. I feel as if I swallowed a pumpkin."

Most of the villagers laughed at her comment but Inge remained serious. Then somebody honked loudly in blowing their nose and people again chuckled.

Cyrus sighed and half-raised an arm. "Alright. We are all thinking of you Inge, and Einar, and hoping you will have a speedy birth and happy baby. Now, can we continue?"

The meeting shifted to reports on food and shelter and furniture-making, and an update on the health of the animals. Robert arose and announced an upcoming story-telling and music night and he encouraged everyone to think about, and rehearse what they wished to contribute. He said he crafted a new story that he thought the children, especially, would enjoy. When these discussions concluded, Cyrus introduced the topic that Heinrich wished to discuss, a trip to the outside.

Heinrich stood up and spoke loudly so that the group would hear him. "I think the time has come to plan a trip to the outside. We need new tools, some of our blades are almost completely worn down. The millwheel on our araster needs replacing and we could use some new harnesses. Right now, the health of our livestock is precarious. We could use some medicine, some seed, some additional breeding stock and I have heard from the women that they would appreciate some new sewing equipment.

"We also need school supplies," Robert spoke up. "New books and pencils and paper."

"We agreed last year that a trip to the outside should be planned,"

Heinrich continued, "and I think now is the time to begin this venture. We will need to construct a boat, and we could plan to travel in late spring or early summer. We will return within one year's time, after working and procuring the items we need."

The air of the meeting suddenly seemed heavier, more somber.

Cyrus pursed his lips before speaking. "Your points are well made, Heinrich. Though I think your planning is premature. As long as we are not careless I believe the tools are able to last for some time yet."

"But why should we put off this trip for only one more year? We have needs, and the sooner we prepare and complete the trip, the sooner our needs are filled."

"I'm with Heinrich," Edmond said in a loud voice. "I think the trip should take place this summer. I think we need to take a vote."

"Take a vote, yes," urged one woman.

Cyrus looked discouraged but relented. "Alright. We will take a vote. I will ask who wishes the trip to be undertaken this spring, who is indifferent to the timing of this trip, and who does not wish for such a trip this year."

People surrounding Cyrus shifted in their chairs and watched him intently.

"Who wishes a trip to the outside to occur this spring or early summer?"

Cyrus counted 23 hands raised into the air.

"Who is indifferent to such a trip and does not care if such a trip occurs this year or next?"

A number of other hands waved, including Cyrus's. "Eighteen," he announced.

"Who does not wish for such a trip to happen this coming summer?"

One lone hand stuck up tentatively in the air. Everyone turned and stared at Robert's wife, Nola, who looked nervous. She turned and looked at her husband then slipped her hand into his.

"Nola," Cyrus said in a muted voice. "You are opposed to this trip?" She nodded. "Will you please share your objection with us."

She took a few seconds to compose herself, continuing to hold Robert's hand. "I can't quite explain it, but I don't want it to go ahead. Not now."

"But you must be able to describe something that is causing you to feel this way," Cyrus urged her.

"I can't really describe anything," she replied. "But I'm afraid."

"Afraid," Cyrus repeated. "Afraid of what, Nola?"

"I don't know," she said. "I'm just afraid."

"What do you mean by 'afraid'", probed Heinrich. "Are you afraid of the journey? We sailed here from Portland didn't we? Our journey this time will only be to the Canadian city of Nanaimo which is much closer."

"I'm not afraid of the journey, Heinrich."

"Well, what then?" he asked harshly.

"I said I can't really explain it."

"This is ridiculous," Edmond said.

"I don't think it is ridiculous," Cyrus countered. "Nola has a reason, even if she can't describe it. This is true for many things in life."

"Like what?"

"Like God," Robert spoke up. "Can you describe God?"

"No, I can't describe God, Robert. Nor do I wish to. But I do want to sail to Nanaimo to purchase supplies that are badly needed in the village. You even said so yourself. And I don't want to put the trip off because one person is afraid of something she can't describe."

Cyrus looked from Heinrich to Edmond to Hazel and pleaded with her.

"Nola, isn't there something..."

"Yes," she cut in. "I can tell you something about my fear. I've felt it ever since those men arrived." The room went quiet. "I don't know what to tell you, but they frighten me."

"How do they frighten you, my love?" Robert asked as he placed his other hand over hers. "We can speak to them."

"No, it's not them exactly. It's something about them." She paused and then held her hands over her heart. "Since we have come here, I have enjoyed the happiest moments of my life. I love our village, whether we are running out of supplies or not. But these men. Since they came here, something has changed. I see they are not like us, and somehow I think if we travel to the outside then we will find more people like them and ...." She looked into Robert's face and suddenly broke into a deep sob. "Oh Robert, I'm so afraid."

Nola threw her arms around Robert who hugged her tightly. "It's okay, my love. It's all right. You are safe with us."

The group remained in silence for a minute.

"I know what Nola is talking about," another woman said. "I

feel the same way about those men. I don't trust them."

"But what is to be afraid of?" asked Anton, who spoke up from within the crowd. "They are only talking about a little progress and science. There is nothing so bad about that. I think maybe we could use a little more of that around here."

"Well, Hilda seems to know them a little better than we do," Cyrus said, looking around. "Perhaps we should ask her. Hilda, what do you think about this business?"

"She's not here tonight," said Edmond. "She's not feeling well."

"Hilda's not here?" Cyrus said, surprised.

"Can we stick to the discussion topic?" Heinrich asked Cyrus. "Are we going to start planning the trip out or not"?

Cyrus slumped in his chair and glared at Heinrich before slowly rolling his eyes over toward Nola.

"Nola," he said in a weary voice. "You have told us you are afraid of the two men, Parrot and Fayne. You know, on such a trip to the outside, we will be able to transport these two men away from here. Will you feel better, then?"

Nola looked toward Cyrus with tears streaming down her cheeks. She nodded her head but continued to sob.

Cyrus looked back at Heinrich and Edmond and Anton. "We will start making plans for such a trip."

Parrot began his exploration by traveling down the beach to Fayne's outpost. Fayne was not there so Parrot ducked inside his shack and retrieved the prospecting pan that he stuffed into his pack. He continued up the shore until he came to a creek that emptied across the sand in long braided rivulets. He reasoned that in tracking up the watershed he could begin exploring tributaries. He knelt at the side of the creek and scooped up a handful of gravel that he traced with his fingers. "Okay darlin', let's meet your family," he said, dropping the gravel from his hand and turning away from the ocean.

Entering the forest, Parrot bushwacked his way beside the creek. The vegetation was extremely thick, overgrown with spiky devil's club vines and underlain with mossy, treacherous boulders and dense clumps of willow and buckbrush. Parrot had to fight his way through the brush, step by step.

The creek Parrot hiked alongside was swollen by the rains of previous weeks into a muddy torrent the color of liquid chocolate that cut into the creek banks and gouged out towering trees. After a couple of days of bushwhacking, his shins were bruised and bleeding and his pants hung in shredded tatters. His hands and arms were also bruised and cut and one hip ached after a nasty fall from a slippery boulder. When Parrot was able to force his way through the brush to the water's edge he had great difficulty in locating an authentic sand bar from which he could obtain a sample of gravel. Discouraged, he retraced his steps and pushed further upstream, hoping that he would have more luck on smaller tributaries though they, too, were transporting an excessive load of sediment and masked the location of their true sand bars.

When the topography began to rise up precipitously, Parrot decided he would turn away from the creek to traverse up and over a ridge and into the adjacent watershed. In the fading light of late afternoon, after he had breached the ridge, Parrot slumped against the roots of a giant fir tree that had toppled to the ground, to stop and rest for the night. He pulled some dead branches and green boughs around him then reached into his pack and yanked out a brown tarp that he arranged over his legs and mid-section. Leaning back against the roots he sighed deeply, then dug in his pack again and retrieved a stub of bread that he began to gnaw on.

Between bites, he yawned widely and closed his eyes, thinking erratically of other prospecting ventures, of splitting rock in quarries, working in mines, sweating, bleeding, hurting, yelling and being so exhausted at the end of a day's work that his body collapsed and he sunk into sleep before his head met a pillow. He was almost that exhausted this evening and began sleeping before he had finished eating.

Into his reverie drifted a noise like a yowling drawl that at first he imagined was a creaking wagon wheel. He ignored it and it went away. He continued to slumber until the noise returned, this time more piercing, drawing him against his will into consciousness. The noise was replaced again by silence, which he monitored until he was comforted and began sliding again into sleep. Then he heard a different noise, louder, more guttural, closer. He felt movement, too, and he forced himself to awaken. Nearby, he heard a growling noise and then felt something yank on his tarp and attempt to pull it away. He stared into the near-darkness, confused by his senses. Suddenly, something bit down through the tarp and grabbed his boot.

"Get away!", Parrot yelled, kicking out and connecting with

something solid that retreated. There was silence then the growling noise filled the air. "Get!" Parrot shouted out as loud as he could. His fingers clawed in the dirt and closed around a rock that he heaved into the blackness. He heard something retreating into the forest followed by an oppressive silence.

Parrot lay awake a long time, his senses alert to the smallest changes in the forest around him. He heard little else save for the wind that swirled in the forest canopy above him and the occasional cone or branch falling to the ground. Eventually, he fell asleep, but his slumber was that of someone listening for a noise, and ready to defend himself against an unseen enemy.

At daybreak Parrot was awakened by ravens squawking nearby. He held his head still while his eyes scanned for danger. Seeing none, he pulled his legs under him and kept them there until there was enough light in the sky for him to arise and travel.

His bread finished, Parrot needed more food, a substantive meal, especially if he were going to continue working hard. He decided he would hike back down to the shore and scavenge for shellfish before trying his luck in the next watershed. The walking was easier along the ridge where the vegetation was less dense than the creek bottom and he made good time.

Parrot arrived at the water's edge in the afternoon. The sky was clearing with a wind blustering from offshore, and his ears readjusted from the silence of the forest to the roar of pounding surf. When the tide fully retreated, Parrot walked out among the cobbles to gather oysters and cockles that he carried in his hat. Rounding a bend high on the beach Parrot suddenly came upon the splintered, weathered fragments of a shipwreck, protruding from the sand like a colossal ribcage. He decided it would make a reasonable shelter and he dropped his pack nearby and tore off some of the planking to begin making a fire. Given the wind and dampness of the wood, it took Parrot more than an hour of chipping with a flint-rock before he was able to coax a flame from a ball of tinder and kindle a fire. In a few minutes, however, Parrot stoked a roaring blaze and was able to balance the oysters and cockles on a rock shelf on which they quickly roasted. After their shells cracked open, Parrot pried them completely open with a shard of driftwood and scraped them into his mouth. He ate until he was completely filled, and then fortified his shelter for the night.

After sleeping soundly, Parrot awoke to a day marked by an ice-blue crystalline sky. Another day of clear weather meant the level of water in the creeks would drop as well, allowing for sandbars to reappear, so he decided to stay another day on the beach, resting and eating before setting out. He kindled another fire in the early afternoon and again roasted a bounty of shellfish and a rockfish that he found trapped in a tidepool. That evening, Parrot built a huge pyre from driftlogs that popped and jettisoned clouds of sparks into the inky blackness. Overhead, the night sky was punctuated by a vast, elegant tapestry of flickering stars and creamy galaxies.

On the same day Parrot rested on the beach, the villagers were also preparing a feast in anticipation of winter solstice, marking the shortest day of the year and the start of what was commonly taken by Europeans and Americans to be the first day of winter. For their celebration, the villagers would hold a special celebratory dinner in the community hall offering mulled cider, candied fruit and smoked fish.

In the late morning, people were completing chores and Hilda and Samuel were gathering some beach plants that continued to grow despite the cold weather.

Across the tidal flats, Fayne emerged from behind a tree and walked toward them.

"Hello," he called out.

His greeting was not returned but he approached them, nonetheless.

"Did you not hear me?" he asked, when he walked up to them.

"What do you want?" Hilda asked. "We're returning to the village soon."

"I am hoping that I can talk with you, privately."

"I have chores to finish," Hilda said. "We are having a feast later this afternoon."

"Really. Am I invited, too?"

There was a moment's silence.

"That isn't for me to decide," Hilda said. "You must ask Cyrus."

"Then I know what the answer will be," Fayne said, smirking. "Cyrus and I are having a fundamental disagreement."

"Please, I would like to continue."

"But I'd like you to walk with me. There is something I wish to discuss with you."

Hilda turned to Samuel. "I will walk with him a short way."

"Why don't you walk on ahead and I'll follow behind," Samuel said.

Hilda glanced at Fayne, nodded her head and began walking up the beach. Fayne grinned at Samuel and turned to join Hilda.

"What is it you want to talk about?"

"You're impatient today," Fayne admonished. Hilda said nothing but pursed her lips. Fayne continued. "You know, sometimes I find it very difficult to live here the way I do. I mean, I'm an educated man and I wish dearly at times for another educated person to talk with."

Hilda stared straight ahead. "The villagers are planning a trip out this coming spring. You will be able to leave us then. It is not so long."

"I know about the trip. But I will return here."

Hilda turned to him, surprised. "What do you mean?"

"Well, I have really just begun my work here. I want to come back to continue my investigations."

Hilda frowned. "I thought you were leaving forever."

"Well, that's what I wanted to talk to you about." Hilda studied Fayne who smiled and started to blush. "This is tricky for me to explain. You know, when I bring back word of my discoveries to the institute, I shall be rather famous, I expect. I will be asked to lecture and attend social functions. A man of my station, however, is not properly ... shall we say, 'set off' without a wife."

"I don't understand," Hilda said, quizzically.

"What is there to understand! I'm asking you to be my wife."

Hilda took a step back in surprise. "Well?" Fayne's voice began to rise. "Why don't you say something? It's a remarkable offer."

"You can't be serious," Hilda said, incredulous, her lips turning up slightly.

Fayne grimaced and grabbed her arm. "You think I am joking?"

Hilda began backing up and tried to wrench her arm free. "But I don't want to marry you."

Fayne was flummoxed. "What do you mean?"

Hilda turned to walk away. "I don't know you. I don't think I like you."

Fayne reached ahead and again grabbed her arm. "Why, you little ingrate," he roared at her. He pulled his arm back to slap her though she pulled away just out of reach. He again lunged for her and pumped his arm to strike her. As Fayne cocked his arm he was grabbed from behind by Samuel who twisted Fayne's arm and clutched him in a choke-hold.

"If you hurt her you'll be a very sorry person, indeed." Fayne was not a match for Samuel's strength and put up only a token struggle.

Hilda took a few seconds to recover. "It's okay, Samuel," she said. Samuel slowly relaxed his grip. Fayne gasped to recover his breath before he looked menacingly at Samuel.

"I just made her an extraordinary offer. She is a fool to turn me down."

Samuel looked at Fayne and then to Hilda.

"He asked me to be his wife."

Samuel stared at Fayne. "Why would Hilda marry you?"

"Why! Because I am going to be famous when I return to Washington and ... oh, why should I bother to explain it to you." Fayne stepped to the side and straightened his jacket before pointing a finger at Hilda. "You'll regret this," he snarled. "I'm used to getting what I want." Then Fayne turned and hiked back into the bush.

Parrot rose the morning after his repast, feeling refreshed and ready to resume prospecting. As early morning sunlight broke over the undulating tidal flats, Parrot rubbed his legs and arms to improve circulation, jammed his tarp into his pack and strode off. Next to the skeletal hull in which he had sheltered, only a faint black smudge remained of Parrot's fire the evening before, the wind having picked up and scattered the ashes and coals.

Parrot headed inland again parallel to a small creek, but giving himself a wide enough berth to avoid the densest vegetation. The forest floor was still damp and spongy but the drier weather had helped to drain away the largest puddles and bogs. Eventually, Parrot turned and thrashed his way down to the creek where he jumped from the bank onto the ridge of a gravel bar. He took off his pack and surveyed the small island to determine where the creek had left behind a tail of sand and he examined a few of the rough-edged boulders poking out of the water. With his pan in hand, Parrot squatted just behind the sand tail where he dug out a half-pan of sand and gravel that he began rocking back and forth in the creek. Working quickly, Parrot soon worked his panload down to a small handful of sandy concentrate. He stood up and took a couple of steps into a sliver of sunlight that penetrated the forest cover and peered into his pan, carefully using a few drops of water remaining in the bottom to roll aside the sand and gravel. On the very bottom of the pan he detected a small tail of black residue and a few fragments of cream-colored gravel.

"Well, there's some quartz in this creek," he said aloud. "And for damn sure that's better than no quartz."

Satisfied, Parrot turned up his pan and spilled out the contents, before picking up his pack and leaping from the sandbar back to the creek bank.

Over the next day and a half, Parrot slowly made his way further upstream, sampling the creek gravel every few hundred yards. Prospecting the creek brought with it an aching back and icy cold hands and feet, made more acute from their repeated plunges into the near-freezing water. Occasionally, Parrot would pick up a boulder and smash it against other rocks until it shattered and he could examine the interior surfaces. Sometimes he accidentally smashed or chipped a finger when attempting to break boulders this way, bruising and bloodying his hands in the process.

Despite the growing discomfort, he was pleased that the creek gravels revealed more quartz the further upstream he hiked. At the intersection of the main creek and a small tributary, he worked down two separate panloads and determined that the quartz was coming in from the tributary, which he selected to explore.

At first, Parrot struggled to walk up the center of the small creek, but as before, there was so much downed wood that he was forever trying to scale massive fallen trunks or crawl under other debris. He was reluctant to abandon the creek bed because despite the dense vegetation, the creek exposed rock outcropping from time to time that Parrot wished to examine, but he was soon forced to revert back to his previous strategy of detouring away from the creek in order to make headway further upstream. Bushwacking in this way was exhausting work and Parrot was soon drenched in sweat despite the chilly, damp air of the forest.

On the second day of prospecting the tributary, Parrot smashed open some angular greenish-grey boulders and was encouraged to find narrow veins of quartz shooting through the rock matrix. His knowledge of geology was limited to the rocks he had seen in mines, but he was confident he had seen this combination with gold, silver and copper. He smashed open several more rocks that yielded the same results before hiking on.

Rain began falling again and Parrot determined to make as much progress upstream as he could before the water level rose significantly. He was scampering from the creek bank to a sand bar when his boot slipped on a mossy, decaying log and he fell heavily onto a rock outcrop below. He yelled out and sprawled full length on the ground, clutching his right leg. On examination, he saw a six-inch long gash in his thigh from which poked pink, frothy tissue. He had twisted his ankle as well. For some time he lay there, moaning and clenching his teeth before he propped himself up. He dragged his leg over to the creek, removed his kerchief and dabbed at the protruding tissue to rinse it off. He winced in pain every time he touched his wound but he eventually worked the kerchief around his leg and affixed it over the gash as a bandage.

Parrot pulled himself to his feet and tried to walk. Again he winced in pain and yelled out. He sat on a log a moment to regain his breath before he reached over and snapped off a long branch that he leaned on with his right arm and tried out as a crutch. It was adequate, and Parrot hobbled over to the end of the sandbar where he carefully knelt down to scoop up a panful of sand and continue his prospecting. In a few minutes he worked his pan down to a concentrate. He rolled over and positioned himself on a log, leg outstretched, to pass final judgment on his panload. Carefully swirling the water and mineral grains into a delicate tail, Parrot suddenly smiled widely. Among the black sand in the bottom of the pan, rested a minute gold nugget, no larger than a water droplet, but immense on an imaginary scale.

"Well, sweet jesus!" Parrot yelled out, his eyes suddenly electrified. "I said I'd find gold and ain't I as good as my word." He put the pan down a moment and laughed aloud, ignoring the rain that washed down his face. "They ain't built the gold mine I can't find once I take a notion to sniff it out." He looked again in the pan to confirm his discovery. "Where are you, you little bitch! Don't go hidin' on me ... Oh, there you are sweet pea. My, but you're just a baby and I really want to meet your mama, so I'll be on my way."

Parrot flicked the pan aside and struggled to his feet, wincing with pain but enthusiastic to continue. He proceeded much slower than before but he made methodical progress through the thick scrub. He eventually hobbled down the creek bank and out onto another sandbar, where he tossed his pack down and sat on a rock for a moment to close his eyes and regain his strength. After a minute he reached into his pack for his pan. "Okay my love, come to daddy," he said, getting to his feet and limping to the end of the bar. After ten minutes work, Parrot revealed a gold nugget the size of a pea in the bottom of his pan.

"Oh, you sweet darling," Parrot said, clenching his teeth and grinning wildly. "Is your mother as sweet as you? I'm a dirty sonofabitch that loves an old whore and I'm sure gonna love the bitch that borned you!" He put the pan down on the gravel and danced about, clumsily, on one leg. "Yessir, Mr. Parrot, is there anything else I can do for you? Oh, you can call me Pat, and, as a matter of fact, you can start by taking off that frilly lace, honey. Go on! Yeehaw!" Parrot twirled a couple of times and collapsed onto the sand, laughing.

A little further upstream, Parrot worked another pan of gravel down and revealed two more nuggets. He sat down on the spot and put his head in his hat. "Oh my! Mother and daughter, bitch and whore, sweet daddy's on his way! Lock 'em up and I'm just gonna break on in! Try and hide and it'll be that much sweeter findin' you out! Soooeeee!"

After resting that night, Parrot's luck extended into the next day, when he continued to turn up coarse gold flakes and small nuggets in his pan. At one mossy outcrop he tugged on a greenish-gray rock before working it loose and smashing it open. The rock inside was streaked with milk-white quartz veinlets and smeared with gold. He had discovered the lode, the source of the creek gold.

Parrot was ecstatic. He knelt on the gravel and ran his hands over the rock surface before pressing his cheek against it. His eyes brimmed with tears. He looked again at the rock fragments in his hand. "As sure as the lamb lies down with the lion I got me one sweet lady now. Them dumb-ass farmers are gonna put their women out to sea when they see what ol' Pat Parrot has been strokin' up here in the hills. Oh, you beautiful baby!" He pressed his face into the rock outcrop and shut his eyes.

Two days later, after hiking out from his discovery site to the beach where he ate another meal of shellfish, Parrot hiked back to the village and limped up the front steps of his cabin. His eyes darted but his face was waxen and drawn with pain. He slung his pack, laden with rock samples, onto the cabin floor and stepped back outside. Some young boys ran by on the gravel trail and stopped to tumble on the ground nearby. They had not observed Parrot, who appeared wild as a banshee in his tattered clothing.

"Yipyipyipyipyipyiyipyipyipyoweeeeee!" Parrot suddenly yelled out.

The boys froze on the spot and stared at Parrot in terror.

Parrot limped up closer to them. "Don't you little tads know that's an Indian holler for GOLD! Huh! You ever seen gold? Well, just you look at these here samples."

He pulled two rocks from his pocket and held them out for the boys, who glanced at the rocks from afar, then scrambled to their feet and ran off.

"Hey!" Parrot yelled after them. "What're you doing, runnin' off like I'm some kinda mad dog. Hey, you dumb ass farmers! Have a look at what old Pat Parrot kicked over back in the hills. Yessir, you'll never forget this day 'cause ain't no person's ever the same after he's sniffed a fresh gold nugget. One minute you're muckin' out pig shit and the next you're an Indian chief! Yipyipyipyipyoweeee!"

Parrot twirled around and then fell to the ground in hysteria. He continued to laugh aloud and didn't notice several adults cautiously approaching him. He sat up to massage his hurt leg but he continued to giggle, even after he spotted the villagers gathered around.

"Hey! You want to make me mayor? Go ahead. I'll be your goddamed mayor! Oh, excuse me, ma'am, I get an awful mouth when I'm talkin' gold. It loosens my tongue and sends bats flyin' in my head. Now, where can a body register a gold mine around here? Heinrich, my friend, how's that horse of yours, still slow as jam?" He laughed aloud and continued grinning as he held out a rock sample for viewing. "See, Heinrich, I found gold, just like I said I would." Heinrich stepped up to look at the rock but said nothing. "Just like I said I would," Parrot emphasized, before collapsing back down on the ground. "But oh, don't that sun look pretty going down tonight. My, my."

The villagers backed off and left Parrot on the ground. They conversed quietly a moment before turning and walking away. Parrot watched them disappear.

"Hey, what the hell's wrong here? I found you people a gold mine! Maybe you need time to think about it, that's okay with me. I can take you up there tomorrow and you can stake claims around mine. Oh, nuts to you. I got me some celebratin' to do tonight, and you can join in if you know the tune," Parrot said as he struggled to his feet and started to dance a jig on his uninjured leg. "'Now have you ever heard of Sweet Betsy from Pike! She crossed the wide ocean with her boyfriend Ike. With a tall shanghai rooster and an old yeller dog, two horny whores and a big spotted hog.'"

Parrot hummed and danced a few more steps before he collapsed again, this time face down on the ground. "Damn," he yelled out rising on his elbows. "Don't nobody know any more words to that song? No? Maybe we could holler a few hymns to the Lord, then. I reckon He'd like that. 'Ezekiel saw a wheel-a-turnin', way in the middle of the air.' And a big golden wheel it was, too!" Parrot sat back, laughing. "Oh, Lordy, I believe I'm drunk though I aint' touched a drop of liquor. And I know I'm gonna have an awful head in the morning."

Parrot slowly pushed himself up from the ground again. "Better lock your doors, everybody. I'm loaded for bear and I just might come looking for girls!" he cackled as he limped up to his cabin and through the door.

The next morning Parrot was sleeping soundly on his bed when there was a loud knock on his cabin door. He stirred and opened his eyes as someone yelled out his name. After looking around, he suddenly jumped out of bed and grabbed his rucksack that he stuffed under a blanket.

"Parrot, are you there?" came the voice again.

"I'm getting to it," he replied. "I'll bet everyone's in a hurry to get stakin' claims today."

Parrot opened the door to Cyrus, Heinrich, Samuel and Edmond, looking somber.

"Well, g'day Cyrus. I guess y'all heard the good news."

Cyrus stepped into the room. "What is it exactly that you have found, Parrot? The villagers are concerned that you have lost your senses."

Parrot grinned widely and chuckled. "Lost my senses!" He shook his head, then reached under the blanket to uncover his rucksack. He stuffed his hand inside and pulled out a rock sample. He blew on it and held it out to Cyrus. "Look here, amigo. It's full of gold. And there's more where I found that. Maybe a whole mountain of gold."

Cyrus had a glance at the rock before passing it to the others. Parrot crossed his arms nervously and snickered.

"Oh, I was feeling mighty high last night. Bet I scared the arse off those young bucks. You know, I didn't mean no harm by it, I just felt like celebratin'."

"I was helping one of the young women who had a very difficult childbirth," Cyrus told him. "But I heard you. We all did."

"Well, I'll bet everybody's excited today knowin' this old powder keg is gonna blow sky high."

"Parrot," Edmond spoke up from the rear of the group clustered around the door. "It is the wish of the community that you do not leave the village again."

Parrot glared at Edmond. "What the hell are you talking?"

Cyrus glanced at Edmond and then at Parrot. "We are willing to provide you with shelter but we want no part of your discovery. We would like your word that when you leave on the trip outside next spring you will tell no one of this gold."

Parrot looked shocked.

"But that don't make no sense. There's enough gold here to make everybody rich. Don't you know that?"

"Parrot," Cyrus said, slowly. "We are simple people. With some small exceptions, we do not contemplate a richer life than we already enjoy."

"We don't want your riches," Heinrich added.

"Well, hell. That's too damn bad," Parrot said, stiffening his back. "I march to a different tune." He reached out and grabbed his rock sample. "Gimme that back." Parrot stuffed the rock sample in his sack and began tugging on his boots. "I'm getting out of here today, and I'll be leading a stampede when I return, mark my words. You best find a different place for your dumb-ass farming."

He pulled his hat around his head and began to shove his way through the crowded door.

"Parrot, don't do this," Cyrus told him, sternly.

"Get out of my way!" Parrot shouted at Heinrich, who blocked the door. Heinrich didn't budge. Parrot pushed against him then pulled a rock sample from his sack and smashed it into Heinrich's face. "Move, you sonofabitch."

Heinrich staggered back and crumpled to the ground. Blood began spurting from his nose as Parrot went to step over him.

"Stop him!" Cyrus yelled out.

Edmond lunged at Parrot and grabbed him around his waist, wrestling him to the ground. Two other men who had arrived ran up and pinned Parrot's flailing arms. He struggled for a moment then stopped, gasping for air.

"You bastards! You got no right keeping me here. Get your

dumb-ass hands off me!" he snarled.

Cyrus reached down and grabbed Parrot's sack from his hands. He stuffed his arm inside and pulled out Parrot's rock samples. One by one, he hurled them far into the bush, then he dropped the empty sack to the ground.

"Let him up."

The men released their grip on Parrot, stood up and backed off a short distance. Parrot stayed on the ground, glaring at the men.

"You will be watched by the men of the village for the rest of your stay here, Parrot. No harm will come to you as long as you do not leave. Forget your gold."

Parrot spat on the ground. "If I was a gamblin' man, I wouldn't bet on that," he replied.

Immediately after his scuffle, Parrot was marshaled back inside his cabin. Soon after, a barricade was nailed across his door and he was forcibly confined. Twice each day, someone arrived with a tray of food and to exchange a wooden bucket containing Parrot's waste. For the first few days, someone was posted as a sentry outside the door, but then it was determined that he was securely confined and a guard was not considered necessary at all times.

Inside the cabin, Parrot was extremely restless, pacing the floor endlessly when he was awake. He muttered and talked to himself and occasionally burst into song. Sometimes he banged on the door and shouted at the villagers and whoever happened to be posted as guard.

One morning, Parrot was stirring on the cabin floor and

ranting. "The boat's going down! My maps, they'll be ruined. I been hired to find gold. On to the Klondike! Never mind the job, ain't nothin' progress can't fix. Even dumb-ass farmers."

He paused and there was a loud knock. He glanced toward the door. "Lucifer, my old friend. Come in."

"It is Hilda," a voice spoke out. "I have brought you some food."

Parrot scuttled to a side wall and pulled himself to his feet as the barricade on the door was lifted. Hilda entered with a tray of food. She looked at Parrot with a mixture of fear and pity and set the tray down on the bed. He ran his fingers through his hair and nervously bobbed his head.

"Me, I'm not getting on badly. Pretty good company for myself, actually. Course, I been locked up for longer than this, though I'm wondering if that boat is leaving anytime soon."

Hilda stared at him. "The boat will not be leaving for a long time yet, Parrot."

He looked incredulous. "No? But I been in here a long time."

"You have been in here less than two weeks. But we have been talking about your problem, Parrot."

He squinted at her. "That right? Well, I only found that gold because I love you, sugar. I know how pretty you'd look in a fancy dress with a drop of gold risin' and fallin' over your heart."

Hilda blushed. "Parott, stop. I have come to ask you if you wish to work outside. Under supervision. We know how difficult it must be for you, in here."

"Work?" Parrot nodded. "Yes, I like to work. Makes a man feel good."

Hilda pursed her lips. "You can do some work today, then." She turned to leave. "Eat first. Someone will come for you soon."

Hilda left the cabin and Parrot watched her walk away through his cabin door. He faced the man guarding the cabin and preparing to barricade the door.

"A little work'll be fine. Just what the doctor ordered."

Later in the morning, two men tied Parrot's hands behind him and led him on a short tether from his cabin through the village. Several people stopped to observe him as he passed by and a gray and white mongrel trotted up behind to sniff and bark out a warning.

"Take a bite of my ass and your teeth'll rot out of your mouth!" Parrot sneered.

The men glanced at each other but led Parrot along in silence to the door of the granary building where a horse was tethered to a railing. One of the men knocked on the door which then rolled open. Edmond stepped out and looked at Parrot disdainfully.

"Well, my old friend, Edmond," Parrot greeted him. "It's a good day for working, I see. Though I believe it'll rain soon. Of course the rain's needed for growing crops."

Edmond sized Parrot up. "You can work in the granary,

Parrot, as long as you cooperate."

"I'll do anything you say, brother. I've always been a working man. Work can't do a body any harm, I always say. Of course my line of work is usually mining or finding ..."

"Enough," Edmond cut him off. "You can start now."

Edmond turned and spoke briefly with the other men. Then he came over and led Parrot inside the building where the horse had been harnessed to the wheel of the araster, the mill stone that ground wheat and other grain crops grown and harvested by the villagers. Edmond tied one of Parrot's hands to a tether affixed to the horse's halter. He tied Parrot's other arm behind his back. He then gave the horse a shove and it began walking slowly around the circle with Parrot alongside.

"Keep the horse walking around, all the time. Somebody will load the hopper and remove the flour after it is ground. Do you understand your job?"

Parrot looked at him incredulously as he walked beside the horse. "You call this work? This ain't work, this ain't nothin' but a Sunday stroll. A church picnic. Get along Nellie!"

The men watched Parrot and the horse going around for a couple of minutes and talked quietly among themselves.

"Now I know for a fact this here work don't take three of you watchin' me," Parrot called out to them.

"Just make sure that horse keeps turning the stone, Parrot," Edmond warned him.

"Oh I can do that, brother! Better'n a nigger, too. And tell the Lord I'm coming. Cuttin' through His fields of golden wheat. 'Ezekiel saw a wheel-a-turnin', Way in the middle of the air!' Yessir, them wheels gotta go round and round." Parrot chuckled as he shuffled in the dust and grit that puffed up in a cloud around his feet.

Parrot worked for several hours at the araster, taking only a short break to eat some food brought to him. Later in the afternoon, Edmond took over the job of loading the grain hopper and collecting the flour. He had very little to say to Parrot until he approached him from the side.

"Well, Parrot. I see you aren't in danger of working too hard."

"I said it before, brother. This here is a Sunday stroll."

Edmond suddenly gripped Parrot by the arm and stared hard into his eyes.

"I want to know, Parrot. What did you do to Hilda?"

Parrot squirmed. "I don't know what you're talking about," he gasped.

He clenched Parrot around his throat and Parrot sunk to the ground. "Tell me what you did, you animal."

"I tell you that girl's crazy for me, brother. Now I got a girl back in town and she can't get enough. But I swear I didn't touch this girl. I swear!"

Edmond stood over Parrot, glaring at him, before he yanked Parrot to his feet. Then he reached behind his back and yanked out a formidable knife that he held at his side.

Parrot looked horror-stricken. Edmond reached over and

cut the tether connecting Parrot to the horse and began pulling him aggressively.

"Where are you taking me?"

"May God have mercy on your soul."

"Look, there's ways of fixing things if that girl is in some kind of trouble," he blurted out. "Hell, where I come from we got doctors that'll fix anything. New technology. Progress ..."

Edmond jerked Parrot around and eyeballed him menacingly. "If you were a dog I would cut your tongue out," he sputtered, before regaining his composure. "We are going to a funeral service for a woman of the village who died. If you know what is good for you, you will shut up."

"My word, brother," Parrot whispered.

Edmond pushed and pulled Parrot to the community hall where the other villagers were filing in quietly.

Inside the hall, the atmosphere was somber and tense. People gathered facing one end where a body was lying on a table atop some cedar boughs. Adjacent to the body, a man sat with his head face down on the table. He lifted his head up after a minute and looked out at the crowd through red-rimmed eyes. The face was Einar's, and it was wrenched in sadness.

Parrot and Edmond sat on a bench behind the villagers. When everybody had arrived, Cyrus slowly walked over and stood alongside Einar. He gently squeezed Einar's shoulder and faced the crowd.

"My friends," he said, barely above a whisper. "We come together today in sorrow at the passing of our dearest Inge. Only a few days ago, we celebrated a child brought into this world by Inge and Einar, and today we mourn the painful loss of this mother, wife and partner, taken from us in the prime of her life."

Einar put his hand up over his eyes and started to sob, rhythmically. Another person in the audience began to cry. Cyrus paused a moment as the full measure of sadness pulsed through the hall.

"The Lord moves in mysterious ways, taking and giving as He sees fit. Why He chose Inge as one of His angels at this time, we cannot know. But we do know that in spite of our deep loss, we remain blessed in many ways, with much to be thankful for. Einar, you have a beautiful new son and you can count on our help in learning the ways of a father. We can also be thankful for receiving a blessing of abundant food, rich, promising land and ..."

Suddenly, Parrot broke away from Edmond's grip and sprang up onto a nearby bench. The commotion startled people and they turned to stare.

"I got something to tell you dumb-ass farmers," he yelled out. "I'll bet that Einar's wife wouldn't have died if your God had provided some medicine for her. But He didn't, did He? You get that medicine in the world I come from where there's doctors to fix ya' up. But you dumb-ass farmers don't know shit about doctors and real medicine, do you. Well? Am I right? How come you're all so goddammed quiet?"

Everyone was shocked and remained motionless.

"Remove him, now!" Cyrus bellowed. Edmond and several

others rushed toward Parrot to grab him and drag him out of the hall.

Two days later, Parrot remained locked inside his cabin. He looked haggard and disheveled pacing the floor and muttering to himself. He occasionally shouted to the sentry posted outside and wrenched on the door, trying to yank it open. When food was brought to him, the barricade was carefully lifted and two or three men blocked the door to prevent Parrot from escaping. One of them carried a musket.

One afternoon, rain drumming on the roof, food arrived for Parrot with Fayne accompanying the men. Fayne stayed inside the cabin to meet with Parrot after the men left. Fayne's long hair hung in matted knots and he wore several shell necklaces around his neck.

"I see they've got you caged, friend," Fayne told Parrot, staring at him.

"Like a rabid coon, partner."

Fayne flopped onto the bed. "Well, they are feeding you anyway. You might even fatten up before spring comes and we get out of here."

"They're not going to let us go anywhere," Parrot huffed.

"What are you talking about?"

Parrot shook his head. "All that college learning and you can't figure it out. These dumb-ass farmers'll do what suits them best, is all. But I know one thing, I'm going to get out of here and head south, soon as I can grab some more gold samples. Look after my own interests before those dumb-asses plan somethin' else." Parrot walked over and wrenched on the door aggressively. "Damn! I just can't figure them out."

"Yes, they are odd. I even asked that girl, Hilda, to marry me but she rejected my offer."

Parrot gawked at Fayne in surprise. "You asked her to marry you, and she turned you down? You must be a hard luck case."

Fayne's face hardened. "What do you mean?"

"Well, hell," Parrot chuckled. "I had my fun with her. On the beach before we went to visit you. She loved it."

Fayne stood up and confronted Parrot. "You're lying! She told me she wanted nothing to do with you," he shouted angrily.

Parrot backed up against the wall, laughing. "I ain't lying, you can ask that girl yourself. She's sneaking round here all the time, looking for more."

Fayne was furious. "You deserve to be chained. You're a dog."

"In a 'dog-eat-dog world', partner. Yipyipyipyipyipyoweeee!"

Fayne pounded on the door. "Open up! I want out," he ordered. The barricade on the door was raised and Fayne stormed away.

Several days later, Parrot received another visit, this time from Cyrus and Anton. Cyrus called to Parrot from outside the door.

"I've come to you with a final offer, Parrot."

"What do you mean, a final offer," Parrot responded from within. "Are you planning to hang me at dawn?"

"You are wearing on my patience, Parrot. I have tried to help you but there are others who are not so kindly disposed toward you."

Parrot tugged angrily on the door. "Bring 'em here and we'll settle our differences."

"Parrot, be reasonable," Anton advised.

"Reasonable? Well, fiddle you farmer! You think you created the Kingdom of Heaven out in this wilderness and then you go and lock me up for speaking my mind. And you want me to be reasonable."

"If you do not settle down and, yes, act reasonably, as Anton suggests, then your fate ... rests in your hands," Cyrus said.

Parrot kicked at the door from the inside and the noise startled the men outside.

"Horse-shit!" Parrot screamed. "Where's my trial? You made me a prisoner here against my will but I ain't stood in front of no judge."

"Our community has judged you on your deeds and intentions."

"That a fact? I figure on helping find some real medicine for Einar's wife instead of that poison ivy you was rubbin' on her, and that makes me a criminal?"

"Parrot, we know your intentions are to share the news of your gold discovery with the outside world. That is not acceptable to us. If you are willing to travel on, without mentioning the gold, that is a different matter."

"Well, fiddle you again! After I get out of here, I'm going to get me an outfit and I'll be leading a damn parade when I come back. With elephants and jugglers and mining equipment! And lots of medicine. Now let me out of here, you sonsabitches!"

Parrot pounded on the door with his fists.

Cyrus' face flushed red and he stepped back from the cabin. "Just remember your fate is cast by your own hands." Then he turned and walked away from the cabin with Anton beside him.

"Oh, I got that right," Parrot yelled, slumping to the ground. "Yipyipyipyipyipyip! Quack, quack, quack, quack! Send your women by and let old Pat Parrot take care of them. Once they get a little sniff of gold, they never go back to farmin'!"

Parrot rested his head against the door. "Oh my, I have my fun. Too bad these dumb-asses ain't got no sense of humor."

Parrot peered out from his cabin through a narrow crack in the wooden siding adjacent to the door. He watched Cyrus talking with several other men, gesticulating back toward the cabin. The men studied the cabin for a few moments before turning and walking away. Parrot's grin melded into a sober frown and he closed his eyes in contemplation. Then he turned around and stared grimly toward the ceiling. A flicker of recognition snicked over his face. "Shit!" he muttered, pounding a fist into the door. "I should've taken care of this before."

He strode across the floor, grabbed his pack and began frantically searching through it. He plunged his hand into the pocket and pulled out a shard of flint rock he had used to make fire out in the bush. He dropped to the floor and began picking and clawing at the boards to gather up splinters of wood and sawdust collected in the cracks. He soon had a small handful of slivers in his hand. Then he grabbed his pillow and ripped it apart, spreading a cloud of dried grass and moss. Parrot next looked under the bed and found a small rock lying there, one that he had brought in weeks before to examine. He palmed the rock in one hand, swept up the sawdust and straw in a small pile and began chipping away at the rock with the shard of flint.

Tiny sparks ricocheted off the rock. In a few minutes a small curl of smoke wisped into the air. Parrot blew gently on the pea-sized coal. A small tendril of grass suddenly lit up. Parrot tenderly fed the flame with another straw and a sliver of wood. In a few seconds a finger-sized tongue of fire flickered. The smoke curled into Parrot's eyes and nose and he backed away. He added another handful of grass and then reached behind him and pulled the blanket from the bed. He slowly fed the blanket into the fire until it, too, curled up in flame. He carefully pulled the blanket across the room and rested it against the door. In less than a minute the blanket was engulfed in flames which began to lick at the door. Parrot jumped up to grab his pack and the rock and stand beside the door. He waited until the door caught fire.

"Help, fire!" he yelled out and pounded his fist on the door just above the flames. "Hey, let me out, there's a fire in here! Help!"

Moments later, Samuel lifted the barricade. Parrot's body tensed and he tightened his fist. As Samuel opened the door and stepped under the lintel, Parrot cocked his arm and slagged him hard in the face with the rock. Samuel sagged to the ground. Parrot added a hard kick in the stomach and pitched him inside the cabin. He turned to attack others but there was no one else around. Parrot grabbed Samuel's musket leaning against the cabin wall and sprinted from the burning cabin into the forest.

Soon after, the villagers gathered outside the community hall, milling about and talking excitedly among themselves. They clustered around Samuel, nursing a swollen, cut face with a wet cloth. Cyrus hurried up to the group and listened to the threads of several conversations before trying to get their attention.

"Please, can we go inside. We need to discuss this," he shouted out.

An older man spoke to Cyrus. "Do you have any ideas on how we are going to stop this crazy man now?"

He was interrupted by Edmond. "There's nothing to talk about. We're wasting time. We must recapture him."

"But whatever we are to do, we must decide on it together," Cyrus intoned.

"That is all very noble," Samuel said, sarcastically. "But while we talk, Parrot escapes."

"That is how we have always done things here," Lucy insisted.

"What do you suggest, Edmond. That we hunt him down like a panther?" Anton asked.

"He must be stopped," Edmond countered. "Our security is threatened."

"Edmond is right," someone yelled out from the crowd. "Parrot is mad."

"Is he?" Anton yelled out. "I agree with some of his ideas."

The crowd was silenced and everyone stared at Anton.

"How can you say that, Anton?" Cyrus sputtered.

"Which of his ideas do you agree with, Anton?" Edmond chided.

Anton glared at Edmond, then he looked around the crowd. "Look, I know Parrot is not very likeable. And I'm sorry that he hurt Samuel today. But I think some of Parrot's ideas about progress are good and I'll bet some of you do, too. Or am I wrong?" The group remained silent. Anton shook his head. "I think I am the only honest one here."

"His ideas are based only on greed," someone spat out. "He cares nothing for our way of life."

There followed another moment of silence. Suddenly Hilda burst into a sob. Everyone turned to stare at her. She was sitting on a bench with her face buried in her hands.

"Hilda, what's wrong? Lucy pleaded, pushing through the crowd to comfort her.

Hilda shook her head and said nothing.

"I'll tell you what is wrong," said Edmond. "Parrot has had his way with her and now he has discarded her. Like a lump of coal."

Everyone was shocked and began muttering.

"What did you say?" asked Cyrus. "Hilda, is this true?"

She bobbed her head in acknowledgement. "I thought he loved me ... but he forced me to do things," she sobbed, balling her hands into fists. "He was so strong, I couldn't escape. Oh, why has this happened? I don't know what to do."

Lucy wrapped her arm around Hilda and hugged her. "There, child. You're safe now. Everything's alright."

Hilda sobbed and stared at Lucy, shaking her head. "No, no,

no," she thrummed.

Again, stony silence pervaded the group.

"This is unbelievable!" Cyrus stammered.

"I am going to find Parrot, now" Edmond announced. "Who is with me?"

Several men raised their hands into the air.

"And you, Anton?" he asked.

Anton's face was tight as stone and drained of color. "He nodded his head, slowly. "Yes," he whispered.

Edmond turned to Cyrus. "Well, what's left to discuss? Are you coming with us?"

Cyrus stared at Edmond before he turned and slowly walked away, his head stooped. He suddenly turned around to face the group. "We have never spilled blood here. That is one of our great strengths," he insisted.

"Why don't we try talking to him again?" Greta spoke up. "If he really sees things our way, he might change his thinking."

"Change his thinking?" Edmond interjected. "Parrot has made his intentions very clear. We must stop deluding ourselves that we are somehow responsible for his thinking and act now to protect what is precious to us."

"But if you hunt Parrot down then you are no better than he is, don't you see that," Lucy said.

"So what other ideas do people propose?" Edmond chided.

The villagers remained mute.

"There is a solution, other than hunting him down," said Lucy.

"If we rush into this situation ..."

"Yes?" Edmond probed.

Lucy's lip quavered before she closed her eyes and quietly sobbed. "We are no better than animals."

"He must be stopped," someone called out.

Cyrus slowly nodded his head and looked at Edmond. "It is getting late. I will meet you at the shed at daybreak tomorrow."

Fayne could hardly believe his eyes nor contain his excitement. He had crawled and fought his way for more than an hour through dense salal and scrub brush toward something poking out above the vegetation that caught his attention, while he had been hiking along a section of the foreshore.

In previous days, after his meeting with Parrot, he was quite discouraged at his situation and rarely ventured far beyond his shack except to gather food and firewood. This morning he had arisen and, after eating some cold fish, determined to shift his lassitude and resume exploring. He was increasingly confident that his collection of Indian artifacts would be considered a significant discovery back at the institution, though he was particularly anxious to make contact with the Indians and reconstruct their history in the region. Quite recently, while hiking the beach, he had come upon a firepit that he hadn't seen before. On close examination he felt it bore signs of fairly recent use and he hoped it presaged contact with the Indians.

Now, his face pressed close to the earth, and his shoulder still supporting a log he had levered out of the way, he stared into the overgrown remains of a large shelter, a longhouse illuminated by a skein of sunlight that filtered through the overhead webwork of branches and thatch. He pulled himself past the log and found he could stand up and look around. A rank, musty smell filled his nostrils, redolent of animal waste. The thatch above shifted in the wind and the light flickered in the room giving an impression of movement that startled him. Fayne felt his heart racing. In the low light he was able to identify several small totem poles, etched with much better detail than any he had previously found. Stones and shells lay scattered in a circle nearby to the totems as well as several woven baskets. He carefully padded his way across the room and knelt to examine a collection of spears. He was further startled when a rat scampered along a wall and emitted a piercing shriek. Backing up, he nearly tripped over a collection of blankets lying on the ground. He nudged the blankets with his toe and felt something solid inside. He reached down and slowly rolled back the blanket until it stuck. He yanked on it a little harder until it suddenly loosened and a skull rolled onto the ground, a few strands of long black hair still clinging to the bone cap.

Fayne dropped the blanket and retreated, his heart cannonading in his chest. He tripped on a rock and stumbled, then crawled across the ground to get away. At the far side of the room he lay prostrate on the ground and closed his eyes. He had previously found many bones and skeletons but this discovery rattled his frayed nerves. After a minute, he cracked his eyes open again and raised himself to his knees. He reassured himself that he had stumbled onto a major discovery, the most important of his career, before he rose and cautiously walked back to the skeleton. He stepped around the skull and then knelt down and carefully pulled the blanket back with two hands. Beneath the shroud lay a full skeleton that Fayne stared at in wonder. Dangling on one side of the rib cage was a spherical silver breastplate adorned with a large, polished stone of turquoise. More silver chains hung around the arm bones, and the bones of the ankles and feet were wrapped in tattered deer-hide moccasins patterned with beads and quills. He felt around the side of the skeleton and found more silver jewelry, including a ring set with a large red stone, probably a ruby. Fayne held the ring up and gazed at it a full minute before closing his palm tightly around it.

Parrot hustled through the forest and down the beach after escaping the village. Anticipating that he would be followed, he purposely left false trail markings leading up a creek valley, hoping to throw off any trackers. He found the location for his trail entrance into the forest marked by a rock cairn he had erected and a tree he had scored with a sharp rock. He dismantled the cairn, hurling the stones into the tidewater, and he swept the sand with a cedar bough to brush over his tracks before he turned inland. His leg wound had healed during his imprisonment and he hiked through the dense forest with ease. He was encumbered, nonetheless, by the musket that he clutched with his right arm, protecting it from rough bumps whenever he tripped so that the barrel and flintlock would remain free from grit and sand. Whatever might happen, Parrot believed the musket would afford him some protection and he was determined to use it rather than face being recaptured.

Parrot planned to procure more rock samples from his showing and then travel south along the shoreline. Though he had little idea about what challenges or impediments he might face, Parrot was confident that he could find food and survive the elements, eventually encountering other people. Maybe he'd find a trapping outpost or signal a passing ship, or maybe he'd have to build a raft and drift down the coast to the nearest settlement. Once he had his gold samples, Parrot was certain he could do anything and go anywhere.

Throughout the rest of the afternoon, Fayne continued exploring the longhouse. He took a stout branch from outside and opened up a hole in the ceiling to let in more light, and he discovered two more skeletons, smaller in stature than the first but likewise adorned with silver jewelry that he surmised had been gained in contact with Spanish explorers. One of the bodies had been dragged about and some of its bones split open, likely by a hungry wolf or cougar. He found other bones and bead trinkets scattered about the floor, as well.

Fayne discovered the location of the main entrance to the longhouse, a door of sorts, which he wedged open. He then worked to clear a trail through the brambles and scrub to the foreshore. Working against the fading light, he hurried to carry out the articles of his discovery, including the blanket and skeleton of the chief that he propped against a drift log. He fingered the silver breastplate dangling over the rib cavity before he lifted the chain from around the protruding vertebrae and hung it around his own neck.

After one more trip in and out of the longhouse, he decided he would return to his shack for the evening and continue exploring the following day. He gathered some articles that he wished to transport back to his shack, including a skull, into a blanket that he rolled up and folded under his arm.

He was about to depart when he heard a footfall on the trail leading to the longhouse. He turned around but saw nothing there. He began walking away but then heard a branch snap nearby.

Fayne whirled around and listened intently. He heard nothing more and took a couple of steps in the direction of the sound. He slowly rotated his head and then, suddenly, his body trembled and he took a wobbly step forward. He wore a look of confusion. His body shuddered again and Fayne lowered his eyes to his chest from which protruded a large spear tip. Fayne's mouth rolled open and he blew out a froth of bloody bubbles before he sagged to the sand.

The men of the village gathered silently by the shed in the pasty light of dawn where Cyrus and Edmond handed out muskets to those who chose to arm themselves. Edmond offered brief instruction on how to load and fire and Cyrus reluctantly advised them to keep their powder dry and to avoid bumping the barrel. Not all of the men chose to carry a musket.

After the firearms had been handed out, the villagers agreed to regroup at tidewater, from where they would travel as a group and commence their search for Parrot. A short time later, the men and women congregated on the beach and made final plans for minding children and carrying food, before the trackers departed in a single line. A wind sidled in from the ocean, carrying with it rain that struck like stinging needles.

They tramped past Fayne's shack an hour after they departed from the village. Cyrus poked his head inside the entrance and yelled out a greeting to which there was no response.

After another hour of walking the group discovered Fayne's corpse lying face down in a tidal pool. Heinrich and Edmond waded into the water and retrieved the body. Hungry crabs had partially devoured him and clung to the corpse like clothespins. The villagers pulled him onto dry ground and puzzled over his death. The men cautiously explored the area but concluded that Fayne had likely drowned in another location and his body drifted here in the current. They agreed to bury him on their return.

Parrot struggled through the forest to locate the site of his gold showing. As before, rain had swollen the level of the creek, changing the appearance of features that he fought to remember in detail. Much of the forest was tediously similar - the giant trees, the moss, the dripping canopy - with barely any outcropping of rock, leading Parrot to question whether his discovery existed only as a dream. He slumped against the bole of a giant douglas fir and carefully reconstructed the details of his discovery in his imagination to confirm whether he had conjured up a fantasy or was truly retracing his steps. He could think of no evidence to prove the existence of his discovery until he remembered his injured leg. He scrambled to his feet and yanked down his trousers to examine his leg where he saw an ugly red and yellow scar.

"It's real!" he whispered, rubbing his fingers over the scarlet, corded skin. "It's real." He sank on his knees into the moss and turned his face into the rain. "There's gold here," he yelled out. "I knew it. I can smell it and I feel it in my bones." He stood up and clenched his musket. "Come on bitch, daddy's here lookin' for a good time."

Soon after, Parrot located his discovery site along the edge of the creek that was spilling over with raging water. He waded into the water to check the outcropping and re-confirm the mineralization. He pried out a sample of quartz vein with his fingers and smashed it into a hundred pieces against a boulder. Half a dozen shards were smeared with visible gold. Parrot gritted his teeth, grinning and laughing.

He hefted a head-sized boulder over his head, struggling to keep his balance. "What do you think of your boy now, daddy, you rotten sonofabitch." He hurled it against a larger boulder resting in the creek where it shattered. "Oh, son," Parrot said, kneeling down and scooping up the fragments, "Don't worry about that bastard. Mama's here and I'm gonna take care of you and make everything right."

Parrot stumbled out of the creek, carrying the rock pieces that he tucked into his rucksack. He leaned against a tree, pale and exhausted, and stared down the creek. "C'mon you dumb-ass farmers!" he hollered. "I'm here. I got what I come for and I'm leaving. Just you try and stop me!" He held the sack in close to his stomach and rested his musket beside him in the moss. He stared down the creek for another minute before his eyelids drooped and he slumped over in deep sleep.

Diaphonous, early morning light barely penetrated the forest canopy. Rain dripped endlessly from branches, needles and trunks, consumed by thick, spongiform moss that swallowed up all sound.

Parrot slept continuously through the night and lay with his face pressed into the moss. He twitched involuntarily and emitted a low rumbling snore with each breath.

Parrot's arm stretched at an angle to his body, draping over his musket.

A hand, not Parrot's, reached down and slowly slid the musket out of his grasp. The slight movement jarred Parrot's consciousness and he struggled to awaken himself. He slowly twisted his head to one side and rolled open an eye. A few seconds later Parrot lifted his head from the moss and propped himself up onto his elbow.

He looked at the villagers who stood in a line in front of him, several of whom trained their muskets on him.

"So, you found me. You're good trackers," he said calmly.

Cyrus gripped a musket in both of his hands. "You were warned not to come back here, Parrot."

Parrot slowly scooted back up against the bole of the tree,

clutching his rucksack. "You're not getting my gold this time."

"And what do you think we are going to do, just let you go and tell the world about this?" Edmond asked abruptly.

Parrot remained stoic.

"You have spoiled something for us, Parrot. We cannot tolerate this situation," Cyrus told him.

The tempo of Parrot's breathing quickened and he looked from man to man. "You can't be serious. Anton, you understand. Make them see."

Anton looked stern and clacked his gums. The tip of his musket barrel swung slightly to the side and he swallowed hard. He turned his head and stared hard at Cyrus who watched him carefully for several seconds before turning back to Parrot.

"You are not afraid, I hope," Cyrus said. "You are quite ... mad with your gold, and perhaps that is the best one should hope for."

"Where I come from you'd be rounded up and hanged for this," Parrot spoke out.

"Where you come from is a very long ways away indeed, my friend," Edmond told him.

"The chance that you will return with other rogues like yourself is too great a risk for us," said Cyrus.

"But my business is finding gold," Parrot said emphatically.

"And so you found it," Cyrus said, in a crystalline voice.

Parrot clenched the rucksack into his chest. "Flesh, stone, eternity," he whispered before squeezing his eyes shut.

There followed a long, heavy silence, suddenly split by a

thundering sound that rose up into a thick forest canopy laden with rain and consumed in swirling clouds. As the reverberation died down, a raven squawked a raucous rebuttal and circled through the fog-bound trees before flying away.

The men of the village began hiking in slow, silent procession back in the direction from which they had come. One of them paused then turned around and looked back up the creek. After a few moments he rejoined the others and continued down the trail.

THE END

CPSIA information can be obtained at www.ICGtesting.com
Printed in the USA
LVOW06s2359211013

357926LV00007B/21/P